DUSTFALL

About the author

Dr Michelle Johnston is a consultant Emergency Physician who works at an inner city hospital. Mostly her days consist of trauma and mess. She studied medicine at UWA, and gained her Fellowship with the Australasian College for Emergency Medicine in 1998. She believes there is a beating heart of humanity, art, and beauty within the sometimes brutal reality of the Emergency Department, and she has dedicated her career to finding that sweet spot between creativity and critical care medicine. Books are her other oxygen, and writing her sustenance.

DUSTFALL

A NOVEL

Michelle Johnston

First published in 2018 by
UWA Publishing
Crawley, Western Australia 6009
www.uwap.uwa.edu.au

UWAP is an imprint of UWA Publishing,
a division of The University of Western Australia.

A catalogue record for this book is available from the National Library of Australia

Cover design by Peter Long
Cover image Paul Mayall Australia / Alamy Stock Photo
Typeset in 11pt Bembo by Lasertype
Printed by McPhersons Printing Group

For

Julian, Isabelle, and Richard

St Agnes' Eve – Ah, bitter chill it was!
The owl, for all its feathers, was a-cold
The hare limp'd trembling through the frozen grass,
And silent was the flock in woolly fold.

John Keats,
The Eve of St Agnes, 1819

Contents

I

When a building dies it cracks open, and new life drifts in on breezes and seeds. A resurrection, blown in from elsewhere. Or perhaps more a rebirth, Lou thinks, reserved solely for things of bricks and mortar, for the never-lived. Not for people, that's for sure. Certainly, not for the little one with the jiggle in her step and the smell of unwashed clothes. No, when humans die they crumble into dust with barely a whisper, and are poured into urns for display on mute mantelpieces, or shelved away silently underground, leaving nothing but official paperwork and vast, endless wreckage.

Lou looks up to the craterous holes in the walls, the yawning openings, where these motes, inklings really, waft in from who knows where. The specks float to the floor without sound, looking like snow, except it's hot. Hotter than she's ever known it, which is something, considering she comes from Perth, a city as baked and dry as forgotten bread.

The hospital is a ruin, without plaque or monument, marked only by a broken *Keep Out* sign, its face canting and creaking on the haunt of a wind, and an entrance flanked by listing pillars that she fancies look like fractured, crippled metacarpals.

Sitting propped up against a half-standing wall, the warmth soaks through her shirt, and the edges of bricks jut on angles into her back. Many of the walls have disintegrated entirely, leaving drifts of grey concrete crumbs which have settled into layers all the way through the building, writing down the story of the place; a chronicle that no one's around to read.

It must have been a large room, this central one. In a corner is a steel contraption, all rusted cylinders and curved pipes. An anaesthetic machine, she guesses, now just a relic – nothing like the modern ones she's been recently spinning the dials of, dispensing their lolly-like vapours of oblivion to the lucky ones under the mask. Lou hauls herself up, wiping her muddy hands on her pants, and walks towards it. She rubs the front of her wrist over one of the canisters. An asinine gesture, she thinks, as if a genie might appear and extinguish this whole episode on the wave of command. A hint of shine emerges – peculiar, after all these years.

On the floor nearby is a bundle of papers, covered in layers of dried muck. She squats next to it and picks off several clods. The top one is an Australian medical journal, dated from sometime in the fifties, although it's difficult to make out the bleached, rippled words. Amazing that they are here, as if waiting patiently to be read. Picking up the paper by its corner, it perishes with a puff, filling the air with the smell of gunpowder. Lying underneath is an envelope, eaten through by the hunger of years and the climate. The writing that remains is faded and barely visible – she can just distinguish an elaborate, looping scrawl. She tries to lift it, but when she does, it also crumbles in her hand, the pieces drifting away like word pollen. Lost to the breeze. Gone. She imagines doing the same herself, dissolving on a breath of air and joining the backlit diaspora.

The wind is lifting. It sounds a lonely squeal as it courses through the holes and the broken windows, and the light is turning granular. Lou realises it's getting late. She has no idea what she'll do now. Perhaps she could camp the night among the ruin and the detritus. She could construct a tent, assembled from the worn seat covers pulled from the rental car, use her socks as a pillow, her change of underwear for decor. Her father would have loved this; she could see him sitting in the middle of it all, shining a torch under his chin for the telling of outlandish ghost stories, always the opportunist. He wouldn't have needed to make up much out here, she thinks. But if her father were present, this would drag her mother into this illogical scenario, and any joy would be stamped out, sprayed with pine-smelling disinfectant, all the stories bulldozed, with Lou and her father forced to feel ashamed of making things up when there was enough rubbish right in front of their eyes. And with him now only keeping the company of cold stone, while her mother sits in a darkened house, waiting for God only knows what in a cloud of synthetic cleaning products, such an image is ridiculous, and she shakes her head. Plus, she has no experience with camping, and joy is no longer hers for the taking.

Scraps of gauze and torn lengths of bandage tumble across the floor. Other items, heavy from rot, lie dumped in corners. A feather, curiously white, floats past her on a draught. She squints and watches the strange thing sail by. Strewn around her are shards of cracked plastic, congealed clumps of paper and fragments of dull metal equipment. It was once new, this hospital; clean, hygienic, presumably painted. Now, it is silent dirt and debris.

At least nobody knows she's here. She thinks her letter of resignation would have been found by now, picked up from where she'd slid it under the door of the Director of Medical Services. He would have opened it and tossed it in with the rest of her dossier, disgusted. They had one on her, she was quite aware. They'd made that clear when she first started working, only a month ago, in that bristling tin-pot of a hospital several hours from here. Made it sound like it was her last chance, her one shot to redeem herself after what went on down in Perth. But a last chance wasn't much use to a body stripped of options; unmuscled and blind as she now felt. She should have known, they all should have known, that exchanging locations was no answer. No popcorn solution, pacifying only to those who liked their schedules blank and their office doors locked by five.

With the oncoming night, the heat starts to drain away and her sodden shirt cools. She pulls it away from her chest. The solitary whine of a dingo twists its way through the rubble. Lou looks up to where there ought to be a ceiling, but there is nothing but the beginnings of distant stars. It's clear that she is gnawingly alone, her only company the fiends who've taken up residence in her skull.

Perhaps she'll have to sleep in the car – it's probably her only option. Early that morning she'd set off, leaving Port Hedland, having planned to drive to Karijini – an unparalleled tourist destination with world-class sparkling gorges, she had read in a glossy brochure, Australia's own Grand Canyon, superior camping grounds et cetera, the perfect place to wash away your troubles, to meditate, to find yourself in nature's beauty. But she hadn't ended up in Karijini, had she? At some non-descript fork in the road, she had seen a sign with the name of a town scratched out. Erased like a mistake. *Wittenoom*, the ghost of the words had said, and in that instant she'd known that this was the turn she should take.

She'd driven into a petrol station near that divergent road, knowing that whatever happened from there, she was going to need supplies. Filling up a bag with cold drinks from the mud-smeared fridge and a handful of packets of nuts and crisps, she'd lugged it to the counter.

The guy behind the register had taken her credit card and turned it over, maybe looking for an explanation.

'You a doctor?' he'd asked, looking at the lonely title next to her name.

She didn't have a lot to show for it, that much she knew.

'Not anymore,' she'd said. Final, like she'd just decided.

'Where're you headed?'

'Wittenoom.'

He'd handed her back the card, shielding his eyes from the blast of the sun. The heat had worked itself into a fury while she'd been driving and she could feel the knife of it slicing through the glass doors into her back.

'I wouldn't. There's nothin' out there. It's bloody Chernobyl.'

She'd shrugged, slung the bag of goods over her shoulder, and walked through the automatic doors into the furnace of noon.

'Only bloody madmen go out there,' he'd called after her, but she didn't turn around.

And by mid-afternoon, she'd arrived.

The air temperature is dropping and it's a disconcerting sensation, as the floor, the fixtures, the crags of furniture are still on the roast, pouring out stored heat like old-fashioned radiators, keeping her legs hot. Is this how it is every night? Her chest is tight, and she's not sure how close the dingoes are, with their mournful, hungry howl. The last of the light is spidery and silhouettes dance on the walls. With a start, she thinks she sees a figure, stiff and seated in a corner, but realises with relief that this too is merely shadow. The stink of dead animal wafts intermittently through to her, coming and going on the curl of the breeze.

She wanders through the last of the rooms, a ward by the look of it, with three low-slung, collapsing iron beds, the mattresses long ago rotted to nothing, still delaying her decision about where to go for the night. Her footsteps splinter the debris underfoot. How much history is she flattening? She knows so little about this spectre of a town. Just asbestos, death and obliteration.

Picking up a pair of rusted metal artery forceps, she can suddenly visualise the hospital peopled, a doctor wielding this instrument, furiously suturing wounds with silk. Perhaps performing operations, or clamping great chest tubes. She lifts up the forceps, making sweeping motions, sensing the rhythm of them, feeling the weighted way they slot into thumb and ring finger, Teutonically engineered and unaltered over decades. The solid metal of them clunks as she opens and closes the ratchets.

But then a more urgent sound becomes apparent and it echoes under the beds. The footsteps belonging to another, crunching up the gravelly front of the hospital. Suddenly she feels loose inside, watery, and puts down the forceps, reaching into her pocket for the jingle of the car keys. She shouldn't be here. She should be back home, but back before. Back before a blink of a job in Port Hedland, back before that mess of a stint in a small suburban Perth hospital, even back before medical school so that she could choose a different career, one with gentle hours and nobody's blood on her uniform. But she's not. She's now crouched behind a carcass of a bed, hoping that the owner of the loping footsteps, the unmistakable sound of a heavy man, will not find her. The swinging light of a torch arcs across from her and she can see bursts of dust in its beam. She remembers that she has parked the stupid little hire car right out the front, a compact Daihatsu that began the day bride white, but is now caked in maroon dust and pockmarked from the ding of rocks. No point hiding, then, she guesses. She stands in time to see a hulk of a man walk in.

He shines the torch right at her and says nothing.

'Hello?' She tries out her dry, croaking voice, surprised at the sound of it, having barely heard it all day.

In the scatter of light she can see a beard of intriguing colour – streaks of black, speckles of orange, and other shades she can't quite make out. It's wiry and full, and he looks like some type of gingery bushranger. On his head, though, his hair is black and thick, and his face is a weathery olive.

'Thought I heard someone out here,' he says after an unsettling pause. 'Don't get many cars like that baby coming through.' He gestures out to the front. His face is Mediterranean, but his voice is pure Australian. 'In fact,' and he lowers the torch, 'we don't get many of anyone coming through. Not since the tourist buses stopped coming. Name's Dave.' And he sticks out his mound of a hand for her to shake. Lou calculates whether she can trust this guy. It used to be one of her talents, sizing things up in a heartbeat.

'Lou,' she says, taking his hand, but has a vision of being clamped in a vice, expecting a taipan strike, and quickly drops it.

'What're you doing here?' he asks, looking around.

How can she answer? 'Just checking it out.'

He looks at her. She knows that look. She starts again. 'Actually, I needed a bit of space. Thought I'd see what's out here.'

'You staying the night?'

'I'm not sure. I'm a bit underprepared.'

He chuckles, and the sound is deep and throaty. It softens her, and she feels her anxiety back off.

'Nobody's ever prepared for here. Do you need somewhere to stay?'

'In Wittenoom? You can stay here?'

'If you want. Not for long, though.' He doesn't explain why, just keeps watching her.

Lou realises he's said *we* earlier on. 'Do you live here? Do others?' She thinks back to when she drove in, bumping up roads that were more suggestions, the few remaining shacks left to cook out their days in the sun. None of the dwellings looked occupied with their shabby rags of curtains, rusted trucks with long flat tyres abandoned in yards, and the quiet of seized-up generators.

He smiles. 'Sure do.' His teeth are white and disarmingly straight. He continues to watch her, a look narrowed to a point somewhere within. She's ashamed – she knows she looks terrible. Her hair is stringy, unwashed, tied back roughly. She had not bothered with makeup when she drove off this morning and her shirt is steeped in sweat and mud. Only twenty-eight and she looks like she's no age. Hardly even human, she thinks, let alone a fair-looking woman.

'But you can't stay with me. Come out and I'll help you get sorted.'

Lou walks behind this hefty man and she can see dust billowing from the ground with each step. He's wearing a checked shirt and heavy, silted-up boots. The pair stand on the slab of concrete that was presumably a verandah of sorts.

'See there,' he points and directs his torch beam to the east, away from where she came in, 'if you drive over, I'll bring around some stuff for you.' And without waiting for her reply, he disappears off down the road to some unknown blackness.

Without Dave's torchlight, things fall to dark, although a glimmer from a half-moon keeps totality at bay. She treads carefully out to her car. The place smells of fresh earth. A dead fence skirts the perimeter of the hospital, and its detached wires poke out in twisted yawns. As she walks through, she goes to close the dilapidated gate, probably just out of habit, but it catches and slides off its rusted hinge, crashing to the ground. A startled spinifex pigeon takes flight and stirs up a whorl of dust. The sound of the wings leaves a ringing in the otherwise empty air.

When she opens the car door and the interior light clicks on, she can see that there are scattered rocks near the front wheel. She picks one up, turning it over. It has a silvery seam cut through the middle, and the fibres pull off with little effort. They look like the grizzled hair of an old man, and she realises this is asbestos, right here in her hand. She knows how dangerous the filaments are; that inhaling a single fibre can sound the march of death, so she drops the rock and wipes her hands on her pants, but then thinks, what does it matter, anyway?

She hops in the car and with the lights on high beam trundles down what she believes are roads. Unseen kerbs and rocks bash at the undercarriage and she hopes the tyres will withstand the jags. Ahead is the row of Nissen huts Dave had pointed out. As she eases the car up close to the first of them, she spies a faded sign over the lean-to door. *Tourist Accommodation*. She has a moment of hope, but when she gets out of the car she realises that these too were abandoned years ago. Hesitating, she smooths down her hair and, after rumbling around in her handbag on the front seat, pulls out her lipstick, just a melted burgundy ingot after today but she slicks some on just the same. *At the very least I'll match the dust*, she thinks.

Leaving the engine running and the lights of the car directed inwards, she creeps inside the first of the huts. The floor is covered in rubbish – empty bottles and cigarette butts interred in dunes of ash and dirt – but good enough for a night.

Lou's bladder calls to her, and she wonders nervously where she is supposed to go to the toilet. So frustrating, her hang-ups about voiding into anything that's not ceramic and disinfected, but some ideas get ingrained young and they're difficult to shake. The travelling she did as a child was demure, her sedate family of four staying in box-like motels booked well in advance. Sure, when they were little they'd go out fishing with their dad, in the little tinny, and they'd pee over the side as if it were a great joke, so when she thinks back on it, it was likely her mother's fear of germs and her great sloshing buckets of Ajax over anything contacting bodily fluid had ruined her for any type of outdoor ablution. But tonight she's got no choice. She slips through a gaping side in the tin wall, where there is still a little light, and squats. Branches brush her face and her haunches and she wees as fast as she can squeeze it out, imagining all sorts of wild Pilbara creatures that might find her white city backside appetising. She stands quickly and zips up her pants, in time to see a lantern swinging up the road. Scrambling back inside, she gets there before Dave does, and he strides through the front entrance, a khaki swag slung over his shoulder.

'Got some bread rolls here.' He starts pulling things out and handing them to Lou. 'Actually, grab this first.' It's a stiff grey army blanket, coarse as bitumen, and she guesses this will be her bedding.

She lays it down and they set out a picnic of sorts, complete with kerosene lantern for mood. He has turned off her car engine on the way through, which leaves only the quiet and the flickering flame. It creates something other-worldly.

'More rolls. Not too stale,' he says, giving them a squeeze. 'Bit of ham, too if you want.' He continues producing items, one at a time, like a magic show. 'Sausages, only cooked yesterday.' He rustles around in the stiff bag. Like everything around here, it is encased in red dust. 'And tada!' He pulls out two cans. 'Beer. Bit warm. But still.'

He passes one to her. She takes it reverentially, like a sacrament.

'Oh, and this.' From the bottom of the swag he removes another blanket, this one a little softer. 'It gets bloody cold here at night. You wouldn't reckon so, but it does.'

'Hang on,' Lou says, and she nips out to the car to grab several packets of salt-and-vinegar chips and some crispy noodle mix, adding them to the rug.

'A banquet.' Dave smiles, and they pull the tops off the beer cans.

Lou takes a great swig and can taste grit from the rim. Even so, it's heavenly and full in her mouth.

'So, what are you really doing here?' He relaxes back on the blanket, propped up by one elbow, the other hand holding the can.

It should be the place, the time, to unload. She wishes she could open up, talk to this hulking, unfurled man who has brought her offerings as though she is worth something. But there's nothing that she'll manage to get out. She'd like to tell him that she feels hunted, her failures following her like a mongrel dog, snarly and vicious, and they won't leave her alone, so she thought the best thing was to keep moving, outrun them. But now she's here in Wittenoom and she knows there can't be anywhere else further to run. She wants to be able to tell him that she's just flushed a career down the toilet, and that she hasn't told anyone back home, least of all her mother, who found enough shame in having a daughter with ambition in the first place, but now that Lou's wholly screwed up everything that had been grudgingly scrimped and saved for, her actions will be deemed unforgiveable. She wants him to hear it all, and have him respond that it's OK, everybody makes mistakes, and to mean it. But she can't. And she knows that once some words come out they can never be put back and things change.

'Travelling,' she says, and tastes the lie smeared on her lips.

She can see he doesn't believe her.

'I'm sorry,' she starts again. 'I just can't.'

He nods – maybe buried truths are entirely expected in this implausible place.

The warm beer emits a yeasty aroma, and it mixes with the fine dust to make each breath dense and strangely tasty. They stay quiet for a bit.

'I had no idea people actually lived here,' she says.

Dave snorts. 'Of course they do. There's not many of us for sure, but why wouldn't you? Best bloody place on the planet. No government interference. No rates. No rules. Most magnificent landscape on God's green earth. Some things are a bit of a hassle it's true, like no electricity, and it's a bit far to get supplies, but when you take all the good things into account I can't understand why everybody doesn't want to live up here.' He sits forward. 'I'm glad they don't though. It's the whole bloody point.'

Lou watches the veins in his neck while he speaks. They are ropes. His hands are muscled, terracotta paws.

'And others?' she asks.

'There's about eight of us. We don't see much of each other. Like to keep to ourselves, really. Occasionally somebody organises a get-together, a few drinks, a barbie, then half of us don't turn up.'

'How long have you been here?'

'About five years. Worked in the pub right until she was closed down. Saw almost everybody leave, then the buildings start to come down. When the government workers come to do it, raze the buildings, they wear all sorts of gear, respirators and whatever other protective kit they've lugged up with them. I like to stand alongside, watching them, having a smoke, just to get up their noses. They're sweating away like bastards, and I'm drinking a cold beer, enjoying the spectacle.' He grins.

'I don't get it,' Lou says. 'I thought asbestos was some of the most dangerous stuff on earth. How are you …?' It feels like prying, asking.

'It is and it isn't,' Dave says. He doesn't offer more.

He hands her a second can of beer. They pick at the food.

'Your turn,' he says.

She carefully chooses her entry point, a small, cordoned-off snippet.

'I've been working in Port Hedland Hospital. They were understaffed so I was given the job at the last minute.' The first real untruth. It was the farthest place from Perth the administrators could think of, she was sure. Somewhere she could clean up her act.

'Routine registrar job,' she continues. 'Wards, looking after the admitted patients, helping out in surgery with the anaesthetics, that sort of thing.' She will leave out the part about being rostered onto the emergency department overnight, the only doctor in the hospital, help not even a phone call away. Not describe those nights lying in the white cage of an on-call room on a thin mattress under papery sheets, with the thud of the ceiling fan overhead. Not tell him how she would lie the whole night, stiff as a shop dummy next to the phone, her eyes unable to close from the drone of fear in her head, and that she couldn't even turn off the light. How she came to know the moment before the phone actually rang, some type of psychic click it must have made, and she'd tense up with terror. Even if she ever managed to doze off, she could sense this sound, and she'd wake, wildly alert, just before the phone rang, and she would stumble like a condemned man approaching his noose, down to the cramped little department, where an unknown, nameless, broken person would be waiting for her to see. She shudders.

'Can't imagine a doctor's job would ever be routine,' he says.

'Hmm. Truth is, I'm taking a bit of a break from it. You know, the stress.'

He nods again, like he understands.

She has nowhere else to go with this conversation. Any further back from Port Hedland and she'll be in Perth, sitting in the director's office on a seat opposite a bare desk, under perfectly straight portraits, next to impeccably manicured pot plants. Well, the desk bare apart from a stack of papers, all relating to complaints and concerns about her, about her work. In an office that smelled of dry-cleaning, where he pushed the pile of words towards her, asking what she had to say for herself, when they'd been so lenient, so *understanding* after the incident. And, of course, any further back from that and they'd be there in that miserable winter, in that suburban emergency department. But she's not going there. She doesn't need to go there. She's done with all that.

'What do you like to do? You know, for fun. Hobbies?' he asks.

She shrugs. 'Not much really. I like to write.'

He becomes visibly interested and inches closer. 'Brilliant.' He sets down his beer. 'Maybe it's fate that's brought you here, then.'

'Really? Ha. But no. Nothing brilliant about it. I haven't written anything decent for years, although I guess ...' An idea shakes her.

He's animated now. 'This place. This story. It needs someone to write it. It needs to be down on paper. I've tried for years. Got some great photos, interviews, stuff like that, but I'm no good at getting it to lie down right on the page. Never sounds any good from my head.'

She looks up at him. 'I know what that's like.'

He's still leaning towards her, blocking out most of the light from the lantern. Off to the side his mammoth shadow is flickering, waltzing.

'This town,' he says again, 'it needs it. Before it all goes. Before we all do.'

The urgency in his voice surprises her. But she understands so little about this place that she doesn't press further.

'Tomorrow,' he says, 'I'll show you round properly. Give you the tour.' He pushes to his feet and dusts himself down.

'Sure,' Lou says. 'I'd like that. And thanks,' she gestures to the remains of the food and the kero lantern.

'My pleasure,' he says, slinging the empty bag over his shoulder. 'Have a peaceful night.' And he smiles and walks off into the night.

Lou arranges the scratchy blankets so they are banked up in one corner, covering as much of the dirt as she can. Dave's departure leaves a void, and the air inside is menacingly quiet. Cold has washed into the shed through its leaks, and she folds the edges of the rug over her. Sporadic caws spear the silence, and once in a while she hears branches scraping, only to then abruptly cease. She can smell campfire, that smoky eucalyptus scent. It's coming from the blanket. It's a smell that never leaves, she thinks. Like having history, a unique Australian history, embroidered into the fabric.

She leans up against the metal corrugations of the wall, knowing she will not sleep. The image of the hospital is stuck firmly in her head, an all-senses blast of that derelict building. A husk, just like her. Her knowledge about anything that happened round here is meagre, but the idea of it is strong. The bell tolled for this place sometime in the sixties, this much she knows. Somehow, though, the building had looked as though it had been abandoned in a hurry, the breath of life suddenly sucked out. And that despite its ossified appearance, and the evaporation of the town around it, life was now germinating back inside. Or is that just her strange, distorted perception? It's an impression, however, that will not leave her alone.

She stands and creeps out to the car, where she knows she has an empty notebook. Maybe Dave has a point. But perhaps it ought to be her own ruin laid out on a page. And if she never leaves, perhaps someone in the future will find it here, pick it up like the papers she saw today. Settling herself back, she begins, and she does not stop until the heat and the horizonless red of the land beyond the shed have woken and have begun to roll themselves out, once again.

The Arrival

Raymond. That was his name, and he emerged from the mire with two small suitcases stuffed to the hinges with items hastily chosen: white shirts (starched, for the last time), several pieces of wintry apparel, a haul of odes, a stethoscope and at least three empty notebooks. Behind him trailed a story and inside him festered the aching tumour of failure.

The bags were placed in lines next to him as the driver saluted him off.

'Good luck, Doc.'

He looked up the path to the hospital and wondered if he might melt before reaching the front door. Too lost to even reply, Raymond looked around, his eyes hurting. Here it was, his future. He picked up the suitcases, one in each hand, and lumbered up to the verandah. Heavy flies stuck to his face, and the sleeves of his thick suitcoat were like cement on his arms. The joins of his shirt grated against his armpits.

A solitary figure stood at the entrance to the hospital. She wore a navy dress that didn't quite hang, more stood to attention upon her, and with her long-sleeved arms crossed and one thin eyebrow arched and expectant, she was a geometry of angles and shadows in contrast to the cavernous wooden door behind her.

'We were expecting you yesterday,' she greeted him.

'I, ah, yes. I rather miscalculated the journey up here. Missed the plane altogether, I'm afraid. Luckily, there was another coming up today. They don't normally fly on a Tuesday, the pilot said. A milk run, he called it. Most fortunate, really.' He was rambling, tripping over lumps of punctuation, and, hearing how indecorous he sounded, he stopped speaking.

'Well, best you come in, then. Without your entourage.' She swished her hand in front of his face, causing the flies to jettison. 'Miss Rosa's my name, although I expect you know that already.' (He didn't. It was one of many nothings he knew, but now was no time to admit it.)

She continued, 'Come in. You've got considerable work to do before we reopen the wards tomorrow.'

He gripped the handles of his bags and followed her through into the airy front room, faint with the slippery weight of it all.

'This is your office. You can leave those in here, for now.'

It was space and light and possibility. 'Oh, it's marvellous.' Raymond looked around after divesting himself of his luggage. It was a huge room, lined with empty bookshelves, and in the centre sat a grand, darkly wooded desk with a leathery chair tucked behind it. Cracked and faded, yes, but leather. An untied gift. Sunlight bounced off the walls. He walked over to the desk and picked up the small brass nameplate that sat at the front. It was hot to the touch, but he turned it over so he could read it.

Dr R.P. Filigree. Medical Superintendent.

The lettering was newly engraved, respectful. He stared at the wonder of it before setting it back down.

'Not what you're used to, Doctor? Back in England?'

'Oh. I was just thinking that these shelves will be perfect for my collection of books. I do love books. Although,' and he pulled out a handkerchief, wiping the back of his neck, 'there was apparently a mix-up at the shipping agency after I left, and it seems that the rest of my library will be somewhat delayed.' He could feel his face flaring, a painful, unseemly red. 'They'll be joining me, soon. The books, that is.' He crunched his teeth. How on God's earth was he going to manage without his reference books? He turned back to Miss Rosa, knowing that he needed to sound learned, authoritative. This was his chance to start again. Wipe the slate clean. 'I do love books.'

Miss Rosa's face softened. 'So do I.'

'You do?' It occurred to him that he did not know what her role was, this turnstile of a woman. All he had was her name. 'How surprising. Miss Rosa you said, didn't you? And if I'm not mistaken, you are the, ah, the caretaker? Or would that be janitor? Cleaner? Or the …' He trailed off, searching for the correct term so as to avoid causing offence to such a formidable creature.

She recoiled but said nothing. Just stared at him.

He looked back at the ferocity of her face and muddled out, 'Oh, goodness. No, what I mean is …'

'Yes. Well, I quite understand, Dr Filigree. Please follow me, then. We can't stand around all day chatting. I shall show you the infirmary.'

Staring at her briskly receding figure, he could feel his entrails slosh, dumping great waves of nausea low inside him.

He'd like to blame a hangover from three piteous weeks of seasickness. Not the consumptive anxiety at the task ahead. Or the emetic fear that he would be exposed. The accusations. The resignation. The mess.

He caught up and followed behind as she strode through, listing off the history of the place in dry, pointed language.

'Built last year. Nineteen sixty-five. March, we opened. Problem is we've had no doctors who have spent any length of time out here. Nurses? They're great. Always have our fill of those.' She turned and glared at him. Perhaps he was supposed to be taking personal responsibility for the captainless wash of the place thus far.

'I'm sorry to hear that,' he said. 'Not about the nurses, obviously,' he clarified.

Outside somewhere, a cockatoo shrieked and he jumped. Miss Rosa turned a stern look on him.

She continued. 'The mines of course, they started up a good few years before we did. But bless our great government, they didn't want anybody crushed to death or dying in their sleep without a proper go in a proper hospital.' She paused, as if daring him to comment. He did not. 'Wittenoom Hospital. Took a while to come up with the name, as you can imagine.' Again she raised her eyebrows. 'But the problem is we've not managed to get any doctors to stay.'

'Oh, that's no good,' was all he could muster.

'Yes. Chap before you was a retired gynaecologist. If you find any jars of clear liquid snuck in corners about the place, you might want to steer clear. That'll be his gin. And before that we had a surgeon over from Newcastle who had a habit of yelling at everything that moved, and liked to parade up and down with a butcher's knife strapped to his belt. Lasted two weeks.' She bent down and picked a piece of gauze off the floor. Her movements were surprisingly agile for a woman who, surely, must have been on the unforgiving side of forty. 'And now you.' She gazed steadily at him. 'All the way from England. It seems we are very fortunate to have you.'

He managed a doubtful nod. The warmth and the stillness inside made him sway, and he was sure his coat squelched as he moved. What was this heat? Was it always like this? It was a brutish heat, a belligerent heat, a heat with no regard for propriety, he thought. Once more he pulled out his handkerchief, now sodden, and wiped his forehead. He would have to embrace it – this much he knew. This glutinous weather would be a small price to pay for this opportunity to start again. And perhaps, the white sun pouring through the windows and the doors was the thing that could scorch away the cold, disastrous, grey life he had left behind. Expunge it, so there would be not a crumb of residue.

'Are you coming, Dr Filigree? I need to show you through the hospital.'

'Of course. Please do lead on, Miss Rosa.'

They walked through the wards, two separate areas, each with three low-set, glossy metal beds.

'First of these is for the menfolk,' Miss Rosa said. 'You'll find they're all quite large around here.'

Were they, Raymond wondered? Did this journey's end have its own unique biology?

The second was obviously for the women and children. The beds were covered in luminously floral sheets, one wall decorated with a raucous and colourful array of motifs. Fishing frogs played with carousel horses and smiling flowers in a hot and incongruous mix, reaching right up to the ceiling.

Miss Rosa observed Raymond as he examined it.

'Oh, how bright,' he said.

'Yes,' Miss Rosa said. 'Money for the decorations was sent up by the Perth chapter of the Country Women's Association, after a particularly bruising bout of fundraising, I'm told.'

'Lovely,' Raymond said, deciding it best to err on the side of polite. 'Although, where are the patients? The nurses?'

She turned to him. 'Without a doctor and with the matron off on leave until tomorrow, we had no choice but to keep the doors closed. Anyone sick would have had to be trundled up the road to Port Hedland.' Again, a pointed look, right into him. 'Three hundred kilometres on gravel. Not very pleasant, as you can imagine. Rather lucky nobody came to misfortune, really.'

She led on. They passed through an assortment of rooms, reaching the back where there was a kitchen, a sluice and several small storage areas.

Miss Rosa pushed open the flywire door to show him the back verandah, and the chickens (chickens? In a hospital?), and they caught sight of a bent man, leaning against the back wall, wearing a prune-like shirt and smoking a limp hand-rolled cigarette. He looked up when he saw Raymond.

'Ah, the doctor. Welcome. Barry's my name. Handyman. Maintenance, that type of thing. Keep the generator going.' He dropped the wet butt on the ground. 'And I drive Maude.'

Raymond startled. 'I beg your pardon?'

Barry motioned out to a van, parked at an angle, near where they stood. It vaguely resembled an ambulance, with a handpainted cross on the outside and uneven lettering pronouncing the name underneath.

'Maude. Saved her from the tip. Knew she'd be good for something.'

'More like mort,' he heard Miss Rosa say quietly, brushing down the front of her dress. Raymond grinned and tried to catch her eye, without success.

'That's what I said, Miss Rosa.'

'So you did, Barry. Now if you'll excuse us, we have work to do.'

Miss Rosa turned, and they walked back through to the centre of the building. She led the way to the clanging, echoing room – the core of the hospital. Inside was a rectangular, steel table, bolted to the floor, its heavy stand flanked by levers. In one corner was a brand-new anaesthetic machine, its metallic gleam so bright it almost sparkled. Raymond walked over and lay a hand on it. Threads of sweat trickled down inside his collar and he swept a finger around underneath to let in the possibility of air. Dear God. The whole place smelled antiseptically new, hardly touched, and here it all was waiting for him, so that he could operate, fix the ill, perform procedures he likely did not yet know the names of. He approached the shelves nearby and ran his finger along them, eyeing off their contents: bandages, IV tubing, urinary catheters, white tin bowls holding sets of shiny surgical equipment – clamps, scalpels, a glittering pair of artery forceps. Clenching his fist, he swallowed – a great abrasive gulp – and spoke. 'Right, then. Tomorrow we start?'

'Tomorrow, Dr Filigree.'

And she showed him to his tiny bungalow, situated a few hundred metres from the infirmary, where he spent the first sleepless night of many, waiting for the eastern glow to bellow into existence – the herald of another febrile day.

II

Lou must have fallen asleep at some point, because she wakes in sweat, crooked and stiff. The tin of the hut is creaking, expanding into the day. She picks up her notebook, intrigued to see how much she has written, all those pages of scrawl, the scenes formed during the granite of night when the only light had come flickering from Dave's lantern.

She stretches her limbs and swallows, not that she's got much saliva to get down. Her tongue is sticky – she hasn't drunk anything since the beer last night. Unsteadily, she gets to her feet and walks to the side of the shed, where the tin sheets are peeled back as though hooked by a monstrous can-opener. The sunlight is dazzling and she shades her eyes. She looks out at the unimaginable expanse of red. Even she, with her barrel of words, can't find the right term for redness on this sort of scale. The mounds of spinifex, contrasting the red with their efficient, modest green, cover up swathes of the richly oxidised soil, and they undulate down the slopes, away into the nether. There is almost perfect silence, like a vacuum might sound, she thinks; just the occasional whistle of wind through the low scrub. Above her, where the sky is a fierce unbroken blue, she sees eagles floating in dozy circles, dots of things lazing on thermals.

She wonders when Dave will turn up – she doesn't feel she can go looking for him. Time is likely to pass differently here, and she supposes she'll just have to wait. She calculates, however, being on the back door of Karijini, that the gorges must be close by, and she'd like to be able to wash off the crust of the last few days. Hopping in her car, she's glad to find the water bottles she'd purchased the day before, and she clunks the car into gear.

She drives with only a vague sense of where the gorges might be, based on an assembly of circling birds. The further she travels, the less the roads resemble anything man-made. Nature is reclaiming it all, it seems, first concealing the tracks under dirt and spinifex and then, eventually, rubbing them out altogether.

Arriving at a dry creek bed, she sees she can take the car no further, so she parks and steps out into the vastness. The air is unruffled, still. Occasionally a bird call punctuates the wide silence, but otherwise there is nothing. A bridge crosses the carved-out waterway, although a third of the way along it has collapsed and fragmented. Huge rocky clumps are piled up in front of it as if they have been swept there by some tidal broom. Fanning down the creek bed is debris, coppery red and brown, and she realises it's a diorama forged by the raging of seasons, seasons which are biblical in their excess. She can picture the staggering tropical flashes, the downpours flattening anything not firmly rooted, and then the torrents which course through these trenches one minute and dry up without a trace the next. There's not a cloud overhead. There'll be no divine flood today. Shame, really – she could open her arms to it and let it take her, or at least ravage her clean.

The stones at the bottom of the bed are worn smooth. They take meandering paths across the bed, and there are trails of vermilion mud snaking between the rocks. It's almost beautiful, although she still has trouble labelling anything that way, and she feels a strand of guilt to be standing here, indulgently lost in such scrutiny.

She picks her way to the other side and she continues to walk, stumbling over the odd rock, stopping occasionally under the scrawny trees and taking advantage of their feeble shade. The trees are some type of gum, she thinks. She doesn't know the name of them, these sad spindly things.

There are warning signs, all the way out here.

Go no further without respirator. Toxic waste present.

Where, she wonders? Here it looks like untouched wilderness, all ancient stripes of metallic rock and rusted earth. Are there still fibres floating around? A name comes to her – crocidolite, the most malign of the asbestos fibres, with its deceptive and cartoonish dumbbell shape. She's never seen a case of mesothelioma, and she's not likely to, now. But she'd learned about it. There were lectures in the hospital basement, complete with archaic pathology specimens imprisoned in thick, yellowing perspex boxes. She remembers seeing a ragged, floating pair of lungs, covered in a dense, mustard blanket – pleural plaques, she recalls being taught. What has stuck in her mind is passing round the weighty container and watching fragments float around in the formalin, the disembodied particles of the killer disease. She flinches at the thought, imagining Dave's lungs growing fat sheets of cancer.

She shakes her head and presses on, ignoring the fatigue in her legs.

Just when she thinks she ought to turn back, she comes to a crumbling red slope and she makes a last push. Reaching the top, she can see the edge of the gorge – a dense, green trim. She clambers over until she can see down inside.

Lou is stunned. It seems impossible that something so lush and astounding could exist anywhere, let alone in this desiccated corner of the world. Succulent trees grow straight out of the cliff sides. Where the walls of the gorge plunge to the bottom, they are hung with heavy vegetation.

A new sound fills the air – a trickling noise where water bubbles over rocks and around the scribbly trees festooning the canyon floor. She inhales all of it. The air rising from down inside is cool and smells of honey.

It's not easy to find a path to the bottom; she slips several times, grappling with branches, lowering herself down frontwards, using stringy vines to help her drop. By the time she reaches the bottom, her limbs are streaked with multicoloured layers of dirt. But she has victory. A stream opens out into a pool nearby. There is running icy water, an impossible magic. Lou peels off her caked shirt and shorts and, after a thought, her underwear, and hangs them all on the arch of a tree root. She is raw, naked, silken down here in this other world, and she runs a hand over her skin, her breasts, her stomach. Suddenly she feels truly, gratifyingly lost. She'd like to howl, but she doesn't want to disturb the quiet. When she steps in, the water is so cold she thinks her blood might freeze, and her bare skin feels flayed. She wades in further, until she is waist-deep. The water is so clear she can see the details of her toes. She squats quickly, submerging herself, and her chest contracts. The pain of the cold stops her every cell. Everything stings, like she's been meted out punishment. A penalty for finding such pleasure in the moment. It's a welcome thought. She stays under for as long as she can.

Afterwards she scrambles, shivering, onto a warm rock. She lies there for an age, letting herself toast. The sun has crept overhead, so that the rays enter directly into the chasm, right down on top of her. The sensation is so transporting that her mind drifts, something she's been trying to prevent.

Her father would have loved to see this place. He adored the surprisingness of the earth, the unexpected. He would pick up rocks of unusual colour, or point out odd-shaped insects, and tell her elaborate stories about their origin, which she only discovered later were made up, falsehoods for who knows what reasons. *Imagine things unpacked, Lou*, he'd advise her. He'd had little formal education, leaving school at fourteen (always a different reason for this, she remembers), and then spent the rest of his adult days working in a haberdasher, which, although he said he hated, never stopped him bringing home tales of delight at the foibles of the customers. He had a mind for mathematics and an eye for the absurd, and she had loved him ferociously and she wondered why her mother never could. Every weekend he fished with a vehemence, and those days, when he took Lou out with her younger brother, when they came home smelling of fish guts and berley, with a bucket full of piddly-sized herring which were all hairy little bones and hardly any flesh, yes, those days were the most wonderful memories she had, and now they were seeping back into her like the warmth from the rock.

She stands, angry that she's allowed herself to remember these small joys, when really, what she deserves is retribution.

It's well into the afternoon. The sun has almost passed the angle of the gorge lip, marking time as if it were a gigantic sundial. Rinsing her clothes, she looks beyond the pool and the lips of the water glistening with sunshine, and she can see an enormous gum tree, bisecting the gorge floor into two paths. It is a colossal thing, with a thick, creamy trunk. In fact, it is two trunks – a pair of trees intertwined around and into each other forming one massive column. The soft folds of its bark are like old skin, and the whole tree is bent and aged. It looks like two lovers have become entombed in each other. Lou shakes her head and pulls on her wrung-out clothes, exasperated at these sentimental thoughts. She needs to get moving, knowing she'd better leave before she too is stuck out here forever.

By the time she manages to climb back out of the gorge and pick her way back to the car, her chest and head are skittery. She wonders if Dave will be waiting for her. Her limbs still buzz from the crashing elements, and she guns the car back to the hut, her foot forcing down the accelerator. She jumps out as soon as she arrives and strides inside. It's empty. Dave has not come. She lets out a quick breath. What was she expecting?

Compared to the clean air of the outdoors, the inside of the hut has the faint whiff of diesel, and the burnt, material odour of dust and ash. It smells of extinction.

Her blankets are heaped up, just as she left them. She lumps over to the pile and reaches under the top for where she'd left her notebook, but discovers it's not there. And then she spies it, behind the cold kerosene lantern. Next to it is a can of lemonade, beads of chilled condensation sliding down the outside, and this is sitting on top of a note. She picks up the can and reads the message through the fuzzed wet ring left behind. The writing is childlike, the words misspelled, the a's printed backwards.

Glad you got out. I'll be back tonight. Care for dinner?

She picks up her journal to see that the paper Dave used was torn from the middle of it. Had he read her outpourings from the night before? She doesn't know how she should feel. Her shores invaded, she thinks, by a trespasser of whom she can't yet see the cut.

Looking around, she discovers that Dave has left a number of other items for her. She could be colonising Mars. A torch, a box of matches, a packet of gingernut biscuits. A container of baby wipes!

Lou picks up one of the blankets, walks outside and shakes it down. Her feet crush the stubble of spinifex poking through the pebbly apron of ground. Overhead the sky has begun to mute – the blue is less glaring, and a gentle wind laps in, making a curl of the mottled grey tin shriek as it flexes its spine.

Settling back, she arranges the things around her, cracks the cold offering, takes a swig, and opens the notebook to the next page. The words have already started to come. Although Dave may have read it, this story is all hers, and she will keep it that way, clutched up close – a world of her very own.

Opening Day

By morning, the inside of Raymond's box of a house had heated up, as if oven notches were being cranked, one by inexorable one. He'd fought with the windows during the night, trying to open them as wide as he could, but this had simply let in a flotilla of flying creatures – midges, mosquitoes, flies – all of which were now claiming the interior as won.

The night before he had unpacked his farcical belongings. Two pairs of shoes, brogues. Four long-sleeved white shirts. Nightwear. Three pairs of trousers, two of them thick, scratchy serge, and one pinstriped. He shook his head. These had been entirely practical for his ward work back home and for blending into rows of austere clinics, but here? He'd hung his coat in the doorframe, where it gave him a start every time he saw it. Three books. Yes, three books only, he discovered with dismay. Pliny, Descartes and his volume of poetry by Keats. They'll be a great help, he thought, and he glanced around before tiptoeing over to his shoebox of a closet, secreting them under his nightshirt. It was time to live without a shadow.

Raymond waved away a lazy fly and blotted sweat from his face with a threadbare towel he had found folded for him on the end of his narrow bed. He'd only left his hard bed and cold kitchenette table of home three weeks ago, when the name of Wittenoom was simply a label on a map. Maps were deceiving things, on their flat, cheerful paper; the names of distant places printed in unvarying fonts, separated by nothing more than an octave of a piano, but in reality as alien as planets in space. And now he was here, on the other side of comprehension.

He fussed around in the swelter of the small living area (actually, it was a mistake to label the layout such. This whole house was simply a single room, pretending to be several; a cramped bedroom, an area for a table and sink, and a tacked-on outhouse). He was delaying the short walk to the hospital, feeling the glare of the spotlight already upon his face. Raymond splashed water from the cold tap (which was not cold, and never likely to be, he realised – it would stay brown, warm and sluggish) over his cheeks for the third time, and then finalised the dressing process, checking his appearance in the fly-specked mirror in the corner. He placed his stethoscope into the side pocket of his suitcoat and a notebook in his portmanteau. At the last minute he went back and fished out his three books, thinking he could find a nonchalant place for them in his office. And when he was solemnly ready, he tucked the bag under his arm and crunched his way across the calculous road, up the front path to the hospital.

Resting his hand on the gate, he turned to look at the expanse of the town and the wild beyond of the Pilbara.

The spray of ramshackle buildings (how on earth was this called a town?) looked as if they were huddling together for protection from the desert, which spread to the horizons on each point of the compass. And the red of it. He'd never seen a colour like it. It was staggering. He took a great lungful of the burning north Australian air, and tried to find some sort of perspective for the red. The soil, kneaded with its minerals and metals, was a mind-boggling red. It was the red of fire. Red the colour of magma, of blood. A red he would need to learn about. The red of forever.

He looked down to see a flowery sprig, an unexpected spritz of white, which he picked, thinking it would suit the light in his office, and he then stepped into the hospital.

On the desk was a watery cup of tea in a chipped mug. Next to it a plate of toast – chewy slabs of rubber smeared with jam. He fished out several small bugs that had suicided in the sugar.

Presuming Miss Rosa had left it for him, he began earnestly working his way through the breakfast. He could hear commotion beyond the door leading into the hospital. Voices, the clanging of metal trays, footsteps. Looking over at the bookshelves, he noticed that they weren't entirely empty. A pile of journals was tucked into the corner of the bottom shelf. He walked over and picked one up. *Advances in Australian Gynaecologic Surgery, 1958*, and then the one underneath it, *A Year of Virchowian Pathology, 1960–1961*. Not greatly useful, he thought, but he brought this last one back to his desk, anyway. The gaunt little flower gave off the unexpected smell of salt. An intrusion of the sea where there ought not be a trace.

Raymond began to plan the day. Was there a standard for the configuring of ward rounds and consultations? Opening up the empty notebook, and titling the first page *Schedule for the running of Wittenoom Hospital*, he realised, in this instant, that he was truly free to begin again. Nobody knew of the man he was a month ago, his career hastily abandoned, the grip on a boy lost. He would meet the staff today and assure them that he was up to date with the latest in methods and process. Despite his lack of reference books (a temporary void, he was confident), he would demonstrate at least a sound knowledge base and a commanding tone of leadership. Once and for all, he would expel the pebbles of apprehension that clogged his gullet and step into this new role. He had the health of this adolescent town in his hands, now – he would not let the good people of Wittenoom down. This was his moment.

The moment, however, was short-lived. Shouts erupted from behind the office, puncturing this reverie with a swift and striking finality. The door swung open and Miss Rosa appeared.

'Doctor. You'd better come quick. Mr Italiano's been brought in. I've called for the matron. She should be back this morning.'

Miss Rosa held the door open as he hurried through, trying not to stumble.

Inside the first of the wards, sitting next to the middle bed, was a mass of a man, hunched over and clutching at his chest. Two nurses in blindingly white uniforms were fussing over him, and a rotund woman was squashed close in, one of her hands on the man's shoulder, the other aggressively smoothing his forehead. The small, twittering congregation stepped aside as he walked in.

'The doctor. Thank God,' the woman said. 'Please, look at my husband.'

'Of course,' Raymond said, and he reached out to grip onto Mr Italiano's pulse, more to steady himself and collect his scattered thoughts, rather than for any good clinical reason.

'What's wrong?' he said. 'Chest pain, is it?'

Mr Italiano nodded, his face contorted and blanched.

'Just started this morning. An hour ago,' Mrs Italiano babbled. 'He's been having little ones for a month, but,' and she reached over to put a hand to her husband's cheek, 'we think he waited until this morning, until you were here, to have the big one.'

The patient smiled weakly and the nurses began unbuttoning his shirt.

Raymond clenched his toes to make sure he remained standing. How could it be this hot so early in the morning? The searing room was silent, except for the rasping sound of Mr Italiano's breathing and the shuffling of his wife's feet.

'Steel band,' was all Mr Italiano could get out.

Raymond nodded. Myocardial infarction. It had to be. He extracted his stethoscope from his pocket and buried the bell of it into the great Italian thickets growing over the front of the man's chest.

While listening intently, he became aware of a woman striding towards them then coming to a dramatic stop. He pulled the earpieces out. In front of him stood a tall, angry-looking woman, with egg-coloured hair and eczematous patches in the crooks of both arms. She was wearing a stiff uniform the colour of cream just turned.

'Dr Filigree, I am presuming.' She pushed aside one of the nurses, and began to manhandle Mr Italiano up onto the bed. 'Girls, please. Get him up.' The two nurses obeyed, one getting behind the man, the other assisting with his legs. Miss Rosa stepped in and helped to push him up onto the mattress, and she spoke as she did so.

'Dr Filigree. This is Margaret. The matron.'

'Why wasn't I called sooner?' She spoke to the cadre in general. 'I arrived back this morning. You know I am to be alerted immediately if anybody sick comes in.' She looked directly at Raymond. 'We have a policy.' She reached over to continue undressing Mr Italiano. 'For good reason,' she added.

'Thank you, Matron. An excellent policy I'm sure. But right now, I'd be grateful if somebody could get some aspirin.' He spoke to one of the girls. 'Nurse, could you do that?' As you mean to continue, he reminded himself. 'I'm sorry, what was your name?'

'Candace, sir. I mean, Doctor.'

'Nurse Randall is her name, Dr Filigree,' Margaret said.

'Thank you, Nurse Randall. Could I also trouble you to get the ECG machine?'

Miss Rosa stepped in. 'I shall collect that for you.'

'Most kind.' He smiled at Miss Rosa. 'And, Matron, oxygen?'

Margaret hesitated a moment, as if wanting to say something, but then spun and marched out of the ward. Raymond returned to Mr Italiano, whose forehead was soaked in glistening sweat.

'It's likely to be a heart attack,' Raymond told the couple.

Mrs Italiano clapped a hand to her mouth.

'We'll make sure, with the electrocardiograph.' God, he hoped he could read it. He'd been quite accomplished with their interpretation for a while, but after the boy, after all those words were said and everybody had watched him like a hawk, he'd lost confidence. His head reeled through knowledge, lectures. Certainly, he'd seen a number of patients with myocardial infarctions, although it was often from a distance in a large teaching hospital whilst swinging past in formation amongst a troupe of other resident medical officers, trying to avoid the humiliation of being singled out for questioning by the tyrant of a consultant. During those days he had learned to stoop, making himself invisible in a crowd.

Margaret wheeled in the heavy oxygen tank and fitted the stiff rubber mask to Mr Italiano. She then pulled the ECG machine off Miss Rosa, and covered Mr Italiano with the leads and electrodes until he was strung up like Christmas lights. Producing a wilted piece of paper, she handed it to Raymond. He held up the thing to the blazing light, trying to decipher it.

'Yes. A heart attack. A big one.'

Mrs Italiano gasped. 'It couldn't be the asbestos dust, could it? He comes home covered in the stuff. And his breathing's got so bad, recently.' She looked up at Raymond. 'I've been trying to tell—'

Mr Italiano shot out a hand and clamped onto his wife's arm. His colour had begun to return with the oxygen. 'Shh, Nancy. Dr Filigree doesn't need to hear about that.'

'But the respirators! Why can't they—'

'Nancy!'

Raymond was preoccupied, however, trying to remember the latest experimental protocol that they had been using for coronary thrombosis. If only he had a formulary. Finally, thanks to a squib of recollection, he said, 'Matron! Please prepare some heparin for infusion. We need to dissolve the clot.'

Margaret looked stony. She paused for several seconds before she replied slowly. 'Doctor. This is the Pilbara.' She stood with her legs slightly apart, her arms again crossed. She said nothing more.

The spark sputtered, his trump card played before the game even began. They didn't have it? What else was in his vaults? The treatment of ischaemic heart disease was all so experimental back home, nothing proven, everything empirical. Quinidine? Nitroglycerin? Would they have any of these things here? If they did he'd be unmasked, having no idea of the dosing. Best just to carry on.

'Of course. Doesn't work so well, anyway.' He folded the ECG in half.

Candace handed Mr Italiano the aspirin and a glass of water.

Over the next half-hour, as they hovered round, Mr Italiano settled. His chest pain abated, leaving only a residue of shallow panting and a dry mouth, for which he requested small sips of water amongst expressing his gratitude to the doctor.

Margaret reminded them all that in her experience, most of these got better by themselves, anyway, and that the last time they had a patient with a heart attack she had managed quite nicely on her own, thank you very much. And then she brushed off the girls, instructing them to go and make sure every bed was in order.

Raymond was simultaneously relieved and reduced, unsure whether he'd sold out for show. But no matter. His first patient had now recovered.

Once Raymond had reassured the grateful husband and wife that Mr Italiano had avoided catastrophe, he excused himself in order to return to his office. He invited Margaret to join him, so that they could together work through the strategies and procedures that would be needed to run the hospital. She replied that she would be too busy this morning, having a lot to catch up on after four days of leave, but that they could perhaps do so later in the day. Miss Rosa quietly watched the exchange.

Raymond retired to his office, removing his heavy coat. He arranged it over the back of the chair. Sweat had soaked through his shirt, and he picked up one of the journals and fanned himself. It cooled him. The Virchowian Pathology might have its uses after all.

He set out several items on the desk – a pen, his notebook and a small clock found in the drawers. In the bottom of these, he discovered a pile of blank death certificates and he shuddered. After the agony of the last he never wanted to fill out another of these; where he'd written those lonely lines of script, the deed completed in the ashen hours of night, on another continent, in a different life. No. As much as he disliked clichés, being a man who had read widely in literature and philosophy, he knew that this here was his clean slate. And onto this clean slate he would write a new story, and he would never, ever have to look back.

Knocking this time, Miss Rosa again appeared at the rear door of the office. Raymond hurried over to keep it open for her, and she stepped through, balancing a tray bearing another cup, full to sloshing, and a small plate of biscuits. She placed it down on the desk and set out the rheumy-looking tea. The biscuits made a wooden clunk on the plate, and she took her time arranging the items on the desk.

How much could she see into him, Raymond wondered, him sitting at this empty desk, with his English shoes and his sweat-stained shirt?

'I wouldn't worry too much about Matron,' Miss Rosa said. 'She'll get used to you. They all will.'

He hadn't thought of things this way, from this angle. It had seemed instead a matter of him having to adjust to the unfamiliarity of all of them.

'This is very kind of you.' Raymond gestured to the offerings, but meaning the words.

'It's understandable there will be a few hiccoughs early on. There always are.'

Only he didn't want hiccoughs. Hiccoughs, and worse, were the hallmark of the man he had left behind, not the director of Wittenoom Hospital.

'The matron,' he asked. 'Does she have a problem with my being here?'

'You have to understand, Dr Filigree. She has got very used to running things her own way. Now we have you, our first permanent appointment, from one of the best medical schools in London.' She picked up the wilted blossom on the desk and examined it. 'I'll find a vase for this.'

Raymond looked down. They certainly had been his words on his job application. Not so much true, more a necessity. But it was a reality that he was free to grow into now that he was here.

And he spent the afternoon doing just that. Raymond wrote out great lists of equipment that he would need, and outlines for the coming days and months, all with the purpose of providing care for Wittenoom's infirm. He planned consulting sessions and educational opportunities for the nursing staff. He wondered whether he could even write a regular newsletter for the people of the town, a health gazette of sorts. Walking through each of the rooms in the hospital, he made notes and imagined uses for every part of that infirmary. His imagination, admittedly, was limited, having been honed in the bleak and archaic corridors of England. However, he had the sense of these days being early, every possibility ahead of him alight.

Margaret only managed to give him ten minutes of her time (and not fruitful ones at that), but still, Raymond realised for the first time that perhaps he had control over his future, and with enough determination, he could mould it the way he wanted. Maybe everything would be alright after all.

A few patients whirled in and out of the hospital that afternoon, none with terribly much wrong. Raymond wondered whether some had come simply to see what new curiosity had turned up in their wild town. Several presented with shortness of breath and hacking coughs, and Raymond's stethoscope was put to frequent use, but nothing posed too great a challenge. He detained people at length, taking the opportunity to learn as much as he could about them and their ills, and in turn testing out his novel ideas about the application of medicine.

'Oh yes,' he said to a rather confused-looking bulk of a man, who complained of an increasingly worrying relationship between exertion and his ability to breathe. 'I wonder if we, in medicine, have been looking at things all wrong.'

Raymond pulled out one earpiece of his stethoscope, so as to talk while he auscultated. 'And instead of the brain of man, the mind of the clinician, trying to reduce the human body in illness to cold, explicable, ordered events and talk over it, we ought to be listening instead, allowing the body to converse with us, as it were. We just need to know how to hear. Even this thing,' Raymond pulled out the other earpiece, holding the whole contraption in his hands, 'designed by the master Laennec, was to hear the lungs *talk* to us. Whispering pectoriloquy, he coined it. A gentle conversation between lungs and physician.'

Margaret stood close by whilst he consulted, looking livid.

Another miner, his lungs bubbling with each breath, was escorted out by the matron while Raymond was mid-sentence. 'It's about respecting and admiring the ferocity, the complexity of humans in the state of disease,' he called out.

Before leaving for the day, Raymond checked on Mr Italiano, who was sitting on the side of his bed, playing Scrabble with his wife. She looked up at him and beamed.

'No more chest pain?' Raymond asked.

'Just a little niggle here and there, Doctor.'

They chatted for fifteen minutes or so. Raymond asked about Mr Italiano's job, the mines, the town. Mrs Italiano answered many of the questions, proud of her husband and his role as mine supervisor. Much loved by all the men, she told Raymond several times. Raymond, in turn, expounded on the wonders of the heart. What a pleasure to sit here doing this, he thought.

Raymond spied Margaret walking by, a small gaggle of white in pursuit. He called out, 'Matron, I wonder if I might ...'

She swung around, and the phalanx marched up to him.

'Yes, Doctor?' Margaret stood stiffly in front of him. The nurses looked down.

'I am wondering who will stay on duty tonight. Perhaps you would? To keep an eye on Mr Italiano?'

Margaret continued to stare at him.

He heard himself prattling on, about his hopes to have twenty-four-hour staffing, regular patient checks and so on. Margaret slung back at him that she hadn't become matron to do night shift. She pointed at another of the nurses and said she supposed Beatrice would do – she was by far the most junior, and this was her first proper job. She could use the experience.

And with that all settled, Raymond took his leave. Miss Rosa had prepared a small dinner for him, packaged up so that he could take it back to his bungalow. Handing it to him, she nodded and stood aside.

He passed through the gate and stopped, halted by the immensity spread out in front of him. Down the hill, amongst the medley of buildings, scattered lights were fizzing into existence. It was fascinating, all these people, going about their domestic business in this brash, teenage town, as though it were quite normal. Which it was, he guessed, for them.

As if a climactic pendulum were swinging back, the air had begun to rapidly cool. And unlike the gentle English twilights he was used to, where the colours would change their hues in a meander, here the sun dropped like a stone. It was the beginning of the dry season, Miss Rosa had told him. No such thing as winter and summer here. As far as he could understand, in these discombobulated seasons, it was fryingly hot during the day, but then the nights turned black in an eyeblink, causing even the silhouettes of the trees to shiver. And then, yes and then, the stars would begin to light up, one by one, burning their position onto this blue-black canvas. He stood and watched this marvel, holding onto his container of food. It was a phenomenon so intense, so overwhelmingly visceral, that it had the unexpected effect of anchoring him, giving him material berth in the world. There must be a sliver of hope for him in a place like this. The cool gentle eddies rippled around him, and he allowed himself the smallest slice of pleasure at where the oceans and roads and inconceivable distances had brought him. He set off for his bungalow to rest up for tomorrow. Tomorrow, he was sure, would be a good day.

III

Dave arrives full of apology as the current of heat ebbs. 'Been busy. Sorry.'

Lou doesn't ask. What could anybody be busy with out here?

They both look down at Lou's notebook where it lies open, more of its pages crammed with her hurried sentences. Skating around its presence glaring up at them, Lou instead tells Dave about the wonders of the gorge, the ghostly beauty of the double-trunked tree, the unthinkable cold of the water.

'See?' he says. 'It's got you, too.'

She smiles and makes a half-shrug, and he extends an arm, gesturing for her to come along – his invitation to dinner.

'It's going to be a beautiful night,' he says as they walk out into the oncoming dusk. 'But then again, it always is.'

They stroll a short way without speaking. The air feels complex, with gentle rips of warmth coiling around her before heading off for the day. Dave is wearing a different shirt from yesterday. It's cleaner, and she sees that he has clipped the wiry edges of his beard. When she strays close she detects the scent of fruit. Peach, maybe, warm from the tree.

Ambling across the patchwork of the old town, they avoid knolls of rubble and clutter, passing several rust-veined water tanks listing on threadbare grass and sidestepping planks of rotting wood. Crippled tractor parts circle a blackened patch on the ground, like they are having some sort of meeting for retired engine parts. She imagines these dregs of habitation positing their own agenda, now that the people have gone. The air smells particulate, somehow alive, and the temperature is perfect, just for those few moments of in-between.

She still can't see anything that resembles civilisation, yet. It's the vestigial lip of everything Lou has ever known, having grown up in the timidity of the suburbs – a new wilderness, sown in the shadow of people's exit. She asks about the names of the trees.

'Most of them are bloodwoods. Eucalypts. Get 'em all through here, all the way out to the desert. They ooze blood when they're cut, poor wounded buggers. Excellent sap, though, bush medicine, great for healing. The Aboriginal people, they use it. They got this land right. They know what works out here. Always have. Shame nobody's bloody listening.'

It seems the vernacular is the same all over, she thinks, made up or not. There is deafness everywhere.

'Feisty things, aren't they,' she says, pulling a leaf off a low-hanging branch and scrunching it up to her nose. It's tough, with sharp edges that don't tear, and it gives off the smell of wintergreen, which remains on her fingers. They are, that's for sure, thriving with a scrappy determination despite the shambles around them.

III

Two ten-gallon drums, glittering with brown rust and corroded through in ragged holes, have curious tentacles of grass running through them. She points this out to Dave, and they laugh at the idea of a turf-octopus lifting the barrels, preparing to hurl them at anyone who walks by.

'People were pretty diligent back then,' Dave says. 'They seeded lawns and planted flowerbeds. A lot of them wanted to make it look like home. Some brought statues up from Perth. You can find the odd lion's head around here, if you look.'

She scouts around, wanting to see ears or limbs or other ornate appendages scattered among the plots, imagining she'd feel rather a kinship with them.

'But they never could,' he continues. 'Turn it into home. Especially the migrant workers. They were completely displaced. A bunch of lost souls.'

'Where did they hail from? The migrants?' Lou asks.

'Italy mostly.' He stops suddenly and picks up a rock. Facing away from her, he lobs it, and it whistles through the silence. He continues, but talks into the distance, his words carrying off in the dark. 'There were hundreds of them up here during the boom.'

'A boom? Really?' She's self-conscious voicing her ignorance about this place while walking among its catacombs, treading on the scraps and the discards of the long gone, maybe even the dead.

'Yeah, not the explosion sort.' He faces her, and Lou hears the change in his voice. He is speaking with an urgency, which is strange in this place that has turned its back on ordinary time. 'Although that would have been a better, quicker death for some of the buggers who mined up here.

No, the asbestos boom was twenty-three long, miserable years. Not quite the glamour of the gold rush. Not at all. Still, it was pretty crazy in the day. People gravitated here from all over the world, most of them under false pretences. And the Italians, they travelled across in droves, expecting some sort of paradise, but found the dusty shitter of hell, instead. The land out here, sure it's beautiful, but the mines were worse than misery's arse. Some of them gave up as soon as they could on that fool of a life and went back to their own country to die.'

'How many?' Lou asks. 'How many would have died because of the mines?' She thinks back to what the guy in the service station said. About this being Chernobyl. Australia's own apocalyptic wasteland.

'Nobody knows,' Dave says, and they start walking again. 'Especially not about the foreign workers. No one's doing a body count.' He shakes his head. 'There's even a cemetery in Italy that the locals call Little Wittenoom.'

Dave stops and puts a hand on her arm. His touch gives her a shock, an electric memory of human contact.

He points out to the west. 'Watch this.'

They stand still and follow the sun melting into the horizon.

'It's like modern bloody art,' he says.

The colours change so fast it does look like a performance. She wonders why she hasn't before appreciated these details – now that Dave has pointed it out, she can see the palette of ochres and vermilions crashing into each other, transforming the canvas in salvos. And, in the space of ten minutes, the sky is wiped clean, leaving a satin blue-black. Such a display is foreign to her, so unique that it reminds her that she's a thousand kilometres away from everything she knows, as well as everything she has done.

As they again pick up pace, Dave points out the parts of the skeleton that once had formed Wittenoom town, some of them concrete; slabs and foundations and remnants of walls, others simply memory. Movie cinema, bowls club, soccer pitch, he tells her as they pass.

They come up to a row of half-standing sheds, and when they walk a little further, Dave says, 'Welcome to my pad.'

It's a ramshackle house with sagging walls. The yard is crammed with rusting objects – shovels, tyres, fuel drums, knotted fencing wire, the metal intestines of machines. An ancient caravan is parked off to one side with its steps pulled down and a light on inside. It's one of those bean-shaped vans, once silver, now a mottled grey, and designed for a single person – a comical thing, like it should be trailing along behind a circus. Lou realises that this is where he lives, and the house is not a house at all, but a shack full of junk.

He motions for her to sit on the stairs. 'I've got some dinner for you.'

He squeezes past her into the van, and comes back out with a foil covered plate. Pulling back the crinkled tin, he reveals a small pie, collapsed in the middle with a puddle of crimson sauce in the well. It smells meaty and delicious.

A broken-off, rusted drum base is nearby, and Dave proceeds to shepherd an entire bonfire inside, growing it from nothing but spindly sticks. It billows into a huge crackling organism, with smoky wisps twisting out from the top of the flames. Lou bites into her pie, watching this outdoor hearth flicker. Through the orange braids of the blaze, she sees a motorbike leaning against the toppling fence.

God, she hates motorbikes. Nothing but devastation, they are. The pie turns dry in her mouth. What if Dave were to have an accident out here? Who would pick up the abraded, bleeding pieces? She squeezes her eyes shut. Out of an empty sky she sees him with a crushed chest, gasping for oxygen, just like the poor guy during her last shift at the big hospital down south. The brutal, broken pieces of a man. They're loathsome, these images coming back uninvited, intruders out here in the quiet.

That last shift, the one down in Perth. The one at least a month after the girl, after everything had become overwhelming, when even turning up for work had been close to impossible, let alone being in charge of a team managing a critically ill trauma. When what had been previously routine had grown into a raging monster of fear and panic, taking hold of her in its teeth and tossing her about like prey.

She remembers this one clearly, the details coming back precise and vicious. A young man on a motorbike, sideswiped proficiently and unseen by a distracted commuter. Routine. Yes, it should have been. But by then, tentative questions were being asked about Lou; the letters and the complaints and the murmurs in corridors were banking up, but still, *she had been so good at this sort of thing.*

Within minutes of his arrival, the boy was trying to haemorrhage his way out of this life and into the next, while Lou fumbled around in her woolly head attempting to locate the right decisions and commands to steer the team. With the boy's life bleeding out she watched him, they all watched him, with his squashed head and skew limbs and gulping breath, this scooped-up and mangled mess that needed her to take charge, and she just stood there blurting out anything, no real instructions, the louder the better, to the junior doctors and the nursing staff, raising her voice while the beeps from the monitors became faster and more erratic and ominously lower in tone. A nervous confusion overtook the assembled team, who were fairly practised at running these things without too much direction, and they had managed to get to work on the boy, minus any great sense from Lou.

Lou, the one they used to look to, the one who had been able to breathe life into those otherwise destined for death, was now the one who stood frozen with little more than a croak and nonsense talk coming from her mouth. The team murmured perplexed words and eventually somebody else senior stepped in, tapping Lou on the shoulder. It was suggested that she might be better off leaving the resuscitation room, maybe she could go and speak to the family, tell them that their boy was critical.

She did not look back as the crowd swarmed around the boy, shutting her out. She did not want to see another life go swirling down the drain, along with the blood and tears and froth from dying lungs, knowing that once again it may well be her omissions that were preening themselves to stamp the death warrant. Because even though this pulverised boy looked nothing like the little girl from a month prior, the thought that somehow it was the same was overpowering. How all the cases in the interim felt the same, and that it was her own choices that had the ability to rip out the marrow of life, just like that, without her even knowing.

She had turned the corner to head to the relatives' room, where the family of the boy would have been sitting on couches, clutching cold polystyrene cups, awaiting word, any word, about their son, but instead, Lou had veered off into the pharmacy to find herself little pills and vials of assistance. When she finally returned to the main department, the boy had been packaged off to the intensive care unit. The remaining staff watched her without speaking. And within hours she had finished her shift there for the last time, leaving via the director's office, where he had spoken bluntly to her. He hadn't said much, just referred her to the piles of notes on the desk. *You need to go elsewhere for a bit. We understand it's been difficult for you after what happened, but you have to get yourself together if you're going to continue being a doctor. Port Hedland,* he had said, *has an opening, it's all been arranged,* and she remembers something about counselling, a card given to her with a psychologist's name, which she had dropped in a bin on the way out.

Dave is watching her, and she knows her brow is furrowed, her jaw clenched. He sits down, squeezing next to her on the narrow steps, picking up a fat stick off the ground.

'If you don't mind me asking, do you have anyone at home?' He has a slight stutter, perhaps just hesitation. 'A boyfriend? Not being nosy, I just wondered.'

Lou shakes her head. More collateral, that was. She'd been so spooked and defensive that it was no surprise that Sam, the guy who had lasted longer than any before, had left. Did it nicely, in a letter, but she read through his euphemistic words. He had described the situation perfectly – she could picture her aura of barbs, damaging anyone who walked too close.

'What about you? Do you have family? Children?' Lou asks. 'Although, I guess this isn't the place to host happy families.'

He smiles. 'No. Had my chance at that. I was engaged for a bit. We – she was pregnant. You know what it's like.' He looks down at the ground, rolling the stick between his hands. She doesn't. No idea at all. 'Are you sure you want to hear? It's not great listening,' he says.

Lou softly touches his arm. It's a great woody plank of a forearm, and the feel of it surprises her in a way she cannot understand. 'Please. It's been a long time since I've heard anybody's story but my own rubbish one.'

'If you're sure, then.'

Lou nods.

'Before I came up here, I had a different life. I had a bit of work here and there. Not much, but enough. And a girlfriend. Lacey was her name. She wasn't so bad, not really. When she got pregnant, we decided we'd get married. Do the right thing.' He pauses, and the pattern of flames chequers across his face. 'But I don't know, she was only halfway along, before we had the chance to get hitched, and something went wrong. We'd been out for the night, over at Mum and Dad's. We didn't see them much, it was always too hard. They were in the process of splitting up and it'd been a pretty tense night – it usually was with them. Lacey'd been mad, cross at something, I can't even remember what. She'd had a few drinks. We knew it wasn't great, but you couldn't ever tell Lacey what to do. When we got home there was a lot of shouting – I remember that. Then she woke up in the night wet from her waters breaking.' He takes a long breath in and leaves a gap between his words. 'Managed to get her into the hospital just in time for our son to slide out. Blue as the sky he was. Machines did the living for him for a few days, but then the docs, they were chucking the word "futile" round like they said it every day at breakfast, and just when Lacey's milk came in they turned off the ventilators. She refused to give him a name. Went a bit crazy and we couldn't ever go back. I'm not even sure now how hard I tried. Plus, I wondered whether it was somehow supposed to be. The sins of the father and all that. It was pretty soon after that I headed up to this place.'

He is frowning, as if the memories are still fresh, unexamined. Lou again briefly lays her hand over his trunk of a forearm, and then retracts it. 'Sorry,' she says, although she means about the horrors of life in general.

'It's OK,' he says, and absently strokes his arm where she has touched it.

'But why up here?' Lou asks. 'And for so long?'

Dave rises, towering over her. 'I want to show you something. Maybe it'll explain things. I don't know,' and he steps inside the van.

While he's gone, her own scenes creep back. The story's writing itself in her head now, but it's shifty and slick and as fugitive as morning dreams, disappearing if she tries to look at it head-on. She's no longer sure who it's about, if she knew at all. She wills herself to remember the images so that they can spill forth later on.

When he comes out he's carrying a tattered shopping bag, straining at the handles. He sits back down and pulls out a file, holding it carefully, as though he's cupping a flame in his hands, and then he lays it out for her, so that she can have a chance to see. At a glance she realises it is heavy history, the deep roots of the place. She delays focusing on the cover, unsure if she's ready to witness it.

Sadly, However, It Was Not

A fierce hammering shook Raymond's front door. He woke, sodden with sweat, disorientated. His heart was pounding, yanked as he was from a short, vivid dream. It sounded like the knock of a policeman with very bad news. He looked at his watch. Four-thirty am.

'Dr Filigree. Wake up.' It was a man's voice, shouting.

Raymond stumbled to the door and wrenched it open. Barry stood there, beckoning for him to follow.

'There's trouble. You need to come.'

Raymond grabbed his suitcoat, pulled it on over his pyjamas, and floundered into his shoes. Both men then broke into an ungainly trot across the short path to the hospital. The infirmary was lit up, all lights blazing.

'Mr Italiano, apparently,' Barry said, as they navigated the office to the wards. Panic incised Raymond as he made his way through. Beatrice stood next to Mr Italiano's bed looking brittle, her face icing white.

Raymond froze. The dead man's fist was clutched up underneath his sternum.

'What?' was all Raymond managed.

'I'm so sorry. I must have been asleep.' Beatrice began to cry. 'And when I came over to check, I found him like this.'

The pebbles clanked over in Raymond's gullet, rocking him off balance. He picked up Mr Italiano's other, already stiff hand to feel for the pulse. Of which there was not.

'Oh. Yes. Dead. That's right,' he responded, as if answering a question. He heard footsteps and looked up to see Miss Rosa walking towards them. A moment later the voice of Margaret could be heard, ferociously making its way up the corridor. Beatrice was flapping around, fussing with the sheets, wiping her eyes with the back of her hand.

'Ah, good morning, Matron.' Raymond was still holding Mr Italiano's wrist, feeling the persistent absence of a pulse.

'What the sweet hell of a good morning? What is this?' she thundered, then turned to Beatrice. 'What happened? Pull yourself together.'

Beatrice was unable to get much out through her sobs. It seemed that the preference for a blink of sleep rather than regular blood pressure and pulse checks might be to blame. Margaret then faced Raymond as he tidily placed the deceased man's hand by his side.

'Well. This is excellent. That's your first patient, then. Dead.'

'Yes, it's terribly shocking, but—'

'You'll have to do an autopsy, you know.' Margaret stared at him. 'That's your job.'

'What, will I?' Raymond asked.

'Today,' she said.

Miss Rosa stood close by, her hand resting on Beatrice's shoulder. Her touch seemed to settle the girl. Raymond looked over at the nurse. The poor thing. As she was new, Raymond guessed she would not have faced the shock of death before, in all its motionless, unbreathing reality.

'Today?' he asked.

'The heat, Doctor,' Margaret enunciated slowly, as if she were explaining something to a child. 'I'm sure you can work out what that does to a body.'

At this Beatrice began once more to cry. Margaret reached out and gripped Beatrice's arm without changing expression, causing the girl to swallow back into silence. Raymond wanted to reach out himself, to console the young woman, perhaps give her hand a reassuring pat, tell her that this horror of seeing a body webbed with rigor mortis, stiff and sightless, with the addition of feeling that one had a hand in the life extinguished, that these things would fade with time and experience. Lose its brutality. But he didn't know how to start, and certainly didn't want to appear irresolute or improper in front of the matron, in front of all of them. Plus, it would be a lie.

'Beatrice,' Raymond said quietly. 'Sometimes, these things can't be prevented. After a heart attack. Arrhythmias, valve dysfunction, and so on.' Half-pages of textbooks some time ago read were reaching out to him; lists, sequelae, complications.

'So on?' Margaret asked, looking hard-boiled. 'Well, I guess that is what your autopsy is for, now isn't it. You'll have to put something legal on the death certificate.'

What was she suggesting? Raymond looked down at his hands. It felt as though his deficiencies were once again opening their jaws, disarticulated and wide, ready to ingest him. It's true, he couldn't be sure. He searched his palms for answers. Where was his finest-medical-school-in-London education now? Should he have foreseen this? Prevented it? God only knew. But he could not asphyxiate, not this soon after the last. He straightened and started anew.

'Then would someone be kind enough to find me a stretcher?'

Nobody answered. The only sound came from Miss Rosa, who appeared to have resumed her duties. She had taken the tray that had contained Mr Italiano's demolished last meal and placed it down by the door with a clatter, after which she had picked up a broom and was now sweeping, her shoes making a clipped noise on the concrete floor. Beatrice swayed. Barry had walked off, grumbling that moving dead bodies was not in his job description.

A buzzing noise interrupted the stand-off, culminating in a quiet 'pop' overhead.

Margaret grumbled. A twist of yolky hair drooped out from under her cap. 'Somebody get Barry, would they? These lights are always blowing.'

Raymond waited a confused moment then started again. 'A stretcher? To move the deceased? The annex behind my office ought to be suitable. It has a table and a small sink.' He squeezed his hands together. 'For the necropsy, I should add.'

Miss Rosa spoke up. 'I'm not sure there is one. A stretcher, that is.' She leaned on her broom. 'Perhaps you might consider doing an inventory of anything you need, at a later date of course, and I would be happy to send it on for requisitioning.'

'Oh, I see.' Raymond scanned around the room, glancing wildly into each corner. 'Sheets, then. Sheets will have to do.'

And after a graceless fifteen minutes, Mr Italiano was twirled up like a macabre bon-bon, the spiralled ends clutched by the unhappy grunting group, and the body was heaved, slipping and jolting down the corridor, and installed in the storage room just behind Raymond's office.

The news reached Mrs Italiano before she set foot in the door of Raymond's office. This much Raymond surmised by the wailing sounds of grief coming down the corridor on the tick of nine.

He opened the door to the newly widowed woman and Miss Rosa, who was acting as Mrs Italiano's crutch. The two of them staggered inside.

Mrs Italiano threw herself to the ground, sobbing and bashing at her chest.

'My Federico! What happened? What happened, Doctor?'

Raymond lowered himself and knelt on the floor beside her. Miss Rosa leaned over, keeping a hand on Mrs Italiano's back.

'Mrs Italiano. I am very sorry. We are all terribly sorry.'

'He was a good man, my husband. A good man!'

Howling sorrow poured from her, and she crouched over further, rocking herself with loss. Her cries were so loud Raymond's explanation could hardly be heard by anyone. He tried to explain about the terrible course of a blockage to the coronary arteries and the relentless complications when a small part of the heart is deprived of oxygen, but his words seemed to just settle on the outside of her, a slick of oil on water. In the end he simply stayed kneeling alongside her, reassuring her that yes, Mr Italiano had been a good man, with a strong heart, but sometimes, illness and death carries with it a deep sense of mystery and unfairness which cannot be predicted, even by those who have some sort of knowledge of it.

At these last words, Mrs Italiano slowly started to quieten, her breath coming in shudders. Raymond did not have much more to offer and felt a stab in what he had just said. Unfairness, this much was true. Raymond despised death, even when it was expected and explicable. At best an insult, and at worst, well, Raymond couldn't face finding the words for it. Death, the sound of it, had such a beastly intimacy. Mr Italiano's death, surely, was more than just the result of a dry coronary thrombosis. How could the richness of existence be reduced to a simple piece of stale sludge, and death have such prosaic impartiality?

He sensed Miss Rosa watching him in that humid fug of a room, the way he was crouched on the floor, undignified and probably looking terminally at sea. But when he looked up at her, he saw a glancing kindness in her eyes. He exhaled privately.

Miss Rosa (again, how surprisingly gracefully she moved) lowered herself to the ground, next to Mrs Italiano. Not a tongue of breeze shifted the air from the widow's face, and her damp hair hung in clots across her eyes, which were puffed and half closed with anguish. Miss Rosa gently pushed back Mrs Italiano's fringe.

Raymond then spoke tactfully of the need for an autopsy, how it was extremely important to determine the exact cause of death.

'Yes, Doctor. You find out. Because you know I think ...' And she dissolved into tears once more. 'Bastards,' was all she managed to get out.

Raymond deflated and then hauled himself to his feet. He knew she meant him and his ilk. And fair enough, too. He felt deceitful, inhabiting these physician's clothes, dressed up in intellectual superiority, directionless in the face of this mess. He was a pretender. An academic imposter. But, somehow, he couldn't claim to be a man of the arts, either. He was no more than an ill-equipped, misguided poet, with no rhymes or quill, simply a stethoscope, a basic medical degree and a plaque on a desk.

He realised that Miss Rosa and Mrs Italiano were staring at him. Had he missed something?

Eventually, Raymond assisted Mrs Italiano to her feet. She limped over to the door, supported by him and Miss Rosa. As she turned to leave, Raymond took both her hands in his. He repeated, 'I really am most awfully sorry for you.'

Mrs Italiano looked directly at him through her red, leaky eyes. 'It's alright, Doctor. I believe you did your best,' and she hobbled off down the path, Miss Rosa helping her along with the crook of her arm.

Those words wrestled in his head, as if fighting for legitimacy. Had he? Had he ever done his best? Was his best watching that small breathless boy limp towards his death only a few months ago? Had he done his best by staying silent when he knew he ought to have spoken up? Or done his best when he booked passage for Australia when he should have faced the iron of that woman? Was his best spending night after night staring up at the stained ceiling of his ship's cabin reading poetry and philosophy, instead of preparing himself for the rigours of sole doctoring in another world? No. These were not words that could be applied to him. All he sensed was his own inadequacy, once more, and it tasted of bile. And he took that sensation, wrapped it in the folds of his coat, and made his cumbersome way into the annex just behind his office.

Raymond looked down at Mr Italiano, a man who had seemed so vital in life, but who was now glassy and blanched and silent. The questions began to come with a roar. What was the final, terminal event here, the true cause of death? Was it somehow Raymond's fault (please, no, not again)? Would he find the answer by cutting Mr Italiano open? How does one even go about performing an autopsy? Such a skill had not been covered in his cachectic training. He had seen one or two, but these also had been from a distance, at the back of a crowd, where he was expected to stand because of his height. Well, he did know a reasonable amount of basic pathology and anatomy. His punishing study of basic science had assured him of that, so really, how hard could it be?

Hard, as it turned out. Lacking a suitable guidebook, and the correct tools (whatever, in fact, they were), Raymond was ginger and tentative and mostly lost. Taking to tracing nerves and arteries like a roadmap, he wended up and down, looking for pointers. He noted several gelatinous lumps beaded through Mr Italiano's coronary arteries, which did resemble the illustrations of ischaemic heart disease in texts previously studied, but then he began second-guessing himself and worried that perhaps they had lodged there, opportunistically, post-mortem. How would he know? The sizzling heat made the entire process slippery and he had to continually mop his brow with the back of his forearm. A coppery smell filled the room. He continued the examination, resorting to lifting organs, peering into pouches and crevices, and becoming increasingly concerned at the lack of definitive answers. The lungs looked strangely fibrous, and made a peculiar crunch when sliced through (what on earth was that?), but in the end, Raymond found he was only left with questions. No truth jumped out. The autopsy was a disaster and after several hot hours, Raymond was forced to concede. At least he had some experience in needlework, and was able to cobble Mr Italiano's exterior so that he looked presentable, as long as he covered the body with strategically positioned sheets.

Raymond looked over at the waxy figure and sagged against the wall. No matter how much he had wished it otherwise, here it was, his new, clean slate. Things were no better than before. Sure, it wasn't the same as a boy, softly spoken and grey-white, snuffed out by ignorance, but still. The amends he had hoped to make seemed so distant he could no longer make them out. He washed his hands in the small sink and left, with a last wonder of who in this town was responsible for the body from there.

He needed a little more time before going back to face the infirmary. The turmoil would still be sitting in there like an unstirred layer, and he slunk back to his office in order not to disturb it. Margaret would know where to find him if a patient turned up.

Reluctantly, he pulled the pristine pile of death certificates from the drawer. The room was molten with the windows closed and the curtains drawn, and he leaned over the top form. A bead of sweat dropped onto the page. He sat, looking at the blank paper with its officious lines, at a wordy impasse. The slow heat gnawed away at him. He pulled out the instructions from the back of the booklet.

The term 'cardiac arrest' is not an acceptable term for the cause of death. Please list the antecedent causes, in no more than two lines.

It's just not possible, he thought. How can life and death be reduced to two lines? The passage of a good man could not be described in terms of pectinous lumps or chalky lungs. Where was the space for uncertainty, for complexity, for the entanglement of existence and, yes, the poetry of truth?

He stared out of the front window. The savage sun was making the glass quiver. For a moment he wished he was back in England. Not the England of the dire final days of his residency that had him skulking out of his hospital with a rent in his soul, cut adrift from everything he knew, but instead, a more genteel and imagined place. A place of cold stone buildings, housing royal colleges and academic discussions over tea while the short misty days drew to a close outside long, elegant, curlicued windows. The heat, however, quickly dissolved this vision. No, he was here for a rebirth, no matter how insurmountable it seemed.

As he stared out the window, he began to absentmindedly draw on the form, creating elaborate doodles of hearts and lungs. Without knocking, Margaret steamed in.

'Ah, Matron. Everything alright? Would you like to sit down? May I offer you a drink? Water?'

She hesitated, perched herself onto the hard-backed chair in front of the desk, and looked down at the pocket watch pinned to the front of her uniform. She then leaned over towards him. Raymond made a particular effort not to look at her breasts, which seemed to resemble sculpted pyramids, held together by wire and architecture, he imagined. She looked fierce up this close, and had deep vertical lines puckered into her lips.

'Yes. A water would do. I have some things to discuss with you.'

'Excellent,' he said, and walked over to the sink in the corner of the room, opening up the recessed cupboards beneath. He fumbled around inside, pulling out odd pieces of surgical equipment and mismatched cups. Pouring a warm, cloudy glass of water, he brought it back and placed it on the desk. She wrinkled her nose, as if she could smell something rotten. Raymond sat down again across from her.

'Dr Filigree.'

'Raymond. Please call me Raymond.'

'Dr Filigree,' she enunciated, 'I'll be honest here. This is a small town.' She looked at him, as if expecting him to know what this signified.

'I realise that, Margaret. Matron. And thus …'

'Word gets around quickly, Doctor.' She gestured back towards the annex. 'In fact, I'd say it already has. I'd be surprised if anybody turns up here, now.'

Raymond stared at her, while several fiery seconds oozed by.

'What do you mean?'

'I'm just saying, Doctor, that I've been here for a while, and we have certain ways of getting things done. The people of this town trust me. For example, normally I would see any patients first, and only decide when we'll call you in. My priorities, you see, are for the wellbeing of the patients here, as well as looking after my nursing staff, and, I would like to add, keeping up standards. I don't think we need to go changing anything, do you?'

'Surely there's room for discussion here, Matron. It sounds as though my aims are very much aligned with yours—'

'That may be, Doctor,' Margaret interrupted, 'but my concern is if people can't have confidence in this hospital—'

Margaret herself was interrupted by the quiet entry of Miss Rosa, bearing another tray laden with wares.

'I am sorry to intrude,' Miss Rosa said, and placed the tray down. Margaret stood abruptly. Raymond could see that the matron was staring pointedly at the death certificate with its pictures and diagrams along the lines instead of words.

Margaret looked back up at him. 'Confidence,' she repeated.

Sweat dripped down the back of Raymond's neck. The word felt like a swipe, a sharp backhander to the face, and all of a sudden, he was back to the same vicious sensation he had when speaking to that woman, that hideous woman, those few months ago. He was sure she too had gone on about confidence. It had been a word of little meaning in the desolate clinics of his training – the grey, concreted, repeating rooms, tacked onto the back of Saint Basil's Hospital, a lead worm of an afterthought. He'd been rostered there after completing his watery basic medical training, along with performing nocturnal ward duties. The whole infirmary had a grubby decay to it, housing miserable staff (many of them at the end of their demoted tenures), and containing all the defective equipment not good enough for hospitals with respectable reputations. It was a place that was perpetually dark inside – even when the tired English sun would peer out elsewhere, the insides of the clinic would remain dank and unlit and unwarmed.

He hadn't taken much notice of her at first. She was just another in a never-ending queue, lined up to get some sort of help from those sitting behind the duplicate desks. Often it was not even clear what the purpose of the visits was, except that the patients would continue to come in their vast, ceaseless lines. They would bring along their aching backs and swollen limbs and pains that had gripped them for weeks, rarely leaving with a diagnosis or cure, as if the effort to achieve these was simply too much for all involved. Yet, they doggedly turned up.

Raymond was part way through his training as a hospitalist, although what the training comprised was never really clear. It seemed be a sort of flailing around in the deep end, lurching from snatches of hope to near-drowning. Nobody ever looked over Raymond's shoulder, advised him, educated him or guided him in any way. He tripped and stumbled his way through the morass of dour unwell, this crowd hunched over with the burden of urban poverty. The masses and his books, that's all he had. Each day he would gaze down the interminable string of patients with dread, determined that this day was the one he would do better. It was only later that he would register the appearance of that woman and her son, somewhere in the midst of this stagnant mob.

And each day he would scrabble around in textbooks, looking for answers to the array of unknowns that presented themselves, patient after patient. He consulted books under the desk, or in the lavatory in order to keep up a façade of knowledge. It was exhausting. He would look across at the other residents in training, or the menacing nurses whose main jobs appeared to be jostling the crowds into order and looking aggressively at their pocket watches. He wanted to ask for help, but knew there'd be little to be had. They were a misfit group of rejection, never destined for the rarefied surrounds of Harley Street, or the leafier London boroughs. At night he would fumble around the hospital wards, seeing the inpatients that the clinic had failed. Some more than others, as it would turn out.

'Dr Filigree,' Miss Rosa spoke. 'Tea. I have brought you some tea.' Margaret was disappearing out the back door. The room was roasting and the heat felt like a claw around his throat. Had she heard Margaret's judgement? 'I wasn't sure if you'd want it, but I made one for you, just in case.' She pushed the cup towards him.

'Oh, Miss Rosa, thank you very much.'

'Do not mention it. It's no trouble.'

Raymond picked up the adorned death certificate and slid it into the bottom drawer of the desk. Miss Rosa held her head on an angle, looking out of the window while he did so. The staccato cluck of chickens milling just beyond the verandah ticked through the window. Of course she'd heard.

She remained standing, smoothing down her skirt, and after a few moments, spoke. 'Dr Filigree, I hope you don't think I'm speaking out of turn, but I think you'll find there's …' she pushed a stray hair behind her ear into her otherwise faultless bun, 'well, I think you'll find that there's something a little bit wrong with all of us. All who've ended up here, in this place, I mean. Things will get better, you have my word. Even if there are a few ups and downs.'

She pulled off her spectacles and polished them on the folds of her skirt. Raymond watched her spare and precise movements. Her face was stretched, pleated by the sun and the years, the supple smile of youth long since departed. But she had an erect bearing, rather a dignified surprise, really, and an unexpectedly elegant curve, starting somewhere underneath the thick twill layers of her dress, continuing up a long neck. Her hair was meticulous, brushed soft and wound with care into a bun. He dropped his gaze.

Peering into the lens, then replacing her glasses, she spoke, 'And I'll ask Barry to contact the men who act as funeral directors. It's not the first time we've needed to bury somebody out here. Problem is the ground's a bit hard, and we need to find the chaps who are good with dynamite. There's a bit of a stash downtown, in a store. Shouldn't be of course, but that's Wittenoom for you. I'll get Barry right on it.' And she slipped off, disappearing back into the heart of the hospital, leaving Raymond to drink his tepid tea, the way Miss Rosa liked to make it, it seemed.

IV

It's a battered file. An old lever-arch thing, bashed in at the corners and coated in dark tangerine dust that masks the original schoolish grey.

Dave opens it to the first page. 'Have a look through. Somewhere in here's the truth. But it deserves to be better put.'

They are sitting close on the step and their knees touch. Lou exhales what she hopes is a normal breath. He's close, and the shape of his legs, even through his jeans, makes them look like wood – so defined they could be carpentered. The file is large enough to rest across them both, and they are able to look at the entries together, the pages a blanket across their laps.

'It's an archive. It started out just for me, well for him, really. But as time has gone on, I reckon it's something that needs to see the light of day. You see the mines, the people in charge of the mines, they killed people. Sure as holding a gun to their head.'

IV

The ring binding is falling apart and some of the pages are torn. The whole file has been ravaged, all the elements having taken a turn. On the first page is a wrinkled newspaper clipping of a broad colonial-style hotel.

'Gorgeous old thing she was, the Fortescue Hotel. I think I miss her the most, that pub and her balconies. Just through here was an open dining room and an endless front bar.' He points out the detail in the photograph. 'Full of colour and light. Too inviting for tourists, they reckoned, so they bulldozed her in front of our eyes.'

The page is corrugated, the creases glutted with ochre. Lou traces her fingers over the bumps, feeling the three-dimensional texture of them.

'Is this all yours?' she asks. The triangle of his elbow rests lightly on her lap, and the gentle pressure stirs confusion inside her.

'I've been collecting it for years,' Dave says, heedless of her heartbeat. 'Newspaper articles, letters, odds and ends. All originals. Interviews I've done with people. The god-awful stuff-ups and the secrets. The people and what this place did to them. I've tried to write it down like a story, but I don't have your way with words. I bet you could do it.'

'You don't know that,' she says, wanting to sound modest, but hears her words sound different on their way out.

Dave stands abruptly, knocking the file from her knees. He picks it up and hands it to her, before disappearing back into the van.

She settles the archive on her lap, once more, and wonders if there will be any secrets in here worse than her own. She doubts it, and turns to the next page.

Droning insects whine circuits round her ears. Apart from that there is no sound but the crackling of the fire and the occasional whoomph of a burnt-out branch collapsing. Dave reappears shortly, squeezing past. He places a can of Coke next to her, a welcome partner to the pie, and then he wanders into the jumbled darkness.

She returns from watching his outline to paging through the file. Peeling photographs are glued haphazardly onto several of the pages, some of them covered by plastic which is now brittle and cracking. Many of these are accompanied by stunted passages written in block-like letters, the spelling disfigured. Lou recognises the backwash of dyslexia. She takes a sip of her icy Coke, the surprise of the fizz explodingly sharp in her nose.

She begins to trawl through. There are loose descriptions of the town, the mine, the everyday lives of the residents of Wittenoom during its heyday. Dave is right – the words are disordered and erratic, but the sentiments are clear. The photos certainly are. The first of the images dates back to the early 1950s. She runs her hand over them, touching the past. There is a lilting optimism in the earliest pieces, in both the images and the words. Some of them, at the start, describe a paradise. It's not much of a stretch. Cobalt skies dotted with eagles, just as she's seen, and that abundant deep red – the soaring red with no end. Brilliant, eternal colours light it up. There are scenes described like the Wild West, and the gorges are mentioned repeatedly, with their sparkling pools in deep-jewelled red recesses. They were seen as huge, welcoming cleavages in the planet, inserted just for the adventure of it, providing somewhere to kick about and cool off. The town of Wittenoom itself was a fantastical alien landscape – the asbestos tailings used for everything: the surface of the airstrip, the pavements, the garden beds, even the play equipment in the schoolyard.

Lou looks up from the file, around at the rust and ataxic mess of Dave's yard, then beyond to the decrepitude of the settlement. He's sitting on a tree stump nearby, staring out into the wilderness, mechanically sipping from his own can of Coke. Something about him, his posture maybe, looks troubled.

She reads on about how extraordinary, how universally useful everybody thought the asbestos was; the unique softness and compliance of the toxic waste was perfect for damping down the dust, and it made everything wondrous and downy underfoot. But then it started to turn up everywhere – in the flour, amongst the folds of people's clothes, in the pores of the concrete floors, in the eyelashes of babies, and crunching between the teeth of those having nightmares. Tailings hung in the trees like cobwebs. It sounded like a land out of fevered dreams, muted and fluffed with blue cottonwool.

Lou calls over to Dave. 'Didn't they know how dangerous the stuff was?'

He takes a while to answer. 'The workers? The families? Nope, they didn't.' He stands and crumples his can, suddenly, violently. Turning towards the dark, he hurls it into a rust heap nearby.

The fire whittles down to a glow, and he comes over carrying an iron rod. When he pokes at the embers, they sputter and shoot off sparks. In the coarse flashes of light his expression looks grim, and she's not sure what she's said that has hit a nerve.

'Keep reading,' he says. 'There's some stuff about the mines you need to see.'

Lou wonders why this determined need for her to read the contents. She who is no longer anything, sitting on his step like it's the final station of the last night train, simply consuming the air and his precious, cold drinks. What is he expecting her to see?

Straining to read the passages, Lou follows the account as it grows bleaker. As time progressed, the adults – the miners and their wives – expressed things differently. They make no mention of beauty – the text is full of heavy, tormented words. Described are houses which were at best utilitarian; lacking flywire, refrigeration, even reliable running water and electricity. The mines, however, were something else altogether.

The reading is hard going. Whole paragraphs tell of the disempowerment the workers felt – references are made to men in clean shirts imposing their will from tidy, dust-free offices somewhere across the Nullarbor. The supervisors on site, seemingly following orders, relentlessly hounded the men back into the ratholes. The workers, it appeared, just had to endure it, having few other options for work in the brutal economic days of the postwar era.

It was a job that would have killed twice, Lou realises. Firstly, from what she can see, hunched over in the stopes, or bashing rock in the mill, every breath thick with asbestos dust. In the mines, she reads, the workers could not even stand, and the heat should have been incompatible with survival. Double shifts were common, and safety equipment non-existent – respirators, fans, hoses, all of them inadequate, missing, or never supplied in the first place. Once in a while a cavalcade of equipment was paraded out, usually when the governmental safety inspectors were visiting, but then they disappeared soon afterwards. The second death, she knows, was to come later, when those who had inhaled the fibres were suffocating, their lungs silting up, or worse, being gnawed away by cancer. But there's not much about that in there. Lou closes the file. It's a lot to take in.

'I had no idea it was this bad,' Lou says.

'There's more.' Dave is staring into the fire. Pops and flashes startle out of it, while he stands motionless.

'Where?'

Dave still doesn't look at her. 'In here.' And he taps his index finger on the side of his head.

Lou waits. He seems to be having difficulty speaking.

'The Italians. You noticed? A lot of the names are Italian.' He walks over to the steps and takes the file from her, putting it back into the bag. 'My dad. I'm a Genovese. He was one of them. Worked here for six years. Recruited from a little paradise in Northern Italy when he was eighteen years old.' He shakes his head, rapidly, like he's trying to dislodge water. 'Apparently, the recruiters came to their village one day like a travelling roadshow. Only wanted the strongest, the fittest. Told them the climate'd be just like home, and that it'd be all milk and honey and riches out here. Paid their way and then plonked them, smack bang in the middle of hell. No way out for them. It broke him, I'm sure. Went from being a racehorse to a hack only good for glue. At least that's what he said in one of the few times he'd talk.' Dave sits heavily back down on the step. 'After working here for as long as he could stand, he hitched a ride down to Perth, married my mum, knocked her up, and then spiralled, as far as I can make out, into a black depression, which only lifted a few times the whole of my life. Those times, the happy ones, were rare, but they were gold. He'd start to talk, but then the edges of the stories about this place would begin to show, and he'd shut up again. I remember craving those times, when he'd talk. Now, I've hardly even got the memories left. I want them back, though, just trying to find a way to do it.' He looks directly at her, as if to gauge her reaction.

She doesn't know what to say – but she feels disorientated, as though she's been grabbed, pushed to move without notice. Motion and transition. And when she moves, she's never sure what to trust. Should she be agreeing? Adding some of her own revelations? She's let down her guard, deceived by the simmer of his looks, the heft of his presence. The northern wind softly shrieks underneath the caravan, whispering what sounds like a warning.

'Anyway, once the asbestosis kicked in and he sounded like he was breathing mud, things slowly got worse. He's spent the last decade plugged into oxygen tubing.'

'But why are you up here, then?' She's apprehensive in asking. He'll turn the same question on her and she'll be forced into truth.

Dave shakes his head. 'Something happened when Lacey and I lost the baby, like he was being strangled. I guess it was his lungs getting worse, but he just stopped talking altogether. It seemed as though the less he could breathe, the more the rage built up inside, and it was silencing him. I got the feeling that he never forgave anything. Not me, not Mum, not a single human on this earth, and I could never figure out why.'

IV

'And that's why you came? To understand?' Lou hears the tentative tone of her voice. She should stopper it before it lets in things she can't manage.

'Yep.' He stands, making the step groan, and walks back to the fire. 'I just wanted answers at first, but then I found something else, entirely. Dad seemed to be an angry man all his life. Coming up here gave me some perspective. I thought I'd give him this archive, but I don't reckon he'll want it like it is. It'll just be another disappointment. So it's just this. An unfinished story for an unfinished man.' He pokes the fire one last time. 'But maybe, in the end, there's no figuring out some people.'

This is something she can agree with. There is no figuring out some people. And forgiveness isn't something easily had; not ordered off a menu, or found in a place, or even written conveniently in a story. Lou knows she won't find hers anywhere. Sitting here in the smoky darkness, it is clear to her that exoneration is reserved, without fail, for the decent. For everybody else, perhaps, just not her.

Reading of the turbulent past has given her a short break from her own recriminations – attention to another man's worries can do that – but now that she has stopped, her focus fissures and images seep back into her head. The flash of dark hair behind curtains, a team turning to her in slow motion, and the sense of her own pupils dilating in the split second of reckoning. She covers her eyes with her hands. The memories have grown another shade more vivid. It's what happens when she tries to shut them out.

'I know,' Dave says, misinterpreting her gesture. 'It was bloody purgatory. The bastards in charge, the snivelling company men from a sugar-refining factory, idiots who knew jack all about sugar let alone mining, they ordered this place to be blasted open, bit by bit, then got their henchmen to fit it out like it was Hades. After that they turned their backs so they couldn't see. The workers were condemned, the poor sods. And that,' he says, returning to the step, squeezing back down next to Lou, 'is why this has to be written.' He runs his hand over the front of the file. 'Properly.'

The fire is now just a glow. With the dearth of light around, the milky way has become luminous – a thick speckled throw across the black sky. Cold seeps into her skin, and her shorts are stiff against her legs. An eerie muted bird coo fills the air with soft, repetitive sounds, coming from a direction she can't figure out. Foreign. Unfamiliar. It's so far from anywhere, this place, so distant from that disaster of a day, and yet.

Dave has turned to her. There is not much room on the step where they sit and his arm is folded up onto itself. Loose strands of her hair have fallen across her face, and he slowly, immeasurably slowly, reaches up and lifts one away. She tenses, but his fingertips lightly graze her face and they are feathery where they make contact. Closing her eyes with the voltage of it, she does not want to move. She's still where she sits, but in her bones is roaring turmoil.

'You could do it,' he says. 'I've seen what you've started.'

She doesn't want to open her eyes, to face what he's asking, and she feels his finger run down the side of her jaw. But keeping her eyes closed is a mistake. His pleas and his fingers disappear and she starts to run through memories like a mantra. Getting dressed in scrubs, hanging her lanyard around her neck, scrabbling around to find her stethoscope, being pleased to find a parking space close to the emergency department, the chill of a fleeting Perth winter, looking up at the clouds of porridge as she walked in, bang on time. The quiet. The deathly quiet.

Her eyes spring open and she starts. Dave withdraws his hand and rests it on the file. Such an eagerness in his face.

He's misled, wrong. There's nothing inside her that he could rely on. It's all corruption and fraudulence in there, and close to the surface at that. And well and truly no room for anything else. No space at all.

Pinpricks begin to puncture her ankles where ants have found her uncovered parts. Then they jab further up her shins. They are feasting on her soft, urban skin, piercing her calves with their needle-like pincers. She stands quickly, hitting her legs and stamping her feet. The file slips to the ground.

'Ants,' is all she says.

He watches, his expression adrift.

Of course he can see into her. Her past is inescapable, as unmistakable as the stars. This is what she is. She is only that day and the avalanche that followed.

'Can I take a lantern with me?' Lou asks.

She doesn't look back as she strides off to the hut, the ant bites throbbing with each step.

What Is Ahead

Raymond remained at the desk, swamped in sweat. Sunlight ricocheted from every surface and its crosshairs were trained right where he sat. He shifted in his chair, trying to find relief for the prickling in his legs and his buttocks. Pulling several sheets of paper from the drawer in order to continue writing out the inventory, he listed a few stuttering items in his curved handwriting. But how could he know what he would need in the future when he didn't know what he needed now? Abandoning the paltry list, he started a fresh page.

In coming to Wittenoom, he had believed that this was his opportunity to understand medicine anew, perhaps even perform some novel research. The unyielding application of the science of it had failed him so terribly back in England, and during the swell of the journey over here he had been playing with ideas, with thoughts, whilst lying in his cabin, the writings of philosophers and poets seeping into his brain like lymph. By the time he'd disembarked into the brilliantined port of Fremantle, where there was sunshine and bustle and possibility, he had fashioned several titles to head up innovative journal articles, the likes of which had not been published before.

A New Approach to Resuscitation and Care. The Filigree Method (was this too bold?).

A Primer for Medicine Incorporating Both Mind and Body, Based on the Meditations of Descartes.

Or, the alternative: *What Pathology Can Learn from Poetry.*

He knew that an academic paper or two would show his predecessors back in England that he was more than the medical bankrupt they thought he was. But as he began to write out the titles, he saw how ridiculous they appeared, written by the hand of a man whose first subject of study was a corpse, and he struck them through. The orangey shafts of sunlight were angling lower, the last of the day. He walked to the window and placed a hand on the baking glass, looking out to the piles of battle-grey tailings and massive mounds of asbestos dust. No. This was not the place for philosophy. Where was there room for verse?

He felt a pecking at his insides, as if he were wood being bored away, a feeling unfamiliar. Perhaps it was simply a craving for company. He wondered about approaching Miss Rosa; maybe they could drink tea together and converse about things both unimportant and profound, but the thought of sitting in her kitchen like a cabbagey confessional discouraged him. What must she think of him, already? And as for Margaret, he wasn't sure how he'd ever face her again.

Dare he venture into the Wittenoom pub? On his brief sojourn through the jumble of streets hoping to find a newspaper or magazine, he had spied the imposing building.

Double-storeyed and stately, its walls were as straight as a backbone, where the rest of the surrounding buildings were simple shacks tossed together with tumbling sides of corrugated iron and dust. She had grace, this edifice, with her impressive balcony wrapped around like a ruffed collar and the enormous potted plants by the door. A seductive sight. A siren for the townsfolk. He feared seeming improper (should the sole doctor ever be seen drinking at a tavern?), but considering his dreadful start, he wondered if there was no place lower to sink. He would have loved to find somewhere in this town to replicate the camaraderie of his resident days, some place reminiscent of those darkly wooded, smoky inns which offered excellent ale and the reassurance of invisibility – but he suspected the Wittenoom pub might provide just the opposite.

Right. That was it. He grabbed his jacket and pulled it on.

He almost tripped over a clucking mess of feathers, and he cursed discreetly. Slipping through the front gate, he marched off down the road. Raymond knew he ought not look back or waver. It felt almost reckless. He marched at a clip, trying to outpace the deep tangled fear that maybe his best days, as appalling as they'd been, might be behind him.

Once he reached the hotel, he stopped outside. He levelled the hem of his jacket. A menu was stuck up on an outside wall, the corner peeling. Raymond didn't stop to peruse its three or four items, knowing he could not give himself a chance to falter. He swung in through the shuttered door, standing still. The room quietened for a few moments, and then the clattering of conversation resumed. He exhaled and wondered what on earth he'd expected – the dramatic entrance into a Western saloon?

Tightening his Windsor knot, he surveyed the scene. In the space of the front room was a loud, raucous mess of men. The bar was lined with grey, heavy workers, all of them caked thick with dust and engaged in very serious drinking from what he could see. Pint beer glasses filled the bench of the bar, many of them empty, each sludged with handprints. Conversations filtered through the air, and Raymond could hear various European accents in addition to the Australian, all of them competing in volume. There were a few colourful round tables in one corner, occupied by small groups of floral women, huddled over short tumblers half full of clear liquid adorned with wedged fragments of lemon. Gin and tonics, Raymond wondered? How civilised.

A few men looked over at him with what appeared to be casual curiosity, and one or two nodded a greeting as if they were old friends. Most returned quickly to their feisty, truncated discourse, although several continued to watch him from behind their drinks.

Raymond slotted into one of the few spaces at the bar and ordered. 'A beer, I think.'

He felt like an actor in a play, hoping he'd get his lines right. Placing his hands on the bar, he waited to see if he'd succeeded.

'Coming right up, Doc.'

He relaxed and observed the scene around him; the men orating brief sentences into their beers before taking a sip, as though they were speaking into their chilled, beaded glasses like microphones. Once in a while he sensed that people were looking his way, speaking words unheard, but when he glanced up, they would drop their gaze and go quiet.

Raymond unwound himself further and was most of the way through his first glass when he turned to see Barry slide into a vacant spot next to him.

'Evening, Doc.'

Buoyed by the airiness of unaccustomed alcohol, Raymond chanced a smile. 'Yes, it's a delightful evening. Quite true. May I buy you a beer, Barry?'

'Don't mind if you do, Doc.'

The two sat in companionable quiet. They meted out sips for a while, before Barry spoke up.

'Sorry about not helping you this morning. Moving Mr Italiano, I mean. Not very keen on corpses, you see.'

'Think nothing of it, Barry. I quite understand.'

Barry looked over at Raymond. 'I appreciate that, Doc,' he said, raising his glass in a gesture of goodwill.

'How long have you worked here, Barry?'

'Well I'm a bit here and there. A working vagrant, really. Came specially for the maintenance job in the hospital, oh, a couple of years ago, but I tend to take extended breaks when I need to. Get out of town. Particularly when the dust gets too much. The job doesn't pay well that way, but hell, what good's a bucket of coins piled on your coffin, eh?'

Raymond found it difficult to hear amongst the dense noise of conversation around them. 'What do you mean?'

'I mean I could make a ton of extra money working in the mill, or even more down the mines, but you'll see, the stuff in there is worse than acid. Can't understand why so many of these guys do it.' He nodded his head towards the crowd. 'But then again, you only believe what you want when there's a salary involved.'

'But don't the safety inspectors come? Hasn't it been all declared safe? There are government inspectors, aren't there? Employed for the protection of the people?' Oddly, he could hear the crunch of Mr Italiano's lungs in the back of his head.

Barry scoffed into his drink, aspirating and spluttering. 'Oh, Doc. You've got a long way to go.'

Several men nearby looked up at the noise and continued to observe Raymond. He became aware of their scrutiny. It felt heavy with judgement. Had everybody figured out that he was floundering? That he was asking the wrong questions? Knowing the wrong things? The beer, however, had managed to loosen his usual self-restraint, and borne on the ease of the moment he was able to ask a question, lightly and effortlessly.

'Barry, do people, will people, trust me? I know it's early days, but after this inauspicious start, I just wonder. Nobody's come to see me after this morning. You haven't heard anyone talking, have you?'

Barry slowly drained his glass, and then set it down on the bar, twirling it several times.

'Doc. I have to be honest. The thing is, they're a pretty superstitious bunch out here. You, you're here with your suit and your fancy talk, and within a day you've got one of the best men in town a dodo, cold and chopped up in a storeroom in the hospital. You could say that these people will be talking. Going to be a bit of an uphill road for you, I reckon.'

Raymond felt vertiginous. He fancied himself swinging, gripping onto the final knot of a long rope, nowhere below him but chasm. He finished the last of his beer and placed it on the counter next to Barry's.

An uphill road, or an impossible one? He was going to be as useful as a doctor in a graveyard, he thought. Perhaps it was pointless to even try, and he felt a resigned sadness that it seemed as though failure, his unique failure, could never be outrun.

Both men looked up at the barman, both preparing to ask whose buy it was next, but were cut short, as the air turned still and time stopped for the briefest of moments.

Right before an explosion there is a temporal flash. A moment of peace. It is a vacuum full of silence, a little like the tide going out before a tsunami, where, for one calm second, there is an unnatural tranquillity, vastly magnified by its brevity. It would be comforting to think that for those who did not survive the blast, this was their final memory, because following this crack in time is the most hideous, drum-bursting, metal-shrieking sound imaginable. A sound that vibrates your chest and shakes your brains. It rips open the earth and bleeds out the soul of anyone in its path.

And in the pub, it was like the collective intake of breath before the scream.

V

Lou sleeps fitfully, taunted by snatches of dreams. She writes short passages then sinks back into the discomfort of the blankets, closing her eyes to the strangeness of the words, and she repeats this cycle well into the bite of morning. Propped up against the tin walls, she eventually writes her pen out of ink. She reads through the pages with a sense of unease, as if the pen had possessed a will of its own, barrelling down a path that even she hadn't foreseen. It's becoming less and less the story that she hoped, and she's determined to find a way to wrestle it back in the direction she needs it to go.

The harbingers of morning have arrived: the long screeching calls of the birds, the high-pitched hum of cicadas, the creaking of the iron sides of the hut under the grill of the sun, followed by phenomenal silences when the noises catch their breath. Her throat feels thick and her neck aches from sleeping at an unnatural angle.

There is another pen in the car, she's sure, and she unfolds herself from the floor. She walks out into the white light and rummages through the back seat, pulling out a change of clothes, a water bottle, a hairbrush. It occurs to her that she ought to make a decision about whether she'll stay any longer. The unsettling attraction she has for Dave will do nothing but complicate things. It'll empty out unwelcome truths, shaking them into the open. Surely it would be better for both of them if she just left. He doesn't deserve the taint of her. But God knows where she'll go from here. Plus, she has summoned her story from the pith of this place. So she'll stay one more day. Write as much as she can while she still smells the grit of the town.

She needs to stretch out – she thinks she'll have a brief walk before putting pen back onto paper, so she takes a swig of water and heads off in a different direction. Tracking over to the other side of the township remains, she's keening for evidence of some of the facts she's now heard. And there they are – great chunks of loss all over. Every rotting foundation, each discarded piece of rubbish, they all had a living hand to them at some point, and likely a dust-covered, dismal one. The stories out here, the graves of the past are everywhere. The bones and ash of people's lives and their endeavours, their houses and pastimes, their lovers and families.

She is gripped suddenly by the thought of her own back home, dispersed and silent. Once her father died, and her mother ratcheted up the blame (*Surely you could have picked up that he had cancer earlier, you're a doctor for God's sake! I don't know why we spent all that money sending you to medical school)*, Lou had stopped talking much to her. Lou's brother, Matthew, younger, quieter, had seen sense to leave home for South Australia, happily losing himself in the wine industry, producing fat, well-adjusted babies. The occasional

Christmas photos she receives are full of smiling people posed in red and green. Lou has nothing to send back.

Any friends had also dissipated. Recently and cleanly. Once the drowning started, after the little girl and then all the things that followed, she shut them all out. None of them tried to fight their way back in and she is grateful for it. Her shame. It's a heavy cloak, and she no longer knows how to take it off.

The place looks different to when she first drove through. At the eastern end of the township, she comes across the remains of a 1960's restaurant. Doc Holiday's Café. How fitting. Truncated graffiti, just disarticulated letters, is scrawled over the torn ringlets of tin making up its walls. Scattered around the building at intervals are the regulation *Keep Out* signs, but their dull, faded surfaces deny them much impact. She steps over a pipe that has fallen off a rusty fuel tank, and dodges snarls of wire sprawling over the flattened path where a driveway once was.

She squeezes in through a side door, which has rusted narrowly ajar. Like the hospital, the interior looks as though the building was deserted precipitously, in some sort of rush. Piles of crockery are heaped up on the dusty benches, and jars of condiments lined in rows contain nothing but black sludge. Everything is submerged, buried under powdery dirt. An industrial fridge swings open at barely a touch, creaking on its busted hinges, and the smell of mould hits her like a wall. Several dented brown cans sit on the shelves. No one has touched these items for decades, and they are now stray, worthless artefacts, their connection to the living severed. A deep metal trough in the corner of the kitchen is full of mouse fur and droppings. Lou tries to turn on the tarnished, seized-up tap, but there is no movement, no water, just a brown rusted circle in the basin.

As she makes to leave, she sees a lone chunk of chalk. She picks it up and scratches onto the bench *Raymond P. Filigree 14/3/66.* It makes her smile, vaguely amused with the madness of it, and she walks out.

It's not hard to cover the length of Wittenoom on foot. It was never very big. Where she had thought that the town was lifeless, the opposite, in fact, is true. The life is just harder to see. Long fronds of weeds snake up and encase the headless signs, and tough tendrils of grass encroach halfway across the roads. Birdsong drops from all corners of the sky and drapes over the rangy branches.

A fire has blazed through sometime in the last few years, torching a segment of the town, and new growth has mushroomed in its aftermath. In a demarcated wedge, young tufts of spinifex flourish, emerging softer than their aged counterparts. Blackened tree trunks have launched juicy shoots of leaves, deep green and serious. It is a verdant explosion, and she can see that the landscape is steadily consuming the settlement. As if nature has laughed, shaking its head at the profane, boorish activities of man, and decided to slowly devour them. How long will it be until there is no trace at all? Maybe if she lay down, right here, she too could be consumed.

Eventually, she rounds to the wreck of the hospital. Dave is sitting on the raised upfront area – the verandah with its osteoporotic struts.

'Hey,' he says. 'Thought you'd come here.' He hands her a bottle of water.

She doesn't know what to say, and gratefully takes the drink.

V

They wander through the rooms, looking down at the medley of remnants littering the floor. Lou picks up a piece of ceramic; a broken triangle – a dirty white wedge rimmed with blue. She shines it with her hand until it gleams.

'How can all this have stayed untouched for so long?' she says. 'Anywhere else ruined like this gets looted. People take stuff as souvenirs.'

'I don't know. I'd say most of those who come gawking are scared stiff of touching anything. They think they'll catch the plague.' He turns to her. 'It's just not like that, you know.'

In one of the remaining walls a rotted, paneless window frame survives, only a rectangle of splintered soft wood. Lou lightly runs a finger along it, forming a trench in the dust.

'You see,' he continues, 'this is why the story has to be written. Address the lies and the misinformation. Get down the facts. I know I started it for Dad, maybe to show him he wasn't the only one to go through it, but then I figured that it shouldn't be just for him, or the people who worked here, but maybe the whole bloody country. Everyone's been robbed by those arseholes in one way or another. Those fibres, let loose on the world.'

He sits down, carefully lowering himself into the place where Lou sat that first night. 'They knew, Lou, they knew. They bloody knew before the mines even opened that asbestos, when it's chopped up and churning in the air like that, will kill you, sure as bloody cyanide. But those prospecting dickheads came up here, and they strutted around like they were saving the world. And then some bumbling sugar-refining company took it all on, a company who thought they'd make a quick buck when they didn't know their arse from dynamite. But they all knew. Took some fairly hard-headed doctors – one guy called Saint, and another McNulty, maybe you've heard of them – men who bashed away for years, writing to everybody they could, who finally got the government to admit it. And when they did, and the whole place closed down, the bastards in charge just washed their own hands and passed the whole bloody thing over to lawyers who sat in air-conditioned offices writing out invoices along with their golf handicaps.'

Lou can't sit down. The air is dense, and she feels like she could choke. She's been watching him speak; his hand movements are graceful, coordinated with his words. It's the Italian in him, she guesses. Persuasive. Impelling. But she doesn't want to be sucked in anywhere, even by these limber hands.

'They were like you, Lou.' It takes a moment for her to understand to whom he's referring. 'Doctors and writers. I read your stuff, you know. Sorry, but I did. I reckon it's the way to do it. Mine, it's just a mess. Photos, articles sure, but it's got no heart. I think people only truly read things with a heart.'

She flinches at his words, these stones flung at her. It's not so much a violation that he's seen her writing, more that she knows he can now see into where it's black and atrophied.

'I don't understand,' he continues, 'why you'd stop being a doctor. After all that training. The investment. You've got the chance to do some good. Why would you throw that away?'

She stays by the gaping socket in the wall, picking splinters out of the frame, the wood like tissue from the decades of furious wet heat. She will not answer this. Cannot.

V

'But what went on out here,' she finally speaks, 'is the past now, surely. It's gone. Done.'

'No. It's not. It's only starting, I can tell you.'

He stands, and the air, which is swimming with motes, moves with him.

'I don't know much, that's true,' says Lou, 'but hasn't this all been through the courts, already? I've seen it in the news – the compensation cases.'

'Compo? Are you kidding?' His words come out jumbled. 'There's hardly been a cent. Not a brass razoo. To anyone. Like getting poisoned blood out of a poisoned stone. It's been a parade of white men in their white shirts keeping the courtroom doors propped open for months, years even, with their files and their photocopies and their technicalities. The sort of people who get a kick out of spending their working days haggling over the price of a man's life. Even when people are dying, murdered more like, the lawyers are arguing between each other, using fucked-up defences dreamed up over drinks in a fancy bar somewhere so that the company can avoid paying a penny to the widows and children.'

He is pacing now, trampling anything underfoot. 'Dad didn't even want to try to get his. Knew too many people who dropped dead on the courtroom steps before they even got inside. More than that, it's hard to know. It's been so bloody difficult to find out about his life up here. There's almost nothing documented. That was part of it, you know. The company destroying documents, left, right and centre. So many secrets concealed in so many papers, just *lost*. Imagine if you did this with your medical notes.'

She swallows. He needs to stop bringing her into it. This is not her story. And some of it sounds implausible, like a massive conspiracy theory. She wonders whether Dave has become unhinged, staying out here for this long.

'Well, why haven't you ever asked him, your dad?'

'I tried.' Dave walks over to where she stands, looking out the window. 'But I think the only time to do that would have been before I was born, when he used to talk. Before he joined the ranks of the walking dead. The only thing he said out loud was that he worked as one of the grey ghosts in the bagging mill, smashing up rocks by hand. A hand he couldn't even see for the dust. For six years. I mean, who could do that?' Dave puts his palms onto the remnants of the sill and stares out. 'By the time he got down to Perth, the damage had set in. Bided its time for a bit, that's what asbestosis does, but I guess you know that. Every year, though, it stole a percentage of his breath. He stopped enjoying anything – food, music, me. He reckoned his lungs were filling up with cement, and he just had to wait until it set for good.'

Lou watches the sweep of his caramel forearms and the clenching of his hands. He is enormous in this bombed-out room. And intimidating, coupled with what he's asking of her.

'I haven't seen him for years. But I'm going to. I want to give him the story when I do though. Show him I cared enough to find out. I'm asking for your help, Lou.'

They are jolting words. Her palms, the backs of her knees, are humid, sweat collecting in fossae. He thinks she can trot out a story about somebody else's buried past, when hers is alive and whipping a tail full of venom.

'Those stories, this history, it's dead,' she says. 'I can't help you.'

V

He looks at her, not understanding. 'Do you mean you won't?'

'No, I can't.' The monopoly on hurt is hers. He's had his time, surely, his chance. Anyway, she'd just screw it up if she tried to help. She always does. She needs to find a way to put him off, so that she can drown alone.

'To be honest, Dave, I don't know if your stuff is salvageable. Some of the parts are OK, but others ...'

He looks like he's taken a hit and he steps back.

'I'm sorry, Dave, I really am. I'm not in the business of fixing the unfixable. Not anymore.' It's been that long since she can remember truly helping anybody, she knows she's no longer capable of it.

'Salvageable?' He takes the water bottle from her hand. Looks hard at her. 'You're unbelievable.'

And he walks off, glass shards cracking underfoot. Out and away through the disjointed corridor, without saying another word.

Lou looks down. She's a fool. But at least she's spared him her involvement. It's better for him this way.

Dave is still visible in the distance. She does know she should have explained things better. This sort of cruelty is foreign to her, and she feels her barbaric behaviour squeezing her ribs.

She calls out his name. He stops momentarily, but doesn't turn around. And then keeps on walking.

And she is alone again, guilty among the ghosts. She stays standing, unmoving, and can hear nothing. The echo of her words has disappeared. Above her head the weightless specks continue to drift, the flakes and the peelings of the past, shedding like squames from who knows where. She waits.

He doesn't return. And thus, in the silence, she walks back to the hut and she collects her things, what few there are. Keys. A bag. A notebook.

But before she leaves, while there is still light, she scribbles more of her unexpectedly explosive sentences. Then she neatly folds the rug and tries to write a note for Dave, except she doesn't know what to say. She gets in the car and drives. She only drives, with no idea where she's headed.

The Misery

In the days to come, days laced with misery and loss, the people of Wittenoom would comment on the curious nature of the blast; how strange it was that only odd windows blew out of certain buildings, forming peculiar patterns, including two on perfectly opposite sides of the Fortescue Hotel. Rather like a puzzle, one of the wives would say later. How a gentle rain of cinders floated delicately up the streets, finding its way into unexpected corners, laying quietly on windowsills and doorsteps, elegant and ornamental in arrangement, and how several wooden beams which fell ended up leaning daintily into each other, poised as if for a kiss.

But in those first few hours, when the town was dense with screams and blood and shards of bone, nobody noticed a thing, except for the frantic desire to locate the ones they loved and the others they needed.

Up through the street and beyond, like the climax of an operatic score, screams rang out. In the pub, where

Raymond had sat just a moment before in congenial reflection, people were reaching out in panic. They grabbed for their friends, their wallets, their hats; others just pushed themselves off the furniture to get out. But where? The street outside was rumbling with fire and the pounding of feet. People, confused about where to exit, crisscrossed and slammed into one another.

Raymond himself stood in robotic fashion, straightened his tie, put several coins on the bar, and walked directly out the front into the hazy street. Without much conscious thought, he advanced down the slope of the road, where he expected to come across the wounded, the injured, the source of the screaming, but all he saw were townsfolk running, crying, crossing the road back and forth. The fuel of hysteria could be felt burning, in the same way as the last struts of the storehouse. As he moved closer to the cloud of smoke and the wafting of ash, he saw a man half carrying, half dragging out another man. They passed Raymond without looking. Another man appeared, staggering out from what was presumably the culprit building, and the xanthous smoke swirled like liquid around him, the fumes closing behind as he went. Billowing black-edged gusts obscured any detail. It was difficult to identify what was building and what was air.

Raymond remained darkly upright, and continued walking towards the epicentre. The smoke filled his nose and dropped acrid beads down the back of his throat. He could taste thick and bitter spice, and could barely swallow. He bore deeper and saw that the buildings on either side of where the repository had sat were now crumpled, imploded into themselves. Girders stood twisted, their skewer-like remains alight and belching toxic black plumes. As for the store itself, it was now a blazing, vaporous nothing. In front of where it had stood, there was no distinction between pavement and road. Both were covered in a homogenous yellow-grey sludge.

Where the heat became too great at the edge of the inferno, Raymond stood still, the paralysing seconds ticking right by. He looked into the sacrificial heart of the fire, wondering whether he might walk straight in – an act that could appear to a bystander as an attempt to render assistance, but the alternative, of course, was simple immolation, a surrender to fiery relief from what was surely to follow. After all, what the devil's worth of good was he going to be?

Close to where he stood, just a mound amongst the piles of ash and debris, the small body of a child began to cry. Tears mixed with soot to form a muddy paste around the boy's eyes and mouth. Raymond squatted and began to wipe gently at the child's face with the edge of his sleeve. He began to feel for a pulse and look for injuries, but stopped himself, knowing that the moment he commenced any sort of medical assessment at this very mouth of hell, he would be consumed by the devastation of it. He crouched in close and supported the boy's filthy head, murmuring words of comfort. Raymond's hands became steeped in mud as he stroked the lad's hair.

As Raymond cowered over the child, he became aware of bulky manly forms, appearing yellow-like through the smoke.

'Doc! You're needed at the hospital. They've started taking the casualties there. Leave this one. We'll sort him out. This is our job. Mick here will take you.' And with that he was manhandled up and out of the venomous cloud, bundled into a firetruck, and raced up the hill to the waiting hospital.

There has been more experience with blast injuries, more research into the medical consequences of explosions, more human hours dedicated to the understanding of those violent fulminations than even the common cold, thanks to the theatre of war. Bloody, explosive battles have provided fertile ground for experimentation and improvisation in surgical care, which has then been transported home and translated (with no small amount of ego by the military surgeons, Raymond recalled) into the more genteel roles of civilian care. It was from one such veteran that Raymond had learned all he knew ('all that someone like you would need to know') about explosions and mass casualties. 'Burst eardrums, lungs popped or ripped off their hinges, shattered bones and ragged amputations good only for the bucket. That's what you need to look out for.'

Raymond jolted around with the movement of the truck, not blinking as he looked through the smeared windows, while the driver ground the gears up the hill. He gripped onto the handle of the door, hoping to still his head full of terror. During the too-brief journey, he focused on trying to calm himself. What good, otherwise, would he be? He attempted to retrieve memories bulldozed away by the flippancy of time, but the bouncing motion and the looming hospital prevented him from locating too many.

'The tools of a good military doctor, in the heat of battle, are several strong tourniquets, a sharp saw, plenty of plasma (use the nurses if you have to – they're strong fillies), and lots of antiseptic. Be ruthless with expectancy. If somebody can't breathe on their own, it's no good hanging around trying to ventilate them. It'll just slow you down. Remember – the greatest good for the greatest number. Better let one half-dead one go, rather than not get to twenty possible survivors.' More than that Raymond could not remember, having preferred the delicate pursuit of an elevated conflation of philosophy, poetry and medicine. Fat lot of good this would be now, he realised.

And thus it was, sitting alone in the back of a firetruck, on a rancid oily seat, rattling closer to the hospital entrance, that Raymond felt the white dread of the imminent. He knew nothing of use. His mind was naught but blank, short-circuiting static.

The truck screamed to a halt outside the hospital gates at the same time as the first injured ones were arriving. Raymond was ejected and propelled to the front of the incoming wash. He braced himself.

'Where shall we put them?' a man supporting a limp, ash-coloured victim asked.

'Anywhere you can,' Raymond responded. 'Anywhere,' he repeated. 'I'll have a look at them as they come, sort them as they arrive. Where are the nurses? Where is the matron?'

As he spoke, he spied Margaret panting, braced at the front door. She looked pale, her face sheened in an unhealthy sweat. Beatrice and Candace also appeared from round the side, running and gasping for breath.

'We've set up what we could. There's not much here, you know. You've not prepared for this,' Margaret yapped at him, her accusations unmistakable.

'Thank you, Matron. Perhaps if you could go in and get started. I'll look at putting the sickest ones in the men's ward. If they can walk they can go to the children's ward. And if they,' he stopped to swallow, 'look like they're in imminent danger, then through to the operating room.'

Margaret glowered at him, and then disappeared back inside. His forceful instructions seemed to bolster the flotsam of helpers who were pouring in through the front gate, some bearing human loads.

The quickest route into the hospital (a most unsatisfactory design feature) was directly through Raymond's front office, and a caravan of patients had begun to traverse it. Several more victims arrived; Raymond counted eight or nine in total, maybe more, coming by every conceivable method – over shoulders, on coats for stretchers, and in the arms of men forming sedan chairs with their mates, the heads of the injured lolling slackly on their shoulders. He gave each of them a destination. Barry and Maude even turned up with one – the small boy that Raymond had seen on the path, by the looks of it. Raymond watched as the victims were taken, one by one, through that oak door, held ajar by a shaking volunteer. They trailed rivulets of blood and other murky secretions through his prized and golden front room.

Margaret appeared again, fighting her way past the current.

'I think that's the last of them,' he said. 'I'll institute a triage system for the casualties.'

She hawked at him. 'A triage system? It's not a bloody Napoleonic war! Get inside, now, and start helping.'

He blanched. 'Matron, I will need you to—'

'Do not even—' she began, saliva flying from her mouth.

He wanted to yell at her, at everybody, *Help*, but instead began to beseech Margaret to form a united front. They were both interrupted.

'What about this one, Doc?' Two men lurched over with a grey body slouched between their hooked arms. 'What shall we do with him?'

This man must have been close to the middle of the blast. His skin was as mottled as old fruit, and the blood that had soaked through his shirt had gone cold. His tongue hung limply from his mouth, and he had the tone of a ragdoll. What little veneer of confidence Raymond had summoned punctured like a stab wound, and he clutched at his stomach, as if to stop his guts spilling out. He put his hand out to feel the man's pulse, and catching the hint of one, whispered, 'God preserve us all.'

The men carrying the broken body looked up at Raymond. 'The operating room,' he told them.

Margaret, who was shouting at somebody pulling a victim off the back of a utility vehicle, screamed that they were just making the injuries worse.

'Matron!' Raymond found minor comfort in raising his voice. 'Will you go in with this one, please. Prepare the instruments and get some oxygen into him. I'll be in there as soon as I can.'

Only one more patient appeared, the last to trickle through the gate. Raymond looked down the hill for an instant, to where the distant glow and muted rumbling sound had melded into an almost peaceful orange backdrop. Between that and the perdition awaiting behind him, he hesitated in this sanctuary, false as it was. He closed his eyes, aware of the thumping of his heart, and conjured up someone he wasn't – a leader, a knowledgeable and capable academic, a commander, striding amongst the patients knowing exactly what to do, wresting out the truth hidden in each of the injured with a competence of which he had only dreamed.

He heard his name being shrieked and the vision vanished. And with that, he followed the trail of leaking fluids through his office and out into the expanse of hell.

It was the noise that struck him first – a seething mass of sound. He found it hard to distinguish between the different sources, between screams of pain, layers of sobbing, and the words bawled out by the young nurses – the unhinged communication flying about the room. The whoosh in his ears simply added to the din. Candace shouted up to him as he strode in.

'Just do the best you can,' he called out to her. 'I've got to start in the operating room. I'll be back as soon as possible and we'll work out what we need to do in here. Staunch any bleeding and cover the burns, whatever you're able.'

And he closed the door behind him, shutting out the pleas. Inside the still procedures room, there was an unpleasant quiet. Margaret had shooed out the helpers and had set to work on the patient, cutting off his sodden clothes and holding an oxygen mask onto the loose folds of his face. His respirations were feeble, and the hiss of gas suggested that little was finding its way into where it was needed.

Realising he still had his coat on, Raymond pulled it off and flung it in the corner, then made straight for the table. He clenched his hands and anchored himself. He had to do what he could.

'Right, what have we got here, Margaret?'

'Can't you see?' Margaret's hair had become loose and wild, and a smear of charcoal had formed a stripe down one side of her face. 'Look at his chest!'

Raymond pulled back the remains of the shirt to see a runty, frayed hole in the right side of the poor man's chest. It was meaty and oozing, and flaccid bubbles gurgled out each time an exhausted breath was attempted. Despite the assistance of oxygen, the grey man gulped without sound, and his pupils were dilated with mute terror.

'There, there, sir. Just try to breathe. We're here to help. We are going to help. Let's see what I can do. Margaret, morphine, please. Then bring me whatever instruments you can find.' He pulled on a pair of rubber gloves and the sound of them snapping echoed off the walls, loud over the hiss and the gush.

He peered into the wound. God, what a mess. Red bubbles frothed up with every breath, spitting out onto Raymond's shirt. He grabbed a clutch of gauze without taking his eyes off the hole and began to wipe away the clots and the muck. This was a sucking chest wound. Long-ago lectures flared somewhere deep. First principles. He pierced his fingers through the floppy, torn flesh, right down into the chest cavity, but there was nothing but space. A hiss of air expelled when he pulled out his finger and Raymond had a moment of hope. He needed to release any trapped air, and perhaps the alveoli could ventilate again, suck oxygen back into the collapsed lung. He plunged his finger back in.

'What are you doing?' Margaret's voice was screeching.

'It's a tension pneumothorax, Margaret. The lung has popped and it's squashing the heart. I need a tube or a catheter of some sort. What have we got? And he also needs some intravenous fluids. I need both. Are you able to start a drip?'

'What do you want me to do first?' she shouted. 'I've only got one set of hands.'

'I understand that, Margaret, it's just that time is paramount. I know this is difficult, but,' he raced over to the shelves on the side, pulling off trays and bowls, 'I just need a chest tube of sorts. It'll help the body fix itself.'

'What do you mean help the body fix itself?' Her voice had heightened to a shrill hysteria. 'Isn't that your job? Oh God …' And she trailed off, looking down at the man, her face contorted with horror. His eyes had closed, but not in the gentle dying way of the end. They had swollen like gaseous blisters and were squashed shut. Air had crept its way out of the lungs and had tracked up and down the man's body until he was puffed up like a blowfish, turning crackly and bloated.

'I can't get a blood pressure!' Margaret scrabbled around, trying to push a stethoscope into the man's now distorted arm. It too had inflated, and the skin resembled pale pork crackling.

'There's no pulse, either.' Raymond had returned to the table and had dug his fingers into the bursting neck. They sank up to his knuckles.

Margaret took a step back. Raymond careened back to the chest, and picturing every image in every textbook he had ever seen, began to compress it, rhythmically, desperately. He threw himself into every pump. 'One, two, three, four.' With each push, dark-red foam spat out of the man's mouth, catching the light of the globe overhead. 'Margaret, can you do mouth to mouth?'

Margaret looked over at the jolting head, blown up and frothing, and slapped a hand to her mouth. She shook her head and backed further to the door. Raymond stumbled over to begin breathing into the man's mouth, which now looked slippery with blood, but then paused, looking down, assessing the horror. The man was bone still. The bubbling was finished. He was inert. All had gone quiet.

Raymond stepped back himself, staring at the stillness on the table. There was a muggy silence, broken only by the heavy dripping of blood onto the floor. But then, other sounds began to trickle into the room. He could hear his name being called. Shouts from the wards behind were filling the air.

'He's gone. Cover him up please, Margaret.' Raymond tried to swallow his dry saliva. 'When you're done, please follow me.' He flicked off his gloves, took a few steps to the sink and washed his hands. Then, without ceremony, he splashed water over his face, gulping down some of it. 'We have a lot of work to do.'

Margaret turned to him, her face devoid of colour, except for a pulsing flush at the base of her throat. 'Are you satisfied now?' She held up an accusatory finger, which was cartilage white. Raymond could see that it was trembling. 'What the hell were you doing in there?'

'What? Margaret, I …' Raymond realised she'd never seen anyone suffer such trauma before. Not that he had, but at least there was a logic to what had happened. She looked splintered, shaking. 'Margaret, that was subcutaneous emphysema. It can just happen after such a huge pneumothorax. It's not likely we could have done much to prevent it.' Although he may not have witnessed it before, the principles did not feel so much a stranger. But as reassuring as those thoughts were, the oncoming practicalities would be another matter, and he could sense them hurling their weight into the door behind them.

'I don't bloody care what you call it,' she wailed. 'You …' She spluttered out her words but couldn't finish.

'Margaret,' Raymond said, and he heard a softness in his tone. 'Let us get back to the rest of the patients. The night ahead of us will be long. We need to approach the situation in an ordered fashion. Let us divide and,' he couldn't bring himself to say 'conquer', so just repeated, 'let's divide up the sickest. Starting with the men's ward. I need your help, Margaret.'

'You're damned right you need help,' she sniffed, but she gathered up some of the equipment and followed him out into the noise.

As soon as he entered the men's ward, Beatrice grabbed him by the arm. 'I'm sorry! I'm so sorry.' She pointed at one of the beds. Slumped at a terrible angle was a man with a head soused in blood, a huge divot out of one side. Cherry-coloured fluid had leaked from one ear, forming a huge halo on the sheets.

'He just slipped away while I was with the man over there. Really, I am sorry.' Tears bulged in her eyes.

Raymond moved closer to the bed and looked at the mess of the head injury. He placed a hand on Beatrice's arm. 'Beatrice, there's nothing you could have done. That sort of head injury – it's not salvageable.' What a dreadful word, salvageable. It sounded judgemental, moralistic. He vowed not to use it again.

The room was heaving. Raymond absorbed it all in an instant – the two other beds occupied and five more casualties lying on sheets on the floor. It was an unthinkable job that lay ahead, a vastness he couldn't begin to calculate. He looked around for Miss Rosa. Where was she? He had an unexpected desire to see her there, efficient and strong, moving through the chaos, holding together the breaking parts like twine.

He spoke loudly, to be heard above the din.

'This is what needs to happen. I will make a brief assessment of each of the patients. Work out what to do. We will try to treat people where they lie. Most people have burns, thus our priorities are pain relief, intravenous fluids and covering the open areas.' He spoke to the two nurses, away from Margaret. 'In circumstances such as this, you will all need to perform duties that you may not feel necessarily trained for.' He wondered to whom he was directing this. Himself?

The cadre attended to each of the victims in an order dictated by Raymond. He himself couldn't have said what that order actually was, simply who appeared the most desperate as he looked.

'Over there!' he'd call, and they would change direction, pounding to the next victim. As he had said, most of the patients were burnt, with glistening sheets of skin pulling away like wet tissue. Several others had been struck by projectiles, and were pierced and bleeding, great chunks of lacerations open to the curdled air. Together they attached bags of fluids to the wounded and administered oxygen. One man had an arm riven through – a mangled mess – and Raymond and Beatrice wheeled him into the operating room so he could be cobbled together, Raymond splashing silvery-brown antiseptic fluid around like water and using the anaesthetic machine as best he could. The pair then brought him back out into the noise. Margaret, a great wadge of red foam clumped behind her right ear, seemed to be yelling a lot of instructions at Candace. Raymond knew he had to be orderly, to think clearly, to assess thoroughly each of the casualties. Who knew what injuries were lurking in the crevices of the patients' bodies? They could be exploded inside like Christmas crackers, and it was imperative he uncover the mutilations, diagnose the damage. He stopped frequently, trying to lumber through memories of lectures and books. But somehow, in the needs and the pandemonium and the clinging heat and the charred smell, a mighty entropy overtook the place, a decline into spattering energy. Raymond surrendered to it, and a previously unknown autopilot switched on.

Townsfolk, loved ones, gawkers, helpers, all had started to trickle into this first ward. Raymond had to squeeze through milling crowds to return to each patient, to check on their progress, and he would again commit himself to the hegemony of each individual in front of him. He intermittently lost sight of the nurses. Carrying on, he hung up more bags, poured fluids into parched bodies, and ensured oxygen was being delivered to those sounding suffocated. He discovered a dog-legged gash running down the lower leg of a waxy adolescent that he'd missed earlier on, with muscle and fascia bulging from its depths. The white flash of shin bone was visible at the bottom end, and oily blood dripped from it as though a tap were left on. He sutured the wound together haphazardly, quickly, knowing the best he could do amongst the circumstances was to approximate edges. And in all of them he checked and covered burns – wrapping them to protect them from the night air seeping through the windows.

Despite this attempt to let in a breeze, the air became thick – laden heavy with lament and blood. The sickly atmosphere cloyed at everyone in the infirmary, and foul viscous sweat clung to their skin. A sweltering heat hung inside, even though the Pilbara sun had long since departed for the day.

The crowd mechanically stepped aside to let Raymond through, watching him, and he would wipe his head with a soaking shirtsleeve and glance around to get his bearings before immersing himself back in the patient in front of him. He still hadn't seen Miss Rosa. Barry wended his way through, grabbing another volunteer, and without fuss, took away the dead man. Raymond watched them disappear; a man whose name he did not know, his deeds in Wittenoom now consigned to history.

Candace slipped through the horde and grabbed Raymond. 'Can you help with this one, Doctor, his breathing's getting worse.'

She led him back to one of the first men to have been brought in, the one with the worst burns. Margaret had him propped up, and had an oxygen mask shoved on his face. His lips were dusky blue, and Raymond could see that he was struggling. Flame had encircled his chest like a hug, but now the burns were turning white and leathery and hard. They were constricting his chest, as sure as a python, and he couldn't breathe. Raymond remembered a phrase – *release the Roman breastplate*, and he shut his eyes for a moment.

'Candace. I need a knife. Iodine. And hurry, please.'

She returned instantly, and, in front of a mob of onlookers, Raymond drew a full breath, sloshed the bowl of coppery fluid over the chest and then sliced a great box shape into the front of the man's chest. Margaret blanched, and several spectators screamed as he cut down far enough to release pale, billowing flesh, but the patient himself was stoic, and within several moments a salmon-pink had returned to his face. His breathing became easier. Raymond looked at his work, a wonky, bleeding, trapezoid shape, covered in ash. Lord only knew what he'd cut into. Despite the temporary reprieve, Raymond couldn't help but see his handiwork as dirt and filth and ineptitude. Margaret, white as death, looked at him with loathing, then simply decamped.

Raymond croaked to Candace, 'Has anyone from the mine turned up? Any other medics? Is there anyone who can help me? I don't even know who to call.' She quietly shook her head.

He saw this and said nothing more.

Inside his head he heard words of vitriol – barbs of criticism and stinging words of disgust – but a curious dichotomy settled itself into his behaviour, and with each swipe directed at himself his outward actions became kinder, softer. His voice became calm and his touch became tender.

After a further hour of toil, the score of painful cries began to subside into a soft blanket of moaning. An opiate calm washed through the room and the mob settled. Raymond, however, had a stew inside of him. He was not sure if he'd managed to do anything decent at all; it was unclear whether he'd sutured tissue to tendon, whether he'd cleaned wounds well enough, if he'd caused harm when all he'd wanted was good. Had he missed injuries that were biding their time in tucked-away viscera, which would jump out and declare themselves later? And, in addition, any foolish ideas of his about the elegance of medicine were in tatters. A dignified truth? Not likely. In one single day, the great philosophers had soured in him, leaving nothing but derision at his former bookish self. He saw his existence for what it was – sawdust. The hot, dry, littered remains of anything he had hoped to achieve by coming out here. He put a hand onto the wall and wondered how he would ever survive himself. Exhaustion suffused into him, down his back, into his thighs.

He saw the taut walk of Miss Rosa passing him by, her arms full of bandages and instruments.

'Miss Rosa.' His voice was weak and dry. 'Where have you been?' He reached out and clutched her arm.

She braced him, transferring her goods to the other arm. 'I've been here all the time.' Gently, she put down her load and supported Raymond with her elbow. 'Let me get you something to drink. You still have several people to see.'

'No, I couldn't. I need to … More patients? Really? Where are they?'

'There are only a few left. We have them down in the children's ward. The walking wounded. Mrs Italiano and I – she came back tonight when she heard the explosion – we've been in there. We could see that you and the nurses were busy, so we just did what we could. None of the patients is very badly injured. They can wait a little longer.'

'Of course. Of course, I'd forgotten, I can't, no I mean they can't …'

'You need to sit yourself down, even if it's just for a moment. Look at how much you've done already. I'm going to get you something. Please just rest here.' And she disappeared off to her kitchen.

Raymond did look at all he'd done and he shook his head. He could taste his deficiencies, the gastric acid of them. Had he been a better man, superiorly trained, more learned, he would have captained this night far more competently. Overseen its command less pitiably. He had relied on a few primitive medical reflexes and some basic knowledge, but these were a pallid skillset for a lone country doctor.

He faltered past the groans, through his office, and out into the night, where the air was deceivingly still. A remote sense of catastrophe continued to smoulder down the end of town – a burnished blur, colour fused with muted noise. The odd shout. Other, strange clanking sounds.

Raymond leaned against the filthy wall and, soundlessly, like a child drowning, slipped to the ground. He felt the hot adult tears of defeat spill out, two or three only, and then they simply stopped, his dehydrated body unable to produce any more.

VI

No idea ends up being back in Port Hedland.

Lou has driven like she's sleepwalking, blindly getting distance between herself and Wittenoom. In a little over three hours, she finds herself rolling into the town that seems to be constructed entirely from sheets of rust, laid out in repeating slabs down the main street like dominoes. Everything is oxidised here. The roads are expansive, wide plains of tar built for ten-tonne trucks, and are lined by blocks of buildings, each of them an identical, coated, flaking brown. It's a ruthless place – the intersection of iron ore, natural gas and fractured families.

She drives aimlessly through the streets and past the hospital, hoping nobody catches sight of her. A somnambulist, with no destination in mind. Soon she'll return the rental, with no plans beyond the handing over of keys.

Carrying on back into the main part of town, she drives in low gear, a sneaking paranoia sitting beside her on the passenger seat. Everyone will be able to see that she doesn't belong. On the street they all wear a uniform – the high-visibility yellow that designates the wearer as being part of a greater whole. At this point it's an inclusion she feels an envy for. A life laid out, planned, preordained. As she drives through, people turn to look at her in a slow, unsmiling way. *They recognise me*, she thinks. The hopeless doctor who couldn't hack it, who came up here with baggage so heavy, all she could do was stumble and fall.

By the time she's done a lap of the central area and looked at the brutish buildings all lined up, she knows she's in the mood to drink.

The pubs are a carbon copy of one another. Utilitarian and unimaginative and there for a purpose. Unappealing advertisements for acts she'd never heard of peel away from their windows, leaving behind triangular, dirty stains.

The first drink is down before it even leaves a ring on the table. By the second she's lightened up enough to pull her notebook out of her bag and clear a spot for it. Nobody bothers her. People hardly bother each other. Disappointed fizzing sounds spray from beer cans opening throughout the room. The drinking here is concerted. Few words are spoken. Most of the light comes from the bain-marie, where the glass steams up in greasy pulses, giving Lou a glimpse of sagging food. She knows she should eat but can't stomach the thought right now. Instead, she orders another drink.

She opens her book to where the words of the last few days have flooded out, exposing her like some dark crime. She's having trouble focusing, and she turns the pages, trying to remember why she wrote the things she did. The cover of the journal sticks to the syrupy remains of beer on the table, left behind by a previous shift of drinkers. A toilet stench sludges out of the bathroom every time the door is opened. It is stagnant inside the main bar area, and the overhead fans do nothing to dispel the swampy air. She looks at the words again and she sees that they are outlandish. What's the point of this exercise? Did she really think she was going to work it out of her, inch out the splinters of hurt, just through her scribble? She takes another slug. As if the getting it out means that it's gone for good, her mistakes erased. Somehow, though, the spilling of words is compulsive. She picks up her pen. Liquid clods dribble onto the page. She reads her lines from before, the pomposity of them – *captaining the night more competently* – and she shakes her head. She tells him, *You're just going to have to sort yourself out.*

'I beg your pardon?'

Lou realises she's spoken aloud. The group sitting at the next table are looking at her. 'Did you say something?' A flint-edged girl with a thin face and heavy eyeliner speaks.

Lou shakes her head, fire in her cheeks, and she picks up her notebook and bag. She heads back to the serving bar. All along the bench are plants in colourful pots. She finds another place to sit and orders her fourth drink. The sentences won't come and her thoughts are fuzzed.

She needs to go to the toilet, so she slides off the stool. On the way down, she puts out a hand and knocks over one of the pots. It clatters to the ground, spilling dirt and pottery fragments in a wide arc over the floor. She sees that the pot had a handpainted motif on it – a smiling flower. The bartender looks up at her, as do most of the people in the room. She brushes herself and attempts to negotiate the tables, which seem to have moved since she sat down, and she makes her way unsteadily to the bathroom. Bloated fumes pour out as she wrenches the door open, and she can feel the roomful of stares. The door slams closed behind her and a sudden urge to vomit shudders deep inside. She tries to get to the sink, but misses by a few inches, slopping her guts onto the tiled floor. Then it keeps coming and it will not stop.

One of the party from the table next to her opens the door, but takes a disgusted look and walks back out. Surveying the floor, Lou pulls brown paper towels from the dispenser with an inaccurate hand, and kneels next to her mess. The moment hangs there, loaded with humiliation and the sour smell. With a fistful of the paper towels, she tries to mop up the gluggy piles, but just ends up moving them from one place to another. Her hair dangles into the liquid. The stink is foul and she retches again. The door opens for a second time. It's the manager. Standing over Lou, her revulsion is obvious.

'You're going to have to leave. We have standards here.'

Lou grabs onto the cool corner of the basin and hauls herself up. 'But I'm a …' She doesn't get any further, as her stomach contracts once more in convulsive waves. She turns back to the sink.

The manager dials a number on her cordless phone and, holding a hand over the mouthpiece, says to Lou, 'Exactly,' then she walks out.

Lou looks at the repellant stranger reflected in the mirror. She turns the tap full on and splashes her face, then her hair, and then she dunks her whole head under the running water. The gush flows and flows, and Lou keeps her eyes closed, as if she's swimming underwater, far away from here. She drinks great gulps of the water, filling her empty belly with its coolness. When she finishes, she straightens up and curls her wet hair around her fingers, tucking the ends into her shirt. She limps out, pays for her last drink and retrieves her notebook. The whole place watches her leave.

The vomiting has cleared her head and she's stopped staggering. The sun is arcing towards the horizon, and she wants to walk, perhaps pace out the disgrace. She heads in the same direction as dusk, hoping to reach the harbour. It would be good to see the ocean. And then, if she's brave, she'll find herself a phone. She'll call home. Let her mother know she's alive. She wonders if anybody has missed her, perhaps questioned where she has disappeared to. She wants to call Dave, to apologise for her parting words, which she knew were lacerating, but she has no number for him. He may well not even have a phone, and thus she is let off her cowardly hook.

Shortly, she arrives at the industrial maw of the town. Hulking constructions fill the skyline and reach their fat fingers into the wharf. The odd palm tree makes the port look vacation-like, as if the thought of leisure was added on by the town planners after all the business was taken care of. It is strangely peaceful in the padded light, with the muted clunking noises of the docks in the distance. A picnic table under one of the trees is clean, and Lou sits on the bench. For a while she watches the far-off bustling activity of ships and trucks and cranes, all engrossed in their own business. There's a world out there, of people chugging through the days of their crammed lives, doing good here, doing bad there. *You're still one of them*, she thinks. But her ledger, the load of it, needs redressing. And the only tool she has is the inky one in her pocket. She just can't think of any other way.

The familiar evening cool is wafting in, and it further soothes her head. The water and the fresh air have revived her. Yes, she'll call home. But she'll just sit here a little longer. She pulls out her pen and lets the words float out to the verandah.

Dawn

Raymond pulled himself to his feet. Words floated out to the verandah – a skein of pleas and commands, and his name being spoken. He put his hand against the wall to steady himself.

Miss Rosa wended her way out and handed him a mug full of sweetened tea. She would be able to see that he'd been crying, and he turned his head away. Humiliation doesn't come more comprehensive than this, he thought.

He took the tea from her with thanks, and they both looked down the hill, inhaling the remission of the night air. Here they were momentarily free from the clammy sweat and horror behind them. Raymond drank from the mug without break, needing to refill his thirsty bones. Miss Rosa made no move, as if waiting for Raymond to collect himself. He eventually gave a nod, returning the mug to her, and they walked back in together, through his office, and then down past the metal row of beds.

They passed the blight of the first ward, the stifling disorder and tumult, the heaped-up sheets, and the patients lying on the floor amongst the horde of helpers. Turning into the children's ward, the counterpoint calm was noticeable, although the gaudy motifs on the wall blared a greeting at him, somehow mocking the anguish of the night. Miss Rosa walked behind him, a net if he should falter.

Three patients occupied the beds, and there was one dusty man, rocking in a chair in the corner. Raymond caught the smell of eucalypt, the scent of old-fashioned balm.

None of the urgency outside could be felt in here. Mrs Italiano sat beside the bed of a child, tenderly stroking his hair. She looked up at Raymond. 'You came,' she said.

He tramped over to them, making dirty footprints on the floor.

'No, you came, Mrs Italiano. After all that has happened today. You came.'

'Well who wouldn't?' she said.

Raymond couldn't be sure, but it looked like her charge was the boy from the path, the paste of his tears cleaned away, unearthing a healthy pink. 'His mum's back through there,' she gestured, 'helping out.'

'We've just now shooed out the rest of the volunteers, too,' Miss Rosa said. 'These people need a bit of quiet.'

Raymond put a hand on the boy's forehead, and was reassured by his hearty breath seesawing away in the thick air. He would have prayed thanks, if he'd believed in the power of it. A good thing he didn't, he admitted, as tonight would have shaken the last of any faith from him.

In the undersized bed opposite a man lay bent in and squashed, sleeping, marking time with his snores. Bandages were wrapped around all four of his limbs, in rather flamboyant and un-nurse-like fashion, the ends tucked in triangles and the tails folded like bows. Miss Rosa looked at Raymond, expectantly.

'You've done an excellent job,' he spoke through his exhaustion. 'Excellent. Both of you.' The two women, who were holding themselves tense, relaxed their posture and emitted a noiseless sigh. He turned to the woman in the bed next to the boy. 'Are you able to tell me what's happened here?' he asked Miss Rosa.

She walked over to the side of a Mrs Flavell, and introduced her to Raymond as the sole teacher of Wittenoom's tiny school.

'Good God,' was all Mrs Flavell said in response.

She still wore her shredded yellow dress, but had most of her wounds already salved and bathed by the self-recruited pair of helpers.

'Lord only knows how she got caught up in all of this,' Miss Rosa said, 'and I certainly can't get a straight answer from her.'

Mrs Flavell looked like she had caught the skirt of the blast.

'What's going on here, then?' She looked up at the colourful animals parading across the walls, her brow contracted with confusion.

Miss Rosa whispered, 'I keep telling her. I think I've explained a dozen times already – she doesn't seem to understand.'

'Mrs Flavell, is it?' Raymond asked. The woman looked up at the doctor, muddled. He said, 'There's been a terrible accident. One of the mining stores in town has blown up and is on fire.' He paused, a distant thud sounding in his head. Accident. An oddly benign word for such incendiary terror. It suggested a mild oversight, like a scraped knee on a misplaced toy.

In the chair opposite, the ruddy man continued to rock. Raymond could hardly hear him, but thought he was saying *accident*, over and over.

Miss Rosa spoke, bringing his attention back to Mrs Flavell. 'I have told her that, she simply doesn't remember.'

'Oh, good God,' Mrs Flavell said.

'It looks like you've been knocked flat,' said Raymond. 'I just need to have a look at some of these wounds.'

Mrs Flavell darted frantic glances down at her dress, each ragged hole fringed with filth, and then back up to the carnival on the wall.

'Good God. What's going on here?'

Miss Rosa had the good manners not to roll her eyes. She gestured to Raymond – see?

Raymond stood alongside, temporarily revived, and they faced the questions together. As they spoke, Raymond repeating the answers, he systematically examined Mrs Flavell, going over her from head to toe, taking his careful time. Underneath the gapes of her dress were myriad puncture marks, tiny bloody divots embroidered into her skin like a quilt. Miss Rosa had cleaned most of them, and had tended to any lacerations where she could.

'Oh my,' Mrs Flavell said, again peeking up at the wall. 'What's happened here? I'd better go and help.' And she hoisted herself up, trying to climb off the bed. Both Raymond and Miss Rosa lay gentle hands on her arms.

'Anterograde amnesia,' he said to Miss Rosa. 'It's a type of concussion where this package of memories has been blasted from her mind. And nothing new will be recorded. The only cure is time. Not a thing we say will be registered at all – it will all simply wash away.'

'Then, Mrs Flavell,' Miss Rosa put a fond hand on the teacher's shoulder, 'we are at the seaside, having a picnic. It's been a bit blowy, but otherwise everything is fine.' Raymond and Miss Rosa glanced directly at each other with the smallest of smiles, just for an instant.

'Oh, that's alright, then,' Mrs Flavell replied. 'Although, why I chose this dress I'll never know. Not suitable for the seaside at all.'

'Do we know when her memory will return?' Miss Rosa wiped a delicate finger underneath the creases of her eye.

'No.' Raymond stood, stretching out his back. 'She's lucky.' He looked towards the door leading back to the rest of the hospital. Moans and cries were still audible from beyond. 'She'll never remember any of this. Whereas we, well we ...'

Miss Rosa lightly touched his arm. 'The worst is over, Dr Filigree. Everything will return to normal, eventually. It's the way of things.' Her words were emollient, and were enough to soothe him.

The man muttering in the corner started up again, and Raymond looked over. 'How is he?' Raymond asked of the women. 'What did he present with?'

'Well, he was a bit staggery when he came in,' Miss Rosa replied. 'He seems to know where he is, but then he keeps repeating himself. We asked him if he was hurt anywhere, but he just shakes his head. He has a few grazes and such, and we've washed them down, but otherwise we're not sure. We were waiting for you.'

'I think it's Arthur Curtis, from down the men's camp,' Mrs Italiano said. 'My Federico knew him. In fact, I thought he was the union leader, although I can't be certain.'

Raymond stepped over. 'Mr Curtis, is it? Are you alright? Are you injured?'

'They're trying to kill us. I tell you, trying to kill us. See what they did?' He stared past Raymond. Mrs Italiano nodded subtly.

'No, Mr Curtis, it was an accident. No one's trying to kill you,' Raymond said. 'Are you alright? Does it hurt anywhere? Is it painful to breathe?'

Shaking his head, the man repeated, 'Won't be long, now, mark my words.'

Raymond spoke to the two women. 'He must have had a knock to the head, too – a concussion. He's not making any sense.'

The two women glanced at each other.

Raymond explained to the man that he would attend to him shortly, and he returned his attention to Mrs Flavell, who was observing the scene with skittish confusion whilst being restrained delicately by Miss Rosa.

At that moment, Margaret strode in, her face streaked with grime and rage, her hair wild, her nurse's cap long missing.

'What's going on in here? Who's done the bandaging of these patients? You're not trained.' She looked beaten, as though the betrayal in this final room had done what the rest of the inferno had not quite managed. Tears spilled out, soaking into the dirt of her cheeks, and a couple took straight, muddied paths down both sides of her face.

She continued to rant and spittle flew from her mouth. Clenching her fists in front of her, she blamed God for this disaster, her nursing contemporaries for their dull incompetence, and Raymond for being instrumental in the leaking away of the lives in the other rooms. She climaxed with a spray of blame in this last ward, hosing insults on the silent women. Margaret looked at Raymond with a wet glare of expectation, as if demanding his support.

'What more do you all want from me?' she wailed.

Everybody else remained silent.

'That's enough now, Matron.' Raymond stepped between Margaret and Miss Rosa. 'Quite enough. I understand how difficult tonight has been, but we're all in this together. Miss Rosa and Mrs Italiano have done an excellent job here, considering the circumstances.'

'Really?' She sniffed. 'You think this is a good job? You think any of this, in this poisoned hellhole is a good job? Well, good luck to all of you.'

'Please, Matron. I need everybody on board tonight. If you would be so kind as to go back through and check on those that are left.' Raymond tilted his head towards the men's ward.

'You've got enough of your lackeys doing that.' She put a hand to the hash of her hair. 'You,' she spat, 'you're welcome to them. To it all. I hope your ridiculous ideas help.' And with that she left. Stomped off to the nurses' quarters, where it was later discovered she had packed her bags and was gone. The dawn had not yet begun its appearance.

Raymond looked at the floor for a few moments, while Miss Rosa hushed the flustered Mrs Flavell, and Mrs Italiano patted the hand of Mr Curtis as he rocked. All Raymond could see was the grime and the patterns; the paths of footprints and the curling tracks of dirt, as if there were some sort of message in them. He could feel the bullseye sting of Margaret's words. There was veracity within them – where *was* his great truth in the filth and pain amongst this disaster? The weight of the dead and the injured hung heavy on him, as if they were stone, as if they were concrete, literal things. His teeth were coated and his legs ached. The room next door continued to thrum, a low and cumbrous noise. And with that he returned quietly to Mrs Flavell, as did Miss Rosa. He ran a hand over the matted back of her head, where the laceration had split into her scalp.

'Let's stitch up this wound, shall we?'

'Good God. What's going on here?'

Miss Rosa made gentle soothing noises, and instructed Mrs Italiano on where to find some of the remaining stashes of equipment to assist in the job.

Underneath the low-wattage globe, Raymond set to repairing the gash, cleaning the wound with a placid rhythm, so at odds with all that had gone before. Mrs Flavell lay remarkably still under the ministrations of Miss Rosa, asking only the occasional, quiet question. At last, in the fragile hours, the hospital fell into silence as the pair worked away. After a short time, they looked over to see Mrs Italiano asleep with her arm curled around the head of the boy, and the bandaged man juddering peacefully. Miss Rosa's movements remained proficient and purposeful, whereas Raymond began to yawn as he pieced together the final corners of the wound. As the last stitch was tied off, he leaned over Mrs Flavell's pillow and fell asleep.

Miss Rosa cleaned up the scissors and the forceps and the bloodied gauze, and sat down herself. The worst was over.

And that same relief floated its way through the breathing of the living and the settling of the fixtures in the infirmary. Surely it was over. Nothing could get any worse than this. Nothing.

VII

Lou books into a hotel on the outskirts of town; a squat, rectangle of a building that serves anonymous breakfasts. She tells the clerk at the front: two, maybe three nights.

It only ends up being one.

She spends that one alone with her notebook. Shutting the door on the rumble of road trains, she pulls the chain across and makes countless cups of scorching, bitter tea from the no-brand teabags found in a basket on the bench.

The cell of a room is a dirty, clingy oatmeal colour. Its walls are stained with freakish, damp shapes, and Lou wonders if anyone has ever ended their life in here, its misery an encouraging backdrop. The fluorescent light on the wall buzzes frenetically once in a while as bugs are zapped to an ozone-reeking death, but even that doesn't mask the smell of rancid butter spilling from an air conditioner set permanently on high.

She continues to write.

VII

As she pushes on, she discovers that letting this peculiar story unravel is exposing unexpected memories of her own, and not just the mechanical occurrences of her past, but ideas she has not revisited for months, maybe years. Emotions, too, maybe because they have been cemented down deep with her recollections, and are now being excavated, hauled up and into the light.

She takes a break and slips into the shower stall, needing to rinse away the dirt that has stubbornly clung on. The water is bitingly hot and she lets it bucket over her. It surprises her, in the hypnotic drum, to suddenly remember something good, a worthwhile moment, when she'd been convinced that all that had gone before was bad. She has the image in her head of an Italian man's heart. The recollection is more feeling than detail. A lost impression of how enchanted she'd been with the wonder of medicine, wrapped in a sense of being esteemed, wanted. It was before, she thinks, before that singular catastrophic day. Before everything good was hosed away. A day of soft sunshine – such a contrast to the gravid cold that blew in soon afterwards. Perhaps though, it's just the unfamiliar feeling of achievement that makes her remember it this way. A male patient, in his fifties, was rushed into the emergency department, hunched over with chest pain, a man the colour of stone, glistening with sweat. It was night-time. Yes, she remembers that because there were few people around. Within seconds of his arrival, he'd crashed – his infarcting, dying heart deteriorating into a fibrillating mess.

The details she can't accurately recall, but she remembers going for hours, a team of hive-efficient nurses at her side, compressing, shocking, responsive to every flat line and jagged lapse of the ECG. The motion of the team was balletic, and the complexity of the pathology keeping the man dangling at the cliff's edge was spectacular. She remembers thinking of the pathological progress as poetry: the rhythms, the grand artistry of the interactions between electricity, myocardial cells, pumps, blood vessels. And he'd survived, eventually having his coronary obstruction ballooned away by another team upstairs. The other thing that stayed with her was the admiration of the staff and the teary gratitude of the corpulent wife, who came down the next day to thank her, bringing a basketful of snacks as a gift, and a bear of a hug that stayed with her for days.

But as she stands there, with the water starting to run cold, sinkholes start to open. Again, she chastises herself for allowing good memories to fill her head. She doesn't deserve this reprieve, as though she is permitted to be all remorse and no redemption. Any further self-congratulatory memories should be banished. Melted down into a hardened clump, all achievements tarnished, dull, forgotten, then tossed.

She towels herself down, and goes back to her untethered words, chewing on the end of her pen. More pages fill. The thing is, if this story is supposed to be some vehicle for atonement, then all she is doing is avoiding the main event. She carries on regardless.

By late afternoon she's hungry, and she creeps out of her room to find food. In a run-down shopping mall nearby, she discovers a delicatessen that sells sandwiches and surprisingly palatable coffee. She lingers, enjoying the invisibility. In a corner of the mall is a makeshift information stand: a couple of tattered banners and a trestle table laid out with scattered pamphlets. She walks closer – there is no one in attendance. Next to the material on the table is a tangle of abandoned knitting – a ball of aqua wool and the beginnings of something that might be a holey scarf, as well as a half-drunk cup of tea. She picks up a brochure. A stylised statue-of-liberty logo proclaims its authorship – the Asbestos Justice Society. Full of enraged information, by the looks of it. It's entitled *The Dust Murders*, and it's printed on cheap paper, as though it has been produced on a home computer by somebody too angry for formatting. The cover picture, however, is compelling. It's an old photo – a grainy blue face wearing a headlight, looking as though he'd seen his own death. There's nobody around to ask, so she takes one back to her hotel.

Settling back at the cramped desk, she flicks through the pamphlet's flimsy few pages. In almost unreadably small font, it outlines the history of the asbestos mines at Wittenoom. Exactly as Dave had told her, with more. She reads dot points about the lawlessness of the town, the brutal, heavy-handed techniques of those in charge, and then the years of savage and deliberate neglect of the workers. A timeline shows a lapse – a latent period during which victims were presumably brewing their demise, and it culminates in the blooded battle for every compensation claim that followed.

There's a small section on the doctors Dave mentioned, both Saint and McNulty, who went back to Wittenoom time after time, the scandal of it revealed slowly to them. Then they began to write – just as Dave had said, and they did not let up. But they were words that were not heard, not at the time, anyway. What would that have been like, she wonders, hurling oneself repeatedly against the doors of this profit-drunk corporation? Brawling for justice, in the form of report after blasting, uncompromising report?

She turns the brochure over. On the back is an odd picture – a rectangular metal opening in the side of a hill, with a façade the colour of coffee grounds, smeared in faded graffiti, a foot or two off ground level. There is no explanation next to it, and Lou guesses its ugliness is some form of anti-advertisement.

Putting down the brochure, she is distracted by the cold sight of the telephone. She'd promised herself to call home. And she finally does.

The conversation is mostly one-sided. Her mother runs through a checklist of Lou's transgressions, related primarily to the worry her daughter has accorded her. Lou is berated for dumping Sam, that boyfriend her mother liked so much, for not contacting her brother, and several other general misdemeanours. Before hanging up, she tells Lou that someone from the Perth hospital has been trying to get in contact with her and she's left a phone number. No, her mother doesn't know what the woman wants, but it would be nice if Lou could ring her so she can stop bothering her, thank you very much. Lou's resignation from Port Hedland doesn't find its way into the discussion.

The phone number is for an administrative assistant; a short, fussy woman who'd been curiously supportive during the month after the incident. She'd steered Lou through the initial minefields, but even her patience wore thin when the waves of complaints began lapping at the doors of the hospital's offices. She'd arranged the details of Lou's job up north, agreeing with the director that it might be useful for Lou to put some distance between herself and Perth.

VII

Lou looks at the piece of paper with the number on it, turning it over in her hand. Eventually she rings it, and makes her way through to the right person.

'It's Lou.'

A silence clogs the end of the line. Lou can hear papers being shuffled.

'Lou Fitzgerald. You wanted me to ring?'

'Yes, I know which Lou. We've been trying to contact you.' The briskness in the woman's voice indicates any friendship the two may have had has evaporated.

'I'm sorry, it's just that I—'

The woman interrupts. 'Where are you currently? We've been told you resigned from your registrar post.'

Lou doesn't know how to explain, and covers the mouthpiece so the wrong sounds won't find their way down the line.

'Anyway,' the woman continues, 'we're going to need you back in Perth. Next week. The coroner's hearing has been announced. It will be in court next Wednesday. You've been summonsed, and are expected to attend.'

Lou looks at the earpiece of the phone. She can hear the woman talking, but she's confused by the words. She makes a few mechanical replies and then the phone clicks off.

A Shakedown

When the morning arrived, Raymond awoke to find himself sitting in a chair under the painted procession of circus animals, covered in a blanket arranged with surgical neatness. Rattling sounds were layered between the knot of voices edging their way through from the ward next door. He stood quickly, letting the blanket drop, and a brief vertigo buffeted him until he found his bearings.

The three patients in the children's ward still slept, and there was no sign of his two helpers. His shirt was filthy and plastered to his chest, and he ran his hand through his hair. A deep ache in his jaw suggested that he must have clenched his way through the hour or so of sleep. The chair that had borne the rocking man, Arthur he remembered, was empty. Where would he have got to? Standing over the boy was a woman in a blue sundress, and she was stroking his hair, humming in a determinedly maternal way. Raymond nodded a quick good morning to her, and stepped out.

In the main ward, a low-level commotion continued to mumble away. Beatrice was checking a blood pressure, and Candace was smoothing out an IV line. They both looked pale and drained of energy. Several of the volunteers still buzzed around. As he appeared, multiple questions were fired at him, a pent-up cohort of confusion. He didn't understand, blaming his sleep-deprived state. Clearing his throat, he began to speak, an uncomfortable task with his larynx like dry toast and his voice just a rasp.

'Our next step is to work out where these patients will go. They can't all stay here. We're overwhelmed as it is.'

'But, Dr Filigree …' Candace started, then looked as though she wasn't sure what to say next.

He moved to the basin and splashed a handful of cool water over his face.

'Now, obviously I am new here, and am not aware of all the proper processes with regard to referring patients to the larger centres. These people will need specialty input – surgeons, respiratory care and so forth. The burns …' he trailed off. Where was the most severely burnt patient? The one on which he'd performed the (horrible, substandard) escharotomies? And there were no patients on the floor. Hadn't they been there just a few hours before?

'Well, that's the thing, Dr Filigree,' Candace said. 'All these ambulances have just turned up. They're lined up out the front, and they've started loading the patients. We presumed you'd called them.'

Raymond strode to the window to see, and sure enough, half a dozen ambulances were there in an orderly queue. In fact, he could see patients being packed into the first couple by ambulance officers, and the back doors slamming shut. He jolted into action and sped out through the front door.

'Ah, hello,' he called out to the men about to climb into the cab of the first vehicle.

'Ah, yes. Doctor. Just sign here, would you?' One of the uniformed men turned and paced over to Raymond with a bundle of papers. His partner started up the engine.

'Oh right, and what is—'

'Just a signature, Doctor. We'll take care of the rest,' the officer interrupted. His shirt was starched and clean, with badges sewn into both blue sleeves. 'Get these patients where they ought to go, eh?'

'Oh. Of course.' Raymond signed the forms, one after the other, barely looking at the garbled content. This must just be the way things are done out here. It felt like a wash of morphine up his veins, a guilty surge of relief – somebody else was helping, another person with responsibility was shouldering the load of this thieving night. The officer shuffled the forms together with a smile, and Raymond did his best to return one, despite the exhaustion that still hung leaden upon him.

A stream of strangers filed in through the front entrance, and then returned, wheeling out the injured one by one. To wedge the great door open, the chair from his office had been pulled out and leaned against the frame. The parade of infirm trundled past him, with their bags of fluid swinging on poles as the ambulance trolleys and stretchers jarred over gravel and bumps.

'Where are they being taken?' Raymond called. 'Out of interest. I'd be most grateful to hear how they all do.' He watched as Mrs Flavell sailed past him. She waved at him without recognition, wriggling herself straight in the chair. Raymond turned to follow her, to explain, but the lead ambulance officer put his fleshy face in front of Raymond's.

'Various places, Doc. You probably wouldn't have heard of them. Don't worry about it. It's all been sorted. Mine executive has been onto it.'

'Oh. Fine. Right. Of course.' Foolish of him to ask.

There was a sudden shift in the orderly evacuation – the young boy from the ward was the last to come out, and his mother was yelling at the officer wheeling the chair.

'He does not need to go anywhere! He's fine.' She spotted Raymond. 'Doctor! Tell them.'

Raymond stood in front of the small cavalcade, bringing it to a halt.

'Steady on here,' he said. 'I don't think this young one needs to be transferred out. There's nothing much wrong with him except a bit of a shake-up.'

The lead officer shook the pile of forms. 'Ah, but you've signed the release, Doctor. Anyway – we've got orders. Everyone injured out.'

'He's not injured,' the mother said, her voice shrill.

At this point, Miss Rosa appeared, marching over from the side of the building. She was immaculately dressed once more, shone and coiffed and fragrant. Joining the deadlock, she stood next to the mother.

'Please pass me his form,' Raymond said slowly, 'and I'll tear it up.'

The officer fixed a gaze on Raymond and the hot seconds ticked by.

'While I don't know whose orders you have,' Raymond continued, his words carefully chosen, 'I can tell you, this boy does not need to be transferred out. Anywhere.' And he looked at Miss Rosa for reassurance. She nodded and clung onto the wheelchair along with the mother.

The officer finally spoke. 'Suit yourself, then,' he said, taking the boy by the arm and pulling him out of the wheelchair. The other officer wheeled the chair away, and a gesture was made for the row of ambulances to start moving out.

While the last of the vans lumbered down the hill, leaving only a shrinking cloud of dust, Raymond stood next to the wire fence, massaging his jaw. The boy let go of his mother's hand and ran off, chasing a concerned-looking chicken who'd strayed into the yard.

Raymond drifted back into the hospital, Miss Rosa following not far behind. His step felt ghostly light.

Inside, a shocked quiet had replaced the discord, as though the building had been shaken down. The empty rooms echoed. Both Candace and Beatrice stood looking bewildered, a cataclysmic gaze in their eyes. He immediately dismissed them.

'I don't have the words to thank you,' Raymond told them. 'You both performed admirably. Way beyond what I should have expected. Please go and rest. And don't give a thought to the matron. We'll sort that out in no time. In fact, I can see one of you stepping into the role.'

The girls smiled, the fog of fatigue lifting for a moment, and they walked off together, arm in arm.

Miss Rosa appraised the aftermath, looking circumspect in the faint metal dust. Despite Raymond's protestations, she began to clean up, a staunch putting to rights of the whole hospital.

'I'll be fine, Dr Filigree. Takes more than a blown-up storeroom to keep these old bones from doing their job.'

Raymond wanted to correct her – they did not appear to be old bones at all. Miss Rosa proved him right by the way she swept through, fluidly gathering up anything in her path. Flotsam was spread throughout the rooms where the maelstrom had shuddered and cracked the place in its wake, and it was going to take some time to return the infirmary to a serviceable state.

Raymond picked up several empty vials, and a thought niggled him.

'Miss Rosa, what about the deceased? The man from the operating room. The other gent with the head injury. Where did they go?'

She did not answer straight away, but looked out to the window.

'They were taken with the first ambulances this morning. Whisked away like a magician's cloak. I've never seen anything like it. It's always taken us days to organise any sort of transfer out from here.'

Raymond leaned against the corridor wall, amazed at the unexpected efficiencies of the region.

Over the next hour, several other helpers turned up to assist with the straightening-out process – Barry, a few relatives and Mrs Italiano. ('What are you doing here?' Raymond beseeched her to go and take care of herself, but she would have none of it, and worked in step with Miss Rosa.) Apart from the indefatigable Miss Rosa, they all took frequent breaks, sitting on chairs and fanning themselves. The heat was particularly unforgiving that morning; Raymond himself could feel it behind his eyeballs. Barry attempted a joke every so often, but these engendered not much more than a weak smile or polite nod from the others. Even the empty beds looked somehow dazed. Great shafts of sunlight angled through the rooms, revealing congealed puddles of blood, runaway scraps of equipment, and torn lengths of bandages and gauze; fragments of the night knocked under beds and chairs during the chaos. Miss Rosa continued to mop and straighten, standing tall once in a while to look around and assess her progress. Apart from the scrapes and the clinks, there was mostly silence. The noises of the birds outside were absent.

Raymond mooched through the disarray, watching it retreat under the labour of the women, picking up the odd thing here or there. He was too unsettled to be constructive, and his mind began to slowly turn to the future. After all this, he wondered how he was going to carry on, let alone return the hospital to normality. He had only been in charge of the hospital for two days. Two days, and this was his offering to Wittenoom. A thought came to him unbidden, that it was his own hands that were venomous. He appreciated that it sounded crazed, but he feared that everything he touched might turn black and shrivel. It frightened him, this superstition, and he fought to quell the possible truth of it.

He was interrupted by Miss Rosa.

'Dr Filigree. There's someone here to see you.' She raised her eyebrows as she spoke.

It was the first of a river of visits. This one was from two bleak managerial types who wore ties and leather shoes in the place of the thick collarless shirts and boulders of boots worn by the rest of the men. Despite the executive look, the red dirt had still snuck its way into every crease of their clothes, and their shoes were dull. The first man, the deputy manager, did most of the speaking. He had voluminous black sideburns that rode further onto his cheekbones than any

Raymond had seen before, and he spoke loudly, enunciating his words as though Raymond might have been dim.

'Terrible business, you'll have to agree.'

His sidekick did nothing but nod.

Raymond did agree. A terrible, sickening business.

'So we're just here,' he said, 'to make sure everything's back to ship-shape, meaning we can get back to full throttle at the mine. Head office were particularly keen for us to make sure that this won't affect production. After all, it really didn't have anything to do with the mines themselves, and the company has just signed off a very important contract to supply asbestos to the Americans, but the government,' a word he pronounced in sarcastic tone, rolling his eyes at the other man, 'say that we can't get back to business unless we have guaranteed medical support on standby.'

He looked directly at Raymond, although it did not feel like an invitation to answer.

'Bit ridiculous, really, when you think about it,' the man said, and his sidekick nodded vigorously, 'when we got by for years without having a hospital at all, but there you go. Government bloody interference. Gets to us all, eh?' And he gave Raymond a conspiratorial wink. It looked wetly unpleasant.

'We're down a few men,' he continued, 'so it'll take us a few days to replace them, but we'd be keen to return to full production as soon as possible. Just need your say-so, Doctor, if you don't mind signing.' And the man thrust out a clipboard with a simple form on it. Raymond skimmed it – it said little, just that he confirmed that they had a staffed hospital with the capability to manage casualties if, in the unlikely event, accidents were to occur. Raymond sighed as he scribbled his name to it – the building may be capable, but himself, the director?

As he returned the clipboard, he felt his circular preoccupation shift, a seismic movement underfoot. He had now given his word – his guarantee. Maybe in here was the real beginning he'd been seeking – not new or heroic, that was certain, but the inchoate prospects of one. To start from scratch, without indulgence or addled ideology. Miss Rosa stood to the side. Her hands were on her hips, and she had not taken her eyes from the men. There was suspicion, a narrow-eyed question in her glare.

Raymond turned back to the deputy manager, who was derisively listing off regulations with numbers and slashes, policies pertaining to the safeguards in place for the mines, and Raymond listened, unsure for whose benefit this was. The sidekick appeared to be smirking. It was growing rather confusing.

Raymond spoke up. 'Will there be an official investigation? An inquiry?' He was picturing the lifeless inflated man, the head-injured worker, all of them. The images were large and raw.

The deputy manager stopped and stared directly at Raymond.

The sidekick was the one to answer. 'It wasn't a mining accident, you know.'

The deputy manager cut in. 'We'll be doing the investigation. Yes. We will. Make sure everything was above board. Don't you worry about that. Now, we need to get back to it.' They prepared to leave.

As they were walking out the door, Raymond caught hold of a thought which had been nagging the periphery of his mind. He called out, 'It's just that it seems rather odd to have gelignite stored in the middle of the town, that's all.'

Both men stopped and looked at each other before the deputy manager answered. 'Doctor, that's really not your business. We run the mining side of things, you look after the sick. Can we make that quite clear.'

Miss Rosa scraped her feet and the noise reverberated. They regarded her for the first time.

'Now, we have work to do. If you'll excuse us, Doctor, Miss.' And they were gone.

Several other official folk from the mine dropped in, but mostly the conversation was the same, comprised of strange soliloquies and uninterruptable monologues. By noon the visits had dried up. Only afterwards, in the quiet of the afternoon, did it occur to Raymond that no one had asked after the patients. Not a one.

With no patients to see and nothing further to do, Raymond settled himself into his office. An update from Miss Rosa, as she brought in another tray of offerings, reassured him that the townsfolk of Wittenoom would rally; they were made of granite these men and women, and already they were back playing soccer on the baking pitch. She hesitated before leaving, and she appeared to want to say something.

'Are you alright, Miss Rosa? You've been magnificent throughout this whole affair, you know.'

This had the effect of making her throat colour, and she put a hand to it. She nodded and hurried out.

He walked to the cavernous bookshelf, empty but for his three ludicrous contributions and the impractical journals left behind by his predecessors. How he craved just one textbook, perhaps his *Imperial Companion for Internal Medicine* with its clear, didactic text and no-nonsense diagrams. He could return to the beginning, consolidate his knowledge, relearn the basics. It would be his crutch, a keystone for his practice. He wouldn't again question the benefit of those dry, unadorned and unpoetic words. If only this repository of knowledge wasn't sailing lost with all the others, untracked, somewhere over the sea. The books here, of prose, philosophy, metaphysics, sonnets – oh these things had as little to do with medicine as a Constable landscape held directions for travel. The readings of a wastrel.

He picked up his book of Pliny the Elder, several volumes in one, and blew the dust off it. How on earth had it become so caked in such a short time? As it was all he had, he resigned himself to it. He read for hours, taking up where he had left off on the ship. Science and technology, written all that time ago. Flicking through the mineral section, he stopped at a page, looking with astonishment. Pliny was describing asbestos. Of all things. Written shortly after the death of Christ. He peered closer. Asbestos – the Greeks called it 'unquenchable' – named for its property of not being flammable, he read. It couldn't be ignited, and it was used to make unburning shrouds for royalty, and fire-resistant plates for kings to impress their subjects when tossed into the flames (saving on washing up, he thought with amusement). The Romans called it 'amiantus', or 'unpolluted'. But what really grabbed Raymond, and he had to read the paragraph several times, was the unambiguous way it was documented that anyone, even the slaves, who worked with the dust of the mineral, had to wear respirators, in the form of sheep bladders. Respirators. Back then. Pliny also discouraged anyone from the purchase of slaves if they'd mined the stuff, because of their unfortunate and expensive habit of dying young from a sickness in the lungs. What had Mrs Italiano said when he had first met her? About breathing equipment? His thoughts snagged as a knock sounded on his door. Miss Rosa entered quietly.

Again she stood there. She made several bird-like movements with her hands. Raymond waited for her to start. He wanted to ask her to furnish him with more information about the mines, but he felt it impolite to push her.

After a minute, he said, 'Miss Rosa, may I ask you a question?'

This seemed to embolden her, and she said, 'Actually Dr Filigree, I'm here to ask you one.'

'Of course. Please.'

'I'm not sure if you knew, but the minister is holding an extra church service tomorrow evening. On account of what happened. Everybody will attend. Perhaps you'd like to come along.'

She found something to do with her hands, brushing through her hair at the back of her neck and coaxing stray strands up into her bun.

'I …'

'With me,' she continued. 'I mean you could accompany me, if you cared to.' She adjusted the pleats of her skirt, then resumed her normally taciturn, formal pose.

Church? Really? He hadn't attended a church service since he was a boy, when he was forced to sit between warring parents, singing songs he didn't understand. It was one of the few pleasures of adulthood, the freedom to choose a path to purgatory if it meant not attending such things. However, this was an invitation, and it sounded warm enough to wash away his cynicism.

'But are you sure I'd be welcome, Miss Rosa. I mean, after all that's happened?'

'Dr Filigree, I ...' A moment hung in the air, teetering on its fulcrum. Miss Rosa appeared to be searching for the appropriate words. 'But of course you would. In fact, I guarantee you'll be expected.'

Raymond blinked. 'Then I'd be delighted to, Miss Rosa. It would be my pleasure to accompany you.'

'Excellent. Then we shall meet here at five-thirty pm. Sharp.' And with a nod she exited, sliding gracefully through the door.

An indelibly altered quiet filled the room. Raymond returned to the works of the Roman naturalist, and continued to read them with growing wonderment. He clutched at his thighs to feel his own solidity, the proportion of his own existence. Here he was, in a remote, charred, stripped-down land, this country that was at the same time both nascent and ancient, and Pliny the Elder was present in the room telling him something. And maybe if this part of the earth could combine the old and the new the way it had, then so, perhaps, could he. Perhaps it wasn't textbooks he needed. He walked out onto the verandah, where the still air was welcoming and a chatter of parrots could be heard again. Leaning on the fence, looking out over the world, here, where there was more sky than anywhere else, he watched the dusk light begin to lap over the populace and into the nether. Raymond felt a spidery optimism brush against him. He would take his example from the tenacious townsfolk. There was always one further step that could be taken. His may simply be to unmask his ears. Let Pliny speak, he thought. Perhaps, indeed, everything might be alright.

VIII

Lou's innards feel like water. The room feels suddenly cold – the whining air conditioner has been icing up the interior, and even the windows are coated in crystals. She sits back heavily onto the olive-green bedcovers, slumping, as though her bones can no longer hold her up.

The coronial inquiry will be dire. Lou sees herself up on a stand, her colleagues giving evidence against her. Not having attended one before, she can only imagine it: a room darkly panelled, ferocious tiers of people handing out damnation from the docks, lawyers, judges, who knows. Would it be wigs and Bible-swearing and cross-examination? Plus, it will be all so bloody pointless. The deed is done. The girl is gone. What's going to change except to bury them, both herself and the girl, even deeper.

She walks to the mirror, a grim short path, and she conjures up segments of conversation. Rehearsing scenarios. Could there be excuses found, or anyone else to blame? How about the bureaucratic erosion of medicine, she wonders.

Surely, that had to shoulder some of the responsibility. When she'd first started working the wards, about five years ago, there had been none of the administrative obstacles that had hindered her later. She recalls her initial and, she guesses, naïve wonder at what medicine could do, a joy in the miracles. But then acronyms and tick-boxes and time-targets hijacked her days, all of their days, people with clipboards checking everything they did, until it became the new normal. Empathy, individuality, all exchanged for numerical efficiency. She watched other doctors, tired of fighting it, morph into hirelings, satisfied with surfaces. And she guesses she had too, slipping into compliance without even a blink. But when she thinks about how this would sound on the stand, calling up administrative initiatives like they were culprits, she knows how feeble it would be.

What about the crash after the girl? Could this mitigate things, or reduce the impact, as though she were already serving sentence? Every action bridled by the fear of her own hand, knowing of what she was capable? How a landslide had been triggered, and she spent more and more time in the director's office, that sterile room with its smell of lime air freshener, fending off accusations that she knew in her heart were true.

The imagined dialogue in her head grows rowdier, and then she hears herself answering questions out loud to queries not yet made. Eventually, it declines into a raging pile of recrimination, and the realisation that she is more than just one unforgiveable mistake. She is the before and the after.

The correct thing to do now would be to book herself on the next plane down to Perth. Go and meet with the hospital's legal team, speak to the director, explain things. Which is exactly why she packs her few things, rings the car-hire office, extends her rental, and heads straight back to Wittenoom.

Arriving in the ghost town, she surprises herself by getting lost. She thought she'd got the measure of the layout, but driving through, looking for Dave's van, she somehow finds herself at the old mine buildings. Further along are the crumbled remains of the mill, with its original layout still visible – boxy sheds cascading down the hillside like a geometrical waterfall, ending up in a dry concrete pond. She hops out of the car and tramps around. In the side of the largest hill she spies a black pocket, and she scrambles up to it. Not much above knee height is a rectangular cleft set apart from the buildings. It's unquestionably man-made – a tinny, square of a mouth, and she recognises it as the access hatch from the photo she saw on the brochure.

This hole is an entrance into the mine itself, a metal mouse hole recessed into the running seams of rock. Bleached planks of wood lean over the opening, a half-hearted attempt to keep the inquisitive out. Lou heaves aside the lumber pieces without too much effort, and she peers in. A light breeze blows onto her face; a curious sensation, cool and musty. It's not clear where the draught could be coming from. She can see further into the tunnel where a shaft of light streams down on an angle, illuminating a gentle shower of powdery particles.

It would be reckless to crawl up inside. Looking around, she figures that even if she were worth rescuing there'd be no one about who could do it. She scrunches herself in, anyway. Her heart beats heavily, palpably deep in the centre of her chest.

The hatch's purpose is not obvious – it's too small for any decent miner-sized man, that's for sure. A little inside the entrance it widens out into a tunnel. It's still not particularly roomy – she can't stand without stooping. It takes a moment for her to become accustomed to the shadowy light. The current of air spirals steadily around her, a slow expiration from somewhere inside the mine. She has no torch with her – she won't be able to advance far – it's nothing but a black hole further on. A dusty tarpaulin, perished in patches, is draped over a large rectangular structure just off the side of the entrance. She pulls away the cover and coughs with the pelt of dirt that explodes off it. The discharged whits float above her, swirling in the fragile light. This thing is a large crank of furniture – electrical racks on the top, with shelves and doors that look like old-fashioned filing cabinets underneath. Pieces of equipment, wrenches, tyre levers, and other unfamiliar items, lie on the open shelving, and they look astonishingly pristine – hardly a scrape of rust on them. She pulls out a lower drawer and the creak of it repeats in the empty space. More dust falls from the shaft that leads someplace upwards. Inside the drawer are five or six face masks – stiff, whitish cups with frayed and disintegrating elastic, fitting snugly together in a row. They haven't been used.

The emptiness crams into her ears, filling them. There is a dead stillness to the scene in here, and a strangeness she can't understand. She wonders if Dave has ever explored this wormcast of a passage.

She stumbles on the uneven ground and stiffens, hoping she hasn't tripped over a bone, or something worse, but when she looks down she sees the start of a rail. Tracing the route of the tracks as far as she is able, she sees a mound of dirt directly under the thin, streaming shaft of light – there must have been a rockfall here some time past. Beyond this again is a flatbed car. Then the tracks disappear around a bend and she can see no further.

The air inside is a funereal cool. Sepulchral and quiet.

Above her the walls curve in, heavy and huddled, and hang claustrophobically close to her head. On the roof of the tunnel to her right are the hieroglyphs of graffiti. Looking more carefully, she sees that it is a faint skull and crossbones. There are other markings nearby, but she can't decipher them. They look desperate, scratched, imploring, although it's possible she's just dressing them in her own unreality and invention. They remind her of the engraving on crypts. Perhaps, she fancies, the epitaphs to the cadavers of stories buried out here. Dave's stories. Dead, yet still needing to claw their way out. The brutal stopes and their raw, memoired walls eat into her.

She needs to find him, and she needs to apologise. This feels like the only thing she's got left – the only thing filling her head, as if the rest of the impending nightmares do not exist. Maybe in some fanciful world he would take her in. Let her explain away her unmending wounds next to the comfort of a fire until they disperse. This universe grows larger in her head until there is no longer a coroner's inquiry, no past, even no Lou as she knows herself. Here, in this cave-like air, without movement or sound, imagining this scenario, she remembers the nectar scent of him. A sense of the humidity of walking close, like the smell of safety.

She squeezes herself back out into the tingling daylight. It's only afternoon – she still has time. She'll look where she's going this time.

Awakening

In the ivory light of morning, Raymond awoke underwater. Sweat had been dripping into his nose and mouth, and he startled, choking. Again, he'd been dreaming of poison. A toxic cloud hanging low over the town of his own childhood, where he'd crept through the badly lit streets of that dour northern hamlet while the residents of the identical, coffin-like, semidetached brick houses pulled their curtains across as he passed. It was palpitatingly real. On the road lay the bodies of small children, each identical in size and shape. He'd blamed the heat, but it was always cold in the dream.

He swung his legs over the side of the bed and wiped his face with the end of his sheet. Dressing quickly, he stepped outside into the glare. It was unexpectedly humid, and he could see monstrous clouds roiling in from the east.

Without much else angling for his time, and the need to shake the nightmarish visions from his head, he headed out to tramp the slopes. Winding his way across the periphery of the settlement, he noted for the first time the extent of asbestos tailings gracing the place. It was everywhere. Like blue-grey felt stuffed into every yard, upholstering each curb, padding down the perimeter of all the public buildings. He felt like he must be missing something – how was this possible if the fibres were so dangerous?

He veered away from the township, and hiked up the rocky path towards the hill not far from the mines. From this vantage point the tiny town looked cramped and stippled, like an oyster shell, but beyond was the unimaginable vastness of the Pilbara. It was henna red, he decided. And the sky, which looked to be slammed down on top, was a searing blue, a glaring, cartoonish colour, as if it ought not be possible in life. The amassing clouds were beginning to cover it, and he watched them squirm and swirl into grotesque shapes.

Standing motionless, he noticed the movement of several animals nearby, creatures visiting on whims, by the looks of it. They paid him no attention. A rock wallaby bounded past in a camouflaged crescent. It stopped, sniffed about and looked up. They stared at each other for an instant, and then the marsupial twitched its nose and hopped away. A jewelled gecko darted by, close to his feet. Further on, Raymond saw a monitor lizard, the gargantuan, lumbering cousin of the gecko, sway through the grass and lower itself onto the sunny side of a rock. It settled in and lay perfectly still, impervious to all the drama and goings-on in the town close by.

The air was tranquil, and the songs of the birds hung gently from the patchy canopy of the snappy gums and bloodwoods, but as Raymond listened, he became aware of another sound – a mechanical vibration, a subdued churning underfoot. He must be close to the mine itself.

He squinted and saw that near where he stood, recessed into the side of the hill, was a rectangular, metal access hatch. How odd. It seemed a good distance from the mine itself. He glanced around – there was no one else about – and he walked close to the aperture so he could see inside. A cool breeze tumbled out, queer and refreshing on his face. The darkness inside precluded him from seeing much, but what he could make out appeared orderly and safe – racks and shelving and stacked piles of equipment. Raymond felt, rather suddenly, that he ought to explore inside. That there were things about the mining in this town that he should learn. Taking a breath, he squashed himself in, curling his limbs and bobbing his head. Once inside, as he tried to unfold himself, he discovered that the chute only opened up a little, and was too low for him to stand upright. He crept, hunched over, to the first rack. Lined up on top was a row of a dozen head torches. All unused. Most had their packaging intact. He picked one up and turned it on. A brilliant beam of light illuminated the entire tunnel, and he peered down the shaft, where the channel of it abruptly vanished around a corner. Pouring from the depths came a noise that sounded like the white roar of a steam engine – clearly ridiculous, he knew, but he looked down to see that he was standing near the buffers of a narrow-gauge rail. Further along were three linked railcars, the flatbed type, and they were stacked to toppling with boxes and crates. He shone his torch to follow the rail, but the tracks retreated around the curve, and he could see no more. Now that he was acclimatised to the space and the light of the torch, he saw that all of the cars were overloaded. He stared. He counted. Dozens of boxes, marked on the outside with their contents. Masks. Respirators. Safety jackets. Torches. Water pouches. All labelled. On most, an address. On many of these Wittenoom had been struck through with a heavy marker, and other addresses had been scribbled on – most Australian, some American, some British. They looked like they were packaged up and ready to leave again. On top, taped down in a clear plastic envelope, were papers with signatures; ledgers, dollar signs up and down columns. Raymond pulled off the top couple and shuffled through them, the implication slowly dawning. He scrabbled into one of the boxes, ripping its sides. Within were hoards of crisp white masks. He grabbed half a dozen of them, knowing he should show them to somebody, perhaps the managers who had visited him yesterday. Surely if they knew about this, that safety equipment was being withheld from the workers, then this would stir up a whirlwind of action and investigation.

Voices became audible from around the bend, and Raymond could see the swinging light of a torch approaching. Panicking, he wondered how he would explain his presence, and he pulled open a low drawer and stuffed the masks inside, thinking it would be difficult to scuttle back out of the chute holding onto them. He planned, however, to return and retrieve them, gathering more evidence when he did. Switching off his own torch, he crouched down and eased back out of the entrance, rolling into the dirt.

A crow wheeled overhead and emitted a single caw; a black, piercing sound in the silence. More clouds had gathered, matted and heavy, and the sky looked like it had been lowered whilst he'd been in there.

Raymond picked himself up and charged down the hill.

Back in his office, his jacket salted with red, he pulled the spines of spinifex from his socks and grappled with what he'd seen. Seizing his notebook from his desk, he opened it up, but then sat for some time bent over its empty pages. He felt he should be pouring out a scree of enlightened insights; however, he did not know where to start. A list of unused equipment would make a fairly pious and unconvincing read, he guessed, and he took to pushing his name plaque around, leaving faint elliptical scratches in the wood.

Five-thirty took its time approaching. Raymond made several trips back to his cottage. He changed shirts twice, cleaned his teeth, and tried to polish his shoes with a thin tea towel.

For the remaining fill of the afternoon he sat at his desk, finally managing to scribble down some oblique thoughts, combing through what he could remember about industrial diseases and their unnatural history; the pneumoconioses of dust and minerals. It wasn't much, and he had no texts to query apart from the ponderings of a pre-Vesuvian Roman philosopher.

Eventually, he heard a precise knock at the door. At exactly the same time, the sky split and a ferocious rain began to tip down on Wittenoom. A laundering of the days past, he thought.

As Raymond stepped onto the verandah, alongside Miss Rosa (who was modestly dressed and customarily silent), the smell of metal filled his throat. He looked out at the sheets of rain and imagined all of the citizens making their wet way, converging onto the chapel like heavy iron filings to a magnet. Humid gossips of birds streaked past, complaining in great squawking groups. The unseasonal weather happily made for an excellent topic of conversation, and prevented Raymond from needing to provide anything too diverting or entertaining.

He concentrated on holding the umbrella, kindly supplied by Miss Rosa, over her. She wore a black dress, perhaps old-fashioned, but who was he to judge. She wore it with such fluency, with a string of pinprick pearls, that he thought she looked extremely striking. He was working through methods of saying so to her, but none of them sounded quite right in his head. As they progressed down the sloping road into the theological heart of the town, they descended into an inscrutable silence. Raymond began to experience a tight fear of meeting the townsfolk, after all that had gone on, and he focused instead on preventing a single drop of rain from landing on Miss Rosa.

On arriving, Raymond was surprised by the *Australianness* of the church. Like the pub, there was little to compare to the experience of his youth. Those childhood memories were of bracing stone vestibules; cold, clanging battlegrounds. A dim recollection of squirming through songs resurfaced, and he remembered sermons that stretched on and on, past any semblance of comprehension and the capability of his young bladder. His parents had sat on either side of him, tight-lipped, seething about something he had no clue about. It was in those cavernous cathedrals that he first had realised he didn't understand adults at all – they seemed to be people who for six days of the week were mercilessly fond of activities such as sitting on their overstuffed backsides, indulging in pernicious commentary on the world, and criticising any person smaller than themselves, yet on the seventh they would stand up and down with vigour, and sing about love and devotion and goodness. At the time, he had wondered how one grew into one of these, and if he would ever do so. He ferreted around in his mind to find out if he had – if the hypocrisy of adulthood had shifted in without him noticing. Perhaps not, he thought, but he had so many other flaws, maybe there was just no room.

But, as Miss Rosa removed her black felt hat and then gently touched his sleeve, he was relieved to see, peeking out from under the umbrella, that this ecumenical place looked different. Its walls were a functional combination of bricks and corrugated iron. The lower edges of them were spattered red, like a lady's skirt walked through mud. The windows, aspiring to be stained glass, consisted of chunky, undecipherable scenes, and it was difficult to tell whether the main one over the entrance depicted a nativity or a crucifixion. Spinifex grew right up to the walls, and encroached upon the stone path leading to the door.

Raymond shook down the umbrella underneath the front eave and scuffed his shoes before entering. He inhaled, unsure how he was going to face the people of Wittenoom, and walked in, Miss Rosa at his side. She led him right down the middle aisle. He would have preferred to creep into the back pew unnoticed, but Miss Rosa was oblivious to his wishes, and carried on straight to the front.

As he did, the congregation rose, person by person, in a scattered pattern across the nave. They reached over to shake his hand, or to nod purposefully at him. Hands weaved between arms the whole way down the aisle. Miss Rosa also received one or two gentle pats on her arm as they passed.

Raymond returned the handshakes of both the men and the women in that little church. He looked around with incredulity. People stretched round each other to connect their hands with his. A murmur undulated through that house of worship, containing words of thanks and gratitude, and sometimes, no more than a supportive humph. Raymond was stunned. Miss Rosa eventually seated herself in the front row and arranged the damp folds of her skirt. She had a warm smile on her face. Raymond slid over the crooked jarrah slats of the pew to sit next to her.

'Welcome to Wittenoom, Dr Filigree.' Everything about Miss Rosa was softened by the humidity. 'Oh, here he is.' She gestured to the minister flowing in, bedecked in robes. 'You'll enjoy this.'

And the sermon began. Raymond heard few of the details, drifting in and out of the thundering words. He snuck a look every so often at Miss Rosa, who was watching the minister attentively.

'Wait for the ecstasy and fire,' she said quietly at one point.

There was scant mention of the explosion, more a fervid urging to care for one another in times of crisis. The minister also recommended that they did not forget their commitment to God (like an insurance policy, Miss Rosa whispered to him), in case death were to visit them at an unexpected and inconvenient time. Raymond did enjoy the whole thing. As the minister drew up to his climax, he blasted off some parting comments about the more earthly supervisors, particularly those in charge of the mines, warning them of the consequences of not caring for their own flocks whilst in this temporary existence. And then, coming to a juddering close, the minister boomed out,

'And yea will the Lord look upon you, and keep you, and will He always lead you down the path of righteousness.' The congregation took in a deep collective breath and then relaxed. A thrum resumed and they rose, moving outside en masse, where they could carry on their presumably less churchly chatter. Raymond and Miss Rosa stayed seated and he felt a few last warm pats on his shoulder as the parish departed.

As well as the pair at the front, one man remained behind after the rest had taken their leave. He was whiskery and in his hand was a dark-grey hat, which he clutched while sidling up to Raymond.

'Arthur Curtis, is it?' Raymond recognised him.

'That's right, Doctor.' Arthur looked pleased. 'I hate to bother you at church, but I was wondering if I could find time to bend your ear.'

'Bend my ...?'

'Have a word,' Miss Rosa explained.

'Do you think I could come and see you? Maybe tomorrow?' Arthur asked.

'Are you unwell?'

'No, Doctor, but I was hoping for your help. In fact, we all were. But I'd rather not talk about it here. Could I come up to the hospital?'

'Certainly, Mr Curtis. I shall look forward to it.' Not quite the right words, Raymond thought, as he watched the man nervously suck in his lips.

Arthur nodded, a tight, sharp gesture, and left. Raymond and Miss Rosa sat for a few moments longer in the quiet, Raymond's head full of speculation. Miss Rosa seemed to be happy just soaking in the muggy ambience.

A lost pigeon flew in through the open door, landing on the pulpit before flitting down into the font with a dainty splash. (Raymond had asked the font's purpose. Miss Rosa had replied, 'Baptismal. Just in case.' Just in case what, he wondered.) The bird bobbed in the holy water, bathing and ruffling its feathers. The seasoned shepherd of a minister shooed it away. He didn't acknowledge the two remaining visitors, each of whom sat consumed, Raymond with a premonition he could not identify. The pigeon hopped around for a minute, then flew out, amplifying the silence in the chapel. The minister began to make abrupt movements, demonstrating that he was a busy man and the period of worship had come to an end. He wiped the sweat from his forehead with his crimson cassock.

'Sermon's over. See you next week. Good evening to you, Miss Rosa.'

'Oh, of course. Apologies,' Raymond said, and he stood, extending a hand to Miss Rosa.

On exiting the church, they saw that the crowd had dispersed and the rain had ceased. The downpour had left the air contused, and the sky overhead had the purplish red of a bruise. Raymond collected the umbrella and they both headed up the hill. They settled on a relaxed pace, both looking at their shoes as they walked, and he wondered if she too continued to feel the unexpected touch of the townsfolk on her sleeve.

They both faltered several times, trying to start off a conversation. Although they were alone on the road, Raymond was self-conscious and unsure of his voice. The red of the dirt rolling off the sides of the road had transformed into wet burgundy banks. Raymond tried again.

'I believe this type of rain is quite unusual for this time of year.' He stepped into a coagulated puddle and hid a grimace.

Miss Rosa smiled. He saw in it a dimple, on one side only. How had he not seen this before? 'Yes. We usually only get this at the height of the wet season. Seems even the weather's disregarding orders.'

Even, Raymond puzzled?

Looming up ahead was the hospital, quiet in its solitude. Above it, the clouds hung low and corpulent, ready to burst once more.

'I do wonder what Mr Curtis wants to discuss,' Raymond said, hoping to appear nonchalant. His voice sounded overloud, and he cleared his throat.

'I have my suspicions, Doctor.' She added nothing else.

Raymond had an unexplained anxiety of emptying his concerns about the mine into the open air. What if he was wrong? If there was another explanation for the virginal equipment he'd found, and he, this interloper, began lobbing accusations where they had no place? But he'd been silent before, and the price for that was unspeakable.

'I do feel I should learn more about asbestos, though, and its implication in health. I don't suppose you'd know where I could locate some information up here?'

Miss Rosa looked over at him. 'I'm sure I could find you something of use.'

Raymond felt unable to ask anything further.

They matched steps up the slope of the road.

'And I did want to say thank you, Miss Rosa, for inviting me along tonight. For many reasons.'

'It was my pleasure, Dr Filigree.'

'I haven't been to a church service for a very long time. Not much seems to have changed. What did you think of the sermon?'

She didn't answer straight away. Instead she looked upwards, a hand on her hat.

'To which part are you referring, Dr Filigree?' she said finally. 'The readings I have heard a hundred times before, the call to alms for the poor souls involved in the incident opportune, and the choice of hymns I couldn't support one way or another.' Their pace was synchronised up the hill. 'Although, I was quite taken with his admonishment of the earthly. I've not heard him do that before. I like that about this one. He's more actuary than minister, the way I see it.'

Raymond smiled. 'Do you think it's an offloading of personal responsibility, though, that last line, expecting that God will lead you down the path to righteousness?'

'Could be,' she said, her voice light, sparkling, 'if you believed in God. Which I don't. I'm not sure why anybody would, with all that brimstone and garbled retribution.'

Raymond stopped. 'Do you not believe in anything overarching? Some greater power?'

'No. Not at all. It's all rubbish.'

'Oh. I see.'

They resumed walking in silence, Raymond absorbing Miss Rosa's words. He was using the umbrella as a cane, and he wondered how they would appear to others. Two figures, him in his absurd outfit, strolling up a steaming Australian road like characters from a Victorian novel instead of the modern people they were, charging through the progressive sixties.

Her frankness gave him a measure of mettle. 'May I ask, Miss Rosa, what brought you up here? To Wittenoom? It seems an unlikely place for a woman of your…' he hesitated, 'capabilities.'

'Capabilities? I would not ever have considered that word as my own.' She turned to him. 'But you are very kind. What brought me up here? I do have a short version I could offer.'

'No, Miss Rosa, if I may insist, I'd like the long.'

She removed her hat and fanned herself slowly, glancing at him as if to gauge the sincerity of his request.

'Well, I grew up in a small country town, about two hundred kilometres in a line directly south-east of Perth. I vowed I'd always move somewhere bigger; that I'd never, ever, end up anywhere smaller.' She summoned a smile, a wistful, sorrowful thing. 'I never fitted in, even as a child. Too strongly spoken, but not pretty enough to get away with it. They called me a trailblazer, but it sounded like a label of contempt, coming from the lips of the townsfolk. I certainly burned a few paths in my desire to get out of there, in order to attend university up in Perth. It was so unseemly for a woman at the time. I think this encouraged me all the more.'

How animated she had become. Her stride picked up pace.

'I attained the highest score ever at the tiny high school in that mealy little town. It was like a punishment for them – me, a woman, and with my, I don't know, plain ways, getting this honour – they had no way of celebrating it. Even my parents felt the shame of it in the corner shop and the petrol station. So I trundled off, with hardly a farewell. I found an egg carton of a flat near the college, and I never went back home. I studied accounting. Bookkeeping. It was all so fascinating, the fluid balance of numbers.'

She stopped talking, seeming a little lost.

Raymond remained silent. It had much left in it, this story.

'I never finished the degree,' she said.

Raymond knew, somehow, that there was a man involved. A disastrous affair, trailblazing gone wrong. He couldn't ask.

'I'm sorry to hear that.'

'It's all in the past, Doctor.' Her long version turned short. 'And, ever since, I've found myself heading further north, to find my home and work, ironically in smaller and smaller places. I don't expect there will be anywhere else left for me after this, with that as my itinerary.'

'Miss Rosa, please call me Raymond.'

She nodded – a graceful assent.

They had reached the deserted entrance to the hospital. The jelly-like clouds sagged close to the roof. Raymond swung open the gate to allow Miss Rosa through.

He stopped on the verandah and spoke. 'Miss Rosa. I want to be of use to this town. Do something that's more than just reactionary for the sick and the injured. Not simply play catch-up. I'd be grateful for any thoughts you might have.'

The sky was so damp it muted out the sounds of the rest of the world.

'Actually, I have had a thought, Doctor.'

'Raymond.'

'Raymond.' They stood at the front door. 'Perhaps we could use this office of yours for something a bit more useful.

Maybe rearrange it into a clinic, somewhere welcoming, where you could chat to patients, without them having to lie in those awful iron beds. A place where people would be free to talk.'

'Miss Rosa. You really are extraordinary.' He reached past her to the door. 'A clinic.' Together they pushed open the door to a rush of light and warmth, and they walked in, a new beginning in the offing.

IX

The dark begins to descend. Lou traces a path she thinks leads back to Dave's place. The crumbling houses all look the same in the receding light, and she's not sure which of them are home to the recluses. In the directionless distance, the rumbling undercurrent of a motor stutters into life and then fades away into the expanse. She parks the car next to a tower of discarded concrete guttering. Wafts of smoke and the dry echo of crackling branches tell her that at least someone is close by, enjoying a fire.

She rehearses her apology. As she walks she realises that her shoulders ache. Her fingernails are still dirty and her hair is knotted underneath – it feels like bundled hay.

Getting closer, she returns to a fantasy where Dave opens the door of his van, its light spilling out, and he invites her in. The van will be soft and clean inside. Surprisingly spacious. Somehow, there will be an open bottle of something, waiting. Maybe wine. They will sit, and after he forgives her, quickly, definitively, knowing she only said those things out of her own hurt, they will clink glasses. Then Lou will find the freedom to open up. And he will understand without question.

Rounding the corner, she sees that the fire is coming from behind the shell of a house she recognises to be Dave's. The caravan alongside has its dingy light dribbling out, and tentatively, hesitant in the gloom, she calls out to him.

Dave doesn't answer. The sting of the night air reaches down the collar of her shirt. She creeps round to the back, where they sat that first night.

Something's different. A number of the tools, the shovels and sledges and rakes, have been dragged over to the side of the fence and tossed into a pile. The fire's a huge raging one, and she can see it's not sticks and kindling that's burning, but chairs and great painted boards and other items that were scattered round the yard only a few days ago. A single chair sits up close to the bonfire and ten, twelve maybe, beer cans lie crumpled and strewn around the base. One can lies on its side, amber liquid dripping from its aluminium mouth.

Lou edges closer to the flames. She stares in and brings her hand up to cover her mouth.

On top of the pyre is Dave's archive. Or what remains of it. The plastic of some of the photograph covers can be seen curling, brown and crumpling in the tips of the flames. Much of the file has disintegrated and falls as embers into the jumble of burning wood. On top, wilting away as she watches, is the phantom image of smiling men, crouching down together, posing with their bare chests and ash-covered faces, but she can't make it out clearly. She's too late to fish it from the blaze and it melts, causing liberated sparks to fly upwards. The file disappears and there's not a thing she can do. She watches her desire to make amends incinerate along with Dave's words. The entire lot of it gone.

Dave. She strides over to the caravan and knocks on the door, calling out his name. There's no response and she panics, pulling on the locked handle. She raps on the windows and yells, in her shamed, breaking voice, but there is nothing. No noise. No movement.

The fire begins to retreat, and she is lost in front of it.

Eventually she blinks, her eyes red and watering from the smoke, and she drops into the chair. It occurs to her – the noise. She looks for the motorbike. It's not there.

She doesn't move until the flames have dwindled to cold ash, and then she too drives away.

The Clinic

Once inside the office, the pair became awkwardly quiet. Miss Rosa tackled this by suggesting her standard solution, her long-honed offering to discomfit.

'May I make you a tea, Raymond?'

'Delightful, Miss Rosa. Thank you.'

She brought back two cups, with saucers, and set them down on the desk.

'We could plan the set-up of the clinic, if you liked,' she said.

'I'd appreciate that.' Raymond looked around the room, imagining its energetic future.

'Funny old furniture, isn't it,' she said. The light from the bulb overhead was a blotched yellow, but it still threw sharp shadows over the chattels decorating the room. 'Everything's cobbled together up here. Second-hand. Begged or borrowed. But it never mattered before. This office was hardly ever used by your predecessors. We were all a bit nervous wondering what sort of doctor would arrive next.' And she made a delicate sound, like the laughter of stars. 'And then you turned up.'

He smiled broadly. 'Yes. What a deal.'

'I think we did rather well,' she said, quickly turning her face from him.

He felt the heat in his cheeks and spoke rapidly to override it. 'I do want to ask you a question if I may. You see, the explosion started me thinking – I have the feeling there may be substandard practices going on, safety issues being disregarded, that sort of thing. I wondered if you were aware of any problems of significance here?'

She drained her tea. 'Substandard? In Wittenoom? Of course. Everything here's substandard.'

'But aren't there rules? Regulations? For example, even I would have thought it unwise to store dynamite in the middle of town. And what about the mineral dust in the mines and the mills that people are breathing like it were fresh country air? Surely, there should be aggressive safety measures to protect the workers. I cannot believe that any company would preside over policies that actively put a man's life at risk.' But as he spoke, he heard his naïveté.

'Raymond,' she said, facing him front on, 'I think it's a good idea for you to talk to Mr Curtis. A very good idea. It's the speaking out that's been the hardest. People know things deep in their heart, but it's bringing them to the surface that's so difficult.'

He heard the words *speaking out*, and in that instant he knew a choice had been made. The future appeared to him in a blaze. The voices of self-censure suddenly left, the pebbles of anxiety gone.

'Then let us put this furniture to good use. Let us organise the room,' he said.

'Yes. And Mrs Italiano has spoken to me – she wants to help out around the hospital. Perhaps she could be a receptionist for the clinic. Man the phone. Help with records, that sort of thing.'

Raymond saw the possibilities ahead, the wax of them setting into a warm, wonderful shape. 'Marvellous. That is indeed marvellous.'

'We could push this desk into the corner. It would make an excellent examination table if we use some of the linen from out the back.'

'Brilliant idea. And I could make do with something much smaller to consult at, without a doubt.'

'Yes. And we could put the chairs up alongside the bookcase. That ought to give you plenty of room.'

'Perfect.' And they both looked around, imagining the business of it to come.

Raymond threw his weight behind the desk and began to heave it.

'Let me help. I'm a good deal stronger than my wretched frame suggests.' Miss Rosa smiled.

'No, I couldn't possibly allow …' But she had turned an angular bottom onto its edge and was pushing it.

'Over there?' she asked.

'Yes. Splendid. A clinic,' he repeated. And together the two of them scraped the table over to its newly assigned corner. With constrained exhilaration, they reclined back on the desk, puffing slightly.

And Miss Rosa leaned over, very close to Raymond, and licked right inside his ear.

X

The car-hire company begrudges Lou an extension, and she fills the tub of a vehicle with fuel until it overflows. It will give her the chance to be alone, encapsulated, with no one to ask her questions.

She drives with the windows wide open. She thinks the roar of air will blast away her clumped-up thoughts. It doesn't work.

It's a two-day monster, this drive from the belly of the Pilbara down to Perth. She hardly stops for the first of them. Not because she's eager to get back, rather this way she can avoid much human interaction. Her hands stay stiff on the wheel. By the second she's grown more resigned to the slough in her head, and she relaxes into the rhythm of driving.

The landscape morphs and changes as she edges southwards. The earth loses the red and the dust, and turns scraggy. Further again the countryside mutates into sepia farmland, its thin paddocks looking like scraps of dull leather, brown and faded and stitched together. The land has been completely appropriated by humans – tenuous, she knows, this hold.

Cramped towns crop up as she continues down the relentless ruler-straight roads – small, huddled places deadened by hard work and a neglectful economy, and she stops to use their tinny toilets and buy their wilted food, which has turned yellow under cheap lights.

Only a few hours out of Perth, the hills begin to roll in gentle undulations and the roads start to curve. The cadence allows her mind to drift, uncoupling it from the tempo of derision that's been beating in her head.

Her father comes to her. As he was, dying in an understaffed hospital room, where they'd waited on a hospice bed that never came. He'd asked her to read poetry to him. Never once in his life had he shown interest in such things, but he'd said that dying does things to a man's heart, and it becomes hungry for beauty. So, she'd dug out her high-school Keats and sat through long evenings, in a four-bedded ward, where cachectic men moaned and the smell of antiseptic and urine circulated through the vents, and read. It was before the incident with the girl, and her voice was strong. The words soothed not only her father, but the other racked men as they lay. Four nights in a row she came to do this, despite her mother complaining that she was keeping him awake, and wasn't she just doing this to get back at her, to wheedle her way into her father's good books before he met his Maker? (What was going to happen up there, Lou wondered? A report card?) On the night he died, he clawed at Lou's hand. His breath reeked of ammonia and he began gurgling in fear. He tried to form all sorts of jumbled words, like he knew his minutes were limited, and Lou fancied he'd told her he was proud of who she'd become, her life as a doctor, telling her to keep going, before her mother bustled in and fell to screaming pieces.

A tear rolls down Lou's cheek.

She slows as she takes a bend into a linear section of road. Some distance ahead of her she sees a car brake, then buckle, then tip off the shoulder of the road. It flips onto its side and sinks into a ditch. Lou yelps in the hermetic hold of her car. A rangy roo just beyond shakes itself down and bounds off into the field beyond. There are no other cars on the road. As she nears the scene, she sees the compact four-wheel drive on its side, one wheel still spinning free in the air. The chassis appears intact. Lou clutches her steering wheel and rolls towards it, adrenaline making her skin prickle and her heart pound. She doesn't want to look, and certainly does not want to stop, knowing that she could be of no possible use to anyone.

Decelerating, she swerves cautiously around the toppled car, but doesn't brake to a stop. She drives on. Further. A hundred metres. Two. But the road ahead, the gaunt rim of forest lining its edges, the sun setting over her right shoulder, the solitude, they all pull her up and speak to her. If she can't even help here, then what else has she left?

She pulls over to the side, makes a U-turn, and heads back.

Parking her car on the side of the road, Lou hops out and walks over. A chute of steam hisses skywards from the damaged bonnet. Sitting scrunched up on the gravel, crying but unmarked, are two slight and fluorescently dressed Asian girls. Japanese, Lou discovers. With some dramatic gesturing, and a check inside the car, Lou sees that nobody else is involved. Nobody is hurt. She walks back to the driver, sits down on the shale alongside, and puts her arm around the girl. Gradually, the young woman's sobbing settles to a whimper, and she leans her head onto Lou's shoulder. They wait, softly connected, until another car comes along, stopping for them, and make plans to enlist uniformed help from the next town. In a way, Lou wishes they could remain this way a little longer, that maybe the sun could stay and time could pause. But she eventually takes her leave and heads off, winding through the last of the paddocks with their golden stubble of wheat. She squints into the sunset.

It's not long before she hits the industrial outer suburbs and she orientates herself. The roads from here are arranged in a no-nonsense grid, with square corners and ordered intersections. She obeys all the traffic signs and makes her way, finally, back home.

What Lies Underneath

Those clinics. Why the very end of hell were they elbowing their way into Raymond's thoughts? Now, of all times, shunting away the pleasure. The recollections of the dark rooms expanded in his head, with their wallpapered damp and the cold that could not be overcome, no matter how many layers he pulled on. And those lugubrious lines of people, queuing and queuing, waiting their turn, finding their plodding way to the front, where the patients would pass through their consultation, substandard as they always were, in order to empty out the other side and return home dissatisfied and no less sullen. What business did these memories have settling themselves down in the front row of his mind, when all the rest of his blood and emotion and wonder were concentrating right inside his ear, bathing in the warm, wet immediacy of a most extraordinary and probing tongue.

It was the boy who kept coming back of course, sneaking into Raymond's brain when there was any opening, any moment of vulnerability, like memories not properly dealt with. Just the way he'd done in real life. And always with his mother.

The first time he saw them in line, nothing seemed out of the ordinary. She was a woman who could at best be described as plain. She wore a stretched cardigan over a green nylon dress, he remembered, and had the thickest bone-coloured stockings he had ever seen. He did not understand why he recalled her clothes in such critical detail, usually giving no thought to fashion whatsoever, but the legs stuck in his mind. They were pillars of stone, hewn smooth by time and weather. And each time she came back she was wearing the same stockings, and he could see them standing out from the crowd. But by then he had started to look out for her, for them, and the unease was building. Even when he tried not to notice, there they were, shuffling along and waiting their turn. He would check himself for his uncharitable thoughts – who would find this woman attractive, with her lemony skin, razor-thin lips and sour, discomfiting scowl? But somebody must have, as evidenced by the son who was always by her side. And there could be no mistaking his lineage – the shape of his face, the frown, the hunch, the way they were weighted similarly as they moved. Their hair may have been the same (dishevelled and mud-coloured in the case of the boy), but the mother's was never revealed from under her scarves, the only piece of apparel that changed day to day. Mind you, when he looked down the line at the others, all mothers, sisters, daughters, sons, they all wore the same uniform of council-flat poverty. The same posture, the same bleak clothing, the same ashen complexions.

He had tried to describe his disquiet about the pair to several of his colleagues. Admittedly his conversation had wandered into the metaphysical, concocting things fanciful, as was his wont, of which they openly reminded him several times over. They dismissed him, most not having the energy at the end of the day to listen to the vagueness of Raymond's paranoia. They'd come to nod blankly at him, or speak curtly when he lapsed into whimsy or meandered into philosophy; really, couldn't he just get on with things? Descartes and Spinoza, Byron and Donne, these had all been very interesting as undergraduates, but what on earth did they have to do with modern medicine? The brain was a brain and the heart was a heart. Blood pumped in one direction and nerves fired in both. Trying to find the mysterious and the enigmatic in the basic mechanics of medicine was the road to lunacy, they all agreed. If he didn't mind, would he put a sock in his codswallop, as they all had a hard enough time trying to get through each day without such nonsense. At one point, James, his oldest friend, told him to stop dithering and just get on with it. Honestly. How difficult could it be?

But it was difficult. While he tried to take James' advice, he still brooded nightly about this particular case. Eventually, however, he surrendered to the wishes of the group and simply stopped making mention of it aloud.

The mother and the son continued to come. Almost every day, with the same story, the same opaque complaints.

'Look at him. He's got no appetite. He's not putting on any weight. And check his skin! Don't tell me that he's just one of those that bruises easily. He's covered in them. Look in his mouth.' She wrenched open the boy's jaw to show

Raymond. 'See? Sick gums.' He was seven, this lad, and did look a little wizened, Raymond agreed – blank of expression and dull in response, although the specific signs, quite obvious to the mother, were not easily visible to Raymond. He continued to scrutinise him, though, making sure he searched carefully when a new symptom was mentioned. Each time Raymond would stand the boy at arm's length in front of him and start again, moving from top to toe, shining lights in his eyes, looking under his tongue, listening to his breath move in and out, and pressing a hand up under his ribcage, feeling for answers. But nothing specific could be found, apart from dry, flaking skin, the occasional bruise tinged with green, and irises with the odd colour of a fading sky and a faint pleading about them.

'I really don't know, Mrs Embleton. We've been over this before. There's nothing to find. His heart sounds unexceptional, his liver and spleen are not enlarged, his blood tests are unrewarding, and I've even done a heart tracing. I showed it to you last week, remember? Plum normal.'

'Well, I want you to do more tests. He should be admitted to the wards. Can't you see how sick he is?'

Raymond was beaten. He resorted to an elaborate method of cross-referencing his textbooks, lying them open on the floor of his cramped room, colour-coding relevant parts with pencil. But nothing stood out, no patterns emerged. The fingers of doubt poked ever more viciously at him, and he grew unsure whether it was the rigid discipline of medicine, or himself, that was wanting.

The next day they would be there, again, and Raymond's stomach would drop. He could taste his shortcomings like bilious reflux, and he was certain that in all likelihood he was missing something. After a week or so of this, he did arrange to admit the child into the hospital proper, a place exponentially more dire than the clinics.

Here inpatients were wedged into nightingale wards – places of unhappy euphemism, evoking songbirds and the legacy of an angelic nurse. The carbolic reality was much bleaker. They were an iron series of thin monotony and noise, with no segregation between the young, the old, the mad, or the dying, and they encouraged the generous sharing of disease and pain between one person and another. Into this Raymond brought the boy. The mute lad was stuck between a jaundiced, cancerous man who cried out every night, thinking it would be his dismal last, and an angry adolescent who habitually cut into his arms until he sawed through the fraying tendons. Both day and night brought with them a cycle of bandaging and hushing and aggressive dishing out of medication. Mrs Embleton took little notice of the stout rules and maintained a vigil that was hard to countenance. She would come in every morning, well before the watery breakfasts were distributed, and thump down in the bare metal chair next to the boy's bed. It would wobble beneath her, and she would slide her handbag between her two pillars of legs. She would not budge for the rest of the day. Several requests were made each night for her to leave – her devotion to the boy was quite clear. Everyone in close proximity, either in passing, or tethered and trussed up nearby, received the burn of her caustic monologues. She griped to the nurses, reproached Raymond, and even fussed away at the consultant who had nominal charge of the boy's care (during the uncommon instances of his presence). She continued to pull up the boy's pyjama sleeves, remonstrating with anybody close, imploring them to look at the rashes which were so difficult to see, and show them clumps of hair, which she claimed were falling from his head like the leaves of a turned season.

'I'm sorry, Mrs Embleton, but we really cannot get a unifying diagnosis here.' The consultant, like every part of this hospital, was a leftover. The remains on a plate once everything else was served to the reputable diners.

'Unifying diagnosis! What does that even mean?' Mrs Embleton could sometimes last hours listening to explanations, but then would erupt, perhaps at having heard one platitude too many.

'I'll thank you not to raise your voice, Mrs Embleton. Your son's symptoms are in none of our textbooks,' the specialist volleyed back at her, clutching the lapels of his jacket, visibly insulted by the conundrum. 'I have consulted every tome I have in this place.'

Raymond, positioned behind the consultant, deflated. Mrs Embleton, on the other hand, perked up.

'I'd suggest you keep looking, then!'

The consultant turned and left, whispering to no one in particular, 'I don't have to put up with this,' and retreated into his office, firmly closing the door behind him.

And each night Raymond would go home spent, all his energy drained. He would try to stay awake over his books and notepads, jotting down increasingly elaborate theories to try to bring sense to the case. He believed that this was the test of him as a doctor, as an academic, of his very intellect. A pivotal moment, and he knew that his relevance would depend upon him succeeding. He walked through every interaction he'd had with the boy and the mother, searching for clues and chinks. There was an answer beyond the categorical, he was convinced, if he could only zoom out to a viewpoint with clearer vision. Turning to Descartes, he tried to see this as an ideological labyrinth. What if this were not a straightforward illness, but a manifestation of some other mind–body–sensory disconnect? Could this lad be falling ill as a result of the power of his own mind? Raymond neglected time with the other patients, was preoccupied through the clinics, and fell behind in every other duty.

Each day, Raymond went back and saw the boy and the mother. Before he walked in, he would steel himself, taking a deep breath. He could hardly look her in the eye. Whatever it was that was amiss seemed to worsen each day. And while the rest of the patients in that grim place got better or worse, at least they did it by the book and under somebody else's bed card. Because while the consultant would drop in, consistently grumbling, it was the unspoken expectation that the responsibility for this one, in the end, would be all Raymond's.

Raymond did not move. Was not sure he could. Miss Rosa's soft tongue was pushed into the folds of his ear, her torso angled and set like marble. The humidity of her breath reached further than just his ear canal – it seeped slowly into his head, soaking into his brain, washing down his neck, melting all the way through each limb, each joint and each bone. As the seconds ticked by, he thought it would be best not to shift at all. This was an unknown pleasure, and it occurred to him, quite suddenly, that he had never understood anything. Nothing. Not pathology, not philosophy, certainly not poetry, and absolutely none of the psychological complexities on this earth. He realised that the world had been keeping most things hidden, and in one sweltering moment, decided now was the time to draw back the curtains. Fearful of even closing his eyes, Raymond was concerned that any movement might disrupt this extraordinary event, thus he remained motionless, chastising himself for wasting these precious moments dwelling on the cold memories of the past. He focused on the luxury swirling into his head.

Slowly, Miss Rosa moved her tongue round, licking the corners and the clefts, exploring every crenellation. It was so much more than a kiss. She held herself perfectly still, apart from her roving tongue. He was hardly aware of her breathing, and certainly had no concept of his own. Raymond listened for any more of her – the rustle of her dress, the beat of her heart, anything at all, but his hearing was overpowered by her touch, deafening him to anything but the movements of her mouth, intimate and warm and invisible to every other human in this world.

He stared at the wall in front of him, trying to keep himself from moving, or even falling. It was a haze. Time carried on. She didn't touch any other part of him. He didn't react. Eventually he closed his eyes, and the bliss showed in his smile.

After many languid minutes, she simply stopped, stood up, walked to the door, picked up a tray from the floor that held some used pieces of crockery, and left.

XI

The hospital has a different personality at night. Lou had always preferred these unsociable hours, when the meetings were finished and their treadmill minutes filed who knows where, the clipboards shelved, and those who wore suits were tucked away at home with their newspapers and regulation evening dinners; when the whole place resprouted, returning to the heart of its trade. Rules became looser, conversations freer, and the medicine more raw. And now is the time when she's least likely to be spotted – that liminal period when those who are exhausted from the day's work leave with their eyes down, and the incoming, unseeing nightshift walk in, trying to clear heads which have been muddied by daytime sleep.

As she's hoped, the code to the library has not been changed since she last worked upstairs in the throng of the hospital proper, and she slips unnoticed into its quiet. Nobody goes there at night. They hardly go during the day – it's arthritic and disapproving – plus, sitting down to read is a fantasy of junior doctors, like sleep minus the squawk of a pager, or clocking off without the consequences of decisions made weighing upon them like rocks. An automatic light flickers on and the front room is thrown into solitary shadows.

She's not sure exactly what she's looking for – she told herself she should read up, prepare for the coroner's case, but now that she's here, between the musty, muted hush of the book-filled shelves, Lou allows herself to be absently distracted by titles and great, avocado-green bound journals, and she perches on stools, picking up books at random. Once she's had enough there she wanders through to the back, lights turning on with a clunk when she passes under door arches, and she reaches the secretive stone steps that lead to the storage area where old journals, state health archives and other items of wildly varying value are stored. It appeals to her, stealing further down into this calcified subterranean world, with its ghostly records and other volumes of ignored words.

Creeping around in the felted silence, Lou slides her fingers along shelving until she finds what perhaps she's been looking for all the time. Occupational health reports from the sixties, all filed without fanfare. She pulls them out and sits down at a narrow table covered with scratched linoleum.

A copy of a letter, faded and barely legible, written in 1948 by Dr Eric Saint, is filed alongside other petitions and reports of the time. It's reverential reading after all she's seen. The letter states plainly that Wittenoom will produce the most lethal crop of asbestosis the world over. In 1948 – eighteen years before the mines were shut down. She checks the date twice.

XI

As an appendix to the reports, there is a list of names of all the men working the Wittenoom mines for the last few years of its operation. Lou runs down the alphabet and finds him.

Back out in the sterile white light of the basement corridor, Lou clutches at her pocket where she's shoved the scribbled piece of paper containing the name and date of birth of Dave's father.

She's almost out, back into the carpark, when she hears her name called, a single command. Instinctively she turns. She sees the white coat and willowed frame of a woman, who's now walking briskly towards her. Lou is crouched inside, ready to run, but she sees that it's Jane approaching – somebody whose friendship she'd clutched onto for years, but whose grip had loosened as Lou was sucked underwater.

'Lou? What on earth are you doing here? We all thought ...'

Lou should hug her, smile, fill her in, but she can't move to do so with the carapace that encases her.

'I'm fine. Just collecting a couple of things.'

The two women stare at each other. Over their heads, on the floor above, noises can be heard – a shout, the bumping wheels of a trolley, the ping of an elevator close by. The night hospital is rumbling on – lives shaking and shuddering in every one of the ward beds overhead, the diligence of nurses and doctors through those lonely hours, the sobbing, loss, wonder, birth. The sounds of her not being needed. A pager in Jane's pocket squeals, aggressively high-pitched, and she puts a hand to it without breaking eye contact.

'Lou,' Jane says. 'Do you need help?'

Lou nods, a thought surprising her, and pulls the name out of her pocket. 'I need to find this man. Can you help me? Can you get me into medical records?'

'That's not what I meant, Lou. Are you okay?'

'I might be,' Lou answers slowly, 'if I can find him. Will you help me in?'

Jane looks resigned. 'Sure,' she says, and Lou follows her.

As they walk Jane says, 'We've heard about the coroner's case. That won't be easy for you.'

Lou tries to make a grunting sound conveying thanks.

Once inside the dreary light of the records room, with Jane hovering nearby and glancing repeatedly towards the door, Lou flicks through a forest of blue cardboard files and locates the information she wants.

She copies out the address and phone number, and then skims the history of hospital visits. They've been frequent in the last three months, and she reads the clinical summaries. And it's there – mesothelioma, diagnosed only six weeks ago, on top of long-standing asbestosis. She searches for Dave's name, but there is only a wife as next of kin.

Lou nods in gratitude to her friend as they leave, murmuring that they'll keep in touch. She senses Jane staring at her back as she walks off.

An Invitation, Answered

By the morning, Raymond was infused with purpose. Overnight he'd fashioned up an information sheet, apprising people of the new clinic. He had stewed over the correct wording, but in the end had decided to tell it straight.

If you have concerns about your health as a result of your occupation, I would be pleased to examine you and make a report. Our clinic hours will be from nine am until four pm.

He didn't think this sounded too insurgent, and he'd copied it out several times, hoping to distribute the handouts somewhere visible. Before heading to the hospital, he detoured through the town and issued a few, leaving one to be taped up on the door of the town hall. Greetings were nodded at all he passed.

Walking by the site of the blast, Raymond was amazed to see that an almighty clean-up had gone on in the short time since the inferno. Although the store itself had mostly vanished, leaving behind not much more than charcoal and shadow, the penumbra had been put to rights. They were indeed a proud people, he thought. And surprisingly efficient, considering the circumstances.

As he strolled though, his thoughts meandered to the sensation of the previous evening, and he wondered how he might orchestrate a situation to allow a similar recurrence. His step was light with the thought, and he dodged the piles of cushiony tailings, sailing past the low sprawl of fibro and tin houses, the red gravel soccer pitch, and the general store with its keeper leaning in the doorframe, smoking wistfully.

By the time he arrived at the infirmary, Arthur Curtis was already sitting in the front room, upright, clutching his hands in his lap. He startled when Raymond swept in. Both Miss Rosa and Mrs Italiano were there. Miss Rosa greeted Raymond as curtly as ever, and he swallowed. Could he have misinterpreted the entire, revealing event of the night before? But what other explanation could there be for a solitary tongue in his ear? For this woman's breath, hot and spirited, spilling onto his shoulder.

'Dr Filigree. You remember Arthur Curtis?' Miss Rosa said.

With an ungainly movement, Arthur rose and reached out his hand to clasp Raymond's. It was wetly cool and slid inside Raymond's firm shake.

The furniture had been further shifted around, and the interior looked even more airy and light. Two Chinese paper partitions with faded blue sea-monster motifs had been set up so that the room was divided into a miniature reception area, the spacious middle with three chairs and a folding card table (his new consulting area; a fine idea), and the discreet examination table up next to the bookshelf. The compact reception desk had been laid out with a regimental line of pens, next to a gleaming black bakelite phone, all at the ready.

Raymond settled across from Arthur, and the two women tactfully withdrew.

'So, Mr Curtis. You said you were not unwell. No after-effects from the blast? Shall we examine you just in case?'

'No, no, Doctor. I'm fully recovered.' He spoke furtively, as if expecting somebody else to be listening. Glancing around, he carried on. 'First thing, though, if anyone asks, I came to you for my gout. Is that alright? It's just that I wouldn't want anyone knowing I'd come up here making noises.'

'You have my assurance, Mr Curtis. I am under oath. What noises do you mean?'

Arthur surveyed the room. 'Looks pretty nice. I've been up here before, you know. Tried to talk to some of the docs before you. Got nowhere though.'

'Where are you trying to get, Mr Curtis? I'd like to understand.'

'I'm actually here on behalf of the men. You see, it's hard to know where to turn. I'm their spokesman, you see. And we all thought you might be able to help.'

'Please go on.'

'I'll get right to it, Doc. We're like lambs to the bloody slaughter. In the mines. And in the mill.'

'Do you mind if I jot some of this down?'

'As long as you don't mention my name, Doc.'

'But I do need to ask, before we go on, are you not the union leader? And if you have concerns about the mine, have you not taken them up with your employers?'

'Ha. I'm more a toothless bit of bloody roadkill for what I'm worth to the workers. It's not even a proper position.

Union.' He shook his head. 'It's just what we call ourselves. My job is mainly to organise the soccer matches and make sure they're umpired fairly. I could complain all I like. All that will do is get my pay docked and get me put on the first bus out of here, then they'd chase up whoever'd spoken to me and they'd do the same to them. We need these jobs, Doc. We have families to feed, but we were hoping to stay alive to do it.' He peered around again. 'If they even found out I'd been up here talking to you about it, I'd be out on my ear.'

'Then let us discuss your gout further, Mr Curtis.'

And they sat for a good half-hour, Raymond listening to the brutal details, convinced that even he could not have conjured such a grim account.

XII

He can only give her half an hour, he says. 'Longer than that I need my oxygen.'

They meet in the café of the retirement village where he now lives.

'I don't know why anyone would want to hear my story. Too many bad stories in this world. Don't need to add mine.'

He looks nothing like Dave – where do those herculean arms come from? Dave's father is crumpled, shrunken, his substance fallen away. Skin hangs loose from his neck and his wrists, and bruises stain his forearms. He doesn't move his head much when he speaks, but it bobs with each breath, and she finds herself fixed on the rhythm. What remains of his black hair is oily, with only a few scattered greys, and it lies uncombed over his head.

'So this is going to have to be short,' he says.

But it doesn't turn out to be short. It's time, he says. Once Giorgio ('not George – it's the only bit of Italy I got left') gets started, his memories spill out. Lou has asked whether she can take notes, yet her pen can't keep up. His tone starts off measured, but it becomes clear that he is brimful of stories and suppressed sadness, and his enemy lungs don't even interrupt as he releases things long hidden away. His accent is still strong, as if Italy never wanted to leave him, either.

'Where I come from, it's beautiful. My family, we grow olives and fresh fruit, you wouldn't believe it. Up on a hilltop, near the Church of Santa Maria. Oh, I remember that place. Like heaven she was, but there were no jobs for young people like me. None. So, when these men come in their hats and their suits and they say, "Men, have we got a job for you!", we say *yes*. No one call me man before. I'm just a boy in my family. Eighteen. They only want the strongest in my village. I tell my mama this and she's so proud. She say, "My boy now a man. He get chosen to go and make us proud." They tell us it's sunny all the time, just like in Italy. We all say yes, and we're packed up and ready in one day. Nineteen fifty-eight, it was. I get to Perth then we all fly up to Wittenoom. On MMA. Oh, you should have seen the air hostesses there. *Mamma Mia*. I want to marry one right away. I think, God must be kind to me, send me all the way over here to find an angel to marry, one with hair the colour of the sun and white, white teeth.'

Lou knows he hasn't spoken about these things for a long time. Something in the way he closes his eyes when he talks. Even though he's wheezing, he does not let up.

'But before I leave Perth, to go up north to work, they make me have chest X-ray. I don't know why, they just do. The men, they say, have you worked in mine before? I say yes. They say can you swing a hammer? I say yes. What do I know? I don't speak any English. I just keep saying yes. We all get up there and step out of the plane, and it so hot we think we might die right there. Like the devil took one big breath in and blew it in our face. We line up in a big queue and they give me boots and socks and a heavy shirt. They don't fit me right, but I haven't worked out how to say no to those people, yet. There's a big man. As big as a bull. He's our foreman, and I think early on that maybe I better not learn how to say no. He takes some of us over to the mill. I go with Giuseppe and Franco and we walk in and I say, "Why it snowing?" It was snowing, I tell you. We so confused. Franco see it straight away and says I no going in there, and I never see him again. Me? I go in.'

Giorgio stops talking. A bouncing, kindly waitress has brought over coffees, and she pats him on the arm. 'It's lovely to see you, Giorgio. You haven't been down here in a while.' The bitter beany smell fills the air and Giorgio inhales from his cup. There are faint tremors in his closed, veiny eyelids.

He looks up at the waitress, and his face has transformed into a beatific smile. She waits a moment, twirling a ring around on her finger. Perhaps she can sense events unravelling, something about to spill from this unknown man. He sips his coffee in silence, holding the cup with both trembling hands. Until the cup is drained, he doesn't utter a word. The waitress smiles and takes her leave. Lou wonders whether he's forgotten where he's up to, and she waits for him to place the cup back down.

'Was that when you became one of the grey ghosts?' she asks.

Giorgio's eyes start to fill and he wipes at them. His skin is so thin she can see it heap up like watery clay beneath his finger.

'Yes. Me, I was grey ghost. The big man, he say, "Giorgio, you strong fellow. We put you on belt." I say yes, yes, yes. I don't know what else to say. The grizzly line, we call it. All day long I smash rock with bat. Smash, smash, smash. That's all I do. Till you fill up the cart and the little train takes him off and a new empty one comes. But you can't see your bat because there's too much dust. You can't even see your own hand. You don't know who is working next to you. We have head torches but no batteries. Every time you bash a piece of rock it explodes and you get cut up. Like, what's the word, bits from bullets, you know?'

'Shrapnel?' Lou asks.

'Yes. Like shrapnel. Any bit not covered gets cut. Over and over. It's so bad, I know for sure I'm in hell.'

'Did you not want to get out?'

'Every night I pray to God. I pray to God every night. I say, God, you must get me out. Please, God. I never miss a night praying. But I got nowhere to go. No one to go to. I even pray to God to send me down the mines, to get me away from the grizzly. But God never hear me. For six years, he never hear me.'

A tear takes an angled track down the sharp cavity of his cheek.

'I go down the mine once in a while, when someone sick, and I'm so happy. Even though you can't stand and you can't breathe, it means I get away from the sacks and the blanket of snow in the air for a day or two. And the money, she's much better down the mine. The more you drill, the more you get paid. But then I keep getting taken back to the grizzly. They don't like me, the big men. I keep getting in trouble. I think it's because I say yes to the wrong things. I sit with the wrong people. I try the drinks they make in their own houses because we don't like the Australian beer in the pub, and the pub owner think we dirty, greasy Italians. I can't sleep in my room because it's too hot, so I find a hose to soak down my mattress every night. Now I can sleep, but my bosses don't like it. They think I try to ruin the things that belong to them. One day, I have enough and I ask for a mask. I ask where they keep the masks. I say I know they have masks, just a little one is all I want.' He shakes his head. 'Just a little one. That's all I ask for.'

Squeezing his eyes shut, the wheezing sounds worsen, audible in the quiet café like broken bellows.

'They don't like me. Not at all.'

'Did anyone ever know that the asbestos dust was this harmful?' Lou asks quietly. 'Didn't anyone say anything?'

'We don't know nothing. Nobody ever say nothing. We know in here,' Giorgio pats at his chest while it works away, 'that the dust is bad. You don't need no big brains to tell you that. I remember a man come up and talk to us. A doctor, he was. Just like you, Lou. He ask a lot of questions. I hear them say that he writing letters, trying to show that the dust bad for us. Going to be very bad, when we were back home, and maybe forever for us. But our bosses say if we go round talking, we can expect a problem with our pay. Plus, they tell us this doctor bad and full of made-up lies. Any time we try to talk, even to each other, they tell us to shut up. I don't get a mask. And I find I don't get pay for two weeks. When I say this to the big man, he laughs and say they fix it sometime. I try to ask someone else for a sack to cover my head, but the big man come back and tell me to keep quiet if I know what's good for me, so we all just keep going. Back on the grizzly. I remember we get ten minutes break and we can't even have a cup of tea because we have to spend time trying to find something to wipe the dust off our face and mouth. And all this time I get acid in my guts and it starts to eat away at everything. By the time I leave and go down to Perth I don't marry the air hostess. I marry the first girl I find, and she doesn't like the way I look or smell. We have our little boy. I want to call him Firenze, but she say his name have to be Dave. I say as long as he gets to be called David, so he close to Firenze, but she say I call him what I bloody want. And then we yell. For a long time. And I know it's the mine that takes out my heart, and now it's going to take out my lungs, too. I pray for mesothelioma so I get to die like my friends. It's the first prayer that God answers.'

He gulps down a sob and chokes on it, spluttering thickly. Lou reaches out and picks up his spotted hand, holding it gently until the episode passes.

'I'm going to die and that's good. But you know, Lou, it would be bad for our story to die out too. Maybe the world does need one more bad story. I watch the television and all I see are government ministers and people who say this country great because of mines. They say we all work together to make this country rich, but all I see is men in fancy suits, with clean hands. They the only stories people hear.'

Lou listens, still holding his hand. 'What about all your friends? Are any of them still alive?' She wants to ask about Dave, but she doesn't know how to broach it. 'Your wife? Is she with you here?'

'My wife? She hate me. She hate me long time ago. She lives with somebody else, now. Someone with good clean lungs and good clean money.'

XII

Lou clasps more firmly to his hand. 'And your son? David?'

But this detonates Giorgio's lungs, triggering a blast of coughing, which lasts for many minutes. His lips turn a blotchy shade of blue, and when he settles, Lou knows her time for questions is over, and she assists him out of the chair and walks him slowly back. He wipes his mouth with the back of his hand, leaving a fine thread of spittle.

He says goodbye to her at the door. 'Don't come in, I can hook myself up back fine,' he insists with his barely recovered strength. He waves away her repeated offers of help, until she gives up. She asks if she can come back, one more time.

The Light of Evening

'Can you explain this?' The deputy manager with the ferocious sideburns had two sidekicks trailing him this time. He held out Raymond's hand-printed notice between his thumb and forefinger.

The largest of the posse, an ox of a man, all hefty and hard, simply stared at Raymond, while the third, a scrawny man clothed in blowsy beige shorts and long socks, with thick-rimmed black glasses, watched silently. The deputy manager did not introduce them.

'Because it looks to me,' he said, 'like you're trying to stir up trouble.'

Raymond stepped back. 'No. Not at all. I have, however, recently become aware that there may be some concerning health issues related to breathing the asbestos dust, and I—'

'Doctor,' the deputy manager interrupted, and the ox-man took a step closer. 'The health of the workers, as it relates to what they do for us, is our business. Which we take seriously. We run a tight ship here, and we've passed every safety inspection we've had. This to me,' and he waggled the wilted piece of paper, 'seems like you're trying to incite unrest.'

'No, no. That is not the case, you have my word. But some of the men have concerns ...' Raymond stopped himself speaking, and moved further back. The air was suffocating in here.

The weedy man spoke. 'We would like, Doctor, very much, to know who these men are. That have these concerns. Their names, if you don't mind.'

Arthur Curtis had just left, and Raymond hoped to God these three had not seen him, striding home after pouring out his worries.

'It's just a general feeling I get. Murmurs,' Raymond said. 'You know the sort of thing. Perhaps that there could be more robust safety procedures, better protective equipment and so on.' He was sweating heavily, and he felt the drops of it in his scalp and like sinkers down his neck.

'You will find, *Doctor*,' the deputy manager spoke the word through curled lips, 'that everything is in order. We have all the documentation, everything properly signed off, all demonstrating that we comply with every safety recommendation.'

'And our recommendation to you, Doctor,' the thin one said, gesturing that the three of them were in agreement, 'is that you leave this right here. Stick to your job, Doctor, and we'll stick to ours. And if anybody comes round here bleating, I suggest you send them in our direction. It's our role to look into these matters.'

'Which of course we'll act upon,' the deputy manager added. 'Are we clear on this?'

Raymond nodded mutely. He knew that he'd stepped onto a battlefield with no weaponry or plan, just the words of a frightened worker, a stream of wheezing lungs, and an image of those virginal masks loaded on a train. But, as limited as his armoury was, he lobbed a final request as the men turned to leave. 'I am. Quite clear. But the thing is, the health of the men, as individuals, is also my responsibility. I'd like to request permission to come and visit the mine site for myself. Just to have a look. Enable me to make sure I'm providing the very best service to the community.'

The three men turned to him in unison.

'None of your predecessors,' said the deputy manager, 'not a one, had a need to do that. They managed to *provide a service* without interfering with our business, or holding up proceedings.'

'Anyway,' the scrawny one said. 'Can't allow it. Safety reasons. You're not certified.' He smiled, a twisted thing. 'You see, we take our regulations *very* seriously.'

They left Raymond clenching the back of his chair. He'd never been a brave man, physically at least, and he couldn't imagine barging into the mine site illegally, demanding to review the goings-on, particularly if the entrance was flanked by oxen. But hadn't his cowardice led him into the dark before; when he'd not defied the burly nurses who prevented him returning to the ward in the coal of night to talk to the boy when the mother had gone home, and then again when he chose passage across the ocean instead of staying and speaking out the truth? No, somehow, he needed to bypass these men, who although may have been large in stature, were surely the small men of the company.

The late afternoon slid quickly into evening as he sat crowding pages with his thoughts. Without solid evidence, his accusations sounded flimsy, and he tore up the sheets as soon as they were filled. The night approached, and, not wanting to lose the comfort of the violet light softening the room, he didn't switch on the overhead globe. Having left the window open, the smell of earth wafted in, a minerally heaviness that he could taste as he worked. But he still wasn't getting anywhere. He needed counsel.

On cue, he heard Miss Rosa coming down the corridor. He moved to turn on the light, but changed his mind. In this shifting air he was conscious of his breathing, his stillness. As the steps grew nearer he stood. Smoothed his coat. Readied himself. She pushed open the door.

'Good evening, Raymond. Your dinner.' And with a smile she unsnarled Raymond's knotted worries. 'It's rather lovely with the light off, isn't it.' She carried the tray over to the table – their oasis from the previous night. Wine-coloured shafts of light poured in, aslant over the desk, and drowsy dust whorls were visible inside of them.

'Thank you. Thank you so very much.' He walked over to where she was laying out her offerings. He felt himself flushing, revisiting an adolescence marked by a fevered mind and inadequate mouth. So little had changed really. He was glad she could not see his face.

'I, er, about last night...'

'I've made some rabbit pie for you,' she said. Definitively. Decisively. 'I hope you like rabbit. Perhaps an acquired taste, but I learned how to make it when we had to trap the things for ourselves. Gave you the impetus to do a good job with the cooking.' She smiled again, this time a distant, lost one. 'But that was when I was much, much younger.'

The thought of Miss Rosa being much, much younger added to the heat inside Raymond's head.

Together they looked down at the tray.

'It looks wonderful. It really does,' he said.

The pie was steaming and attractive, and arranged neatly over a bed of vegetables. It could be pomegranate and caviar, for its allure.

'It's quite hot,' she said. 'Might be worth leaving it for a bit.'

'Yes, I'll do that.' And they both stared at the plate.

The wisps of steam curled into the last beams of light, mesmerising to both of them.

Eventually Raymond spoke. 'Miss Rosa, you know I feel that I am meant to be more than just the doctor here. I didn't come over here with much, I know. In fact, I myself wasn't very much. Less even. But things can change. I don't know exactly what I can offer, but somehow, I need to go beyond the patching up of people. The mines, the dust, surely if this is making people sick that don't need to be, then it is my place to intervene. I wondered, if you wouldn't be too averse, whether you could help me. It might carry with it some risk, though.'

Miss Rosa said nothing, but nodded slowly. She raised her head to him before finally speaking. 'You're right, of course. I think it's something people know in their hearts. And naturally I will help. There's never very much for me to lose, anyway.'

He watched her say this, her tensile strength, her certainty, on display as though they were physical supports, the struts of her.

'I'm not sure of the most effective way, however,' he said. 'The bosses here in Wittenoom seem to be oafs, and malicious ones at that, if I may say so.'

She laughed, agreeing. 'Indeed. Then perhaps you should simply go above them. Contact the head office over in Sydney, and at the same time invite the officers of the Government Department of Mines to take a tour. A surprise visit even.'

'Yes. I'd wondered that myself. And I think I'll make a little surprise visit, too.' As he said this his entrails churned a little. 'If I'm able,' he added.

'Of course you'll be able, Raymond.' She looked directly at him. 'Whatever you were before, here you are another man.'

Raymond dropped his head at her words. Intention was a vastly different beast to fruition, that much he knew.

'Raymond.' She lowered her own head, to speak in tune with him. 'It seems as though you're running from something, and that maybe you need a friend to which to tell it. So here I am.'

He swallowed. She left the silence open.

'I need to …'

'Tell me, Raymond.' She spoke clear and exact in the hush of the room. 'Let me inside your secret.' Raymond remained mute. She repeated, 'Let me inside.'

XIII

Lou returns the following day, telling herself it's to check on Giorgio, to ensure that he's recovered from her interrogation. It's also a distraction from the impending hearing, the thoughts of which have tangled so wildly in her belly that she physically feels her nerves rummaging through the mess when she walks. His front door is unlocked, and when there is no reply to her knock she lets herself in. He is sitting half dressed in a torrent of a living room, a stained singlet hanging from his bony frame. His shirt has fallen to the floor. He is gasping for breath, trying to extract whatever oxygen he can from the nasal prongs that he is crushing into his nostrils, the flecked sinews of his hands tenting his skin.

Lou strides over to him, and realises that the oxygen bottle is empty. No soothing hiss comes from its tubing. She explains this to Giorgio, and his eyes again water. He points to a cupboard nearby, and she picks her way through the clutter and chaos and finds another cylinder.

XIII

For the next hour she busies herself. The kitchen, his living area, the cramped bedroom, are all a neglected mess – a tide of living unable to be held back. He watches her sorrowfully, wordlessly. There is the occasional apology murmured into the air, but apart from that he simply sucks in the fresh flow of gas, wheezing with pain on exhalation.

After she has tidied what she can, Lou makes them both a cup of tea. Black, unhappily, as the milk in the otherwise empty fridge is curdled.

'Giorgio. Have you thought about getting help in?'

He shakes his head. 'No one want to come and help me. There's no point.'

There are bubbles in his voice and a crackling in his chest as he makes the effort to speak.

'But there are services …'

He forcefully shakes his head. Specks of saliva fling from his chin. 'The people come once a week to give me more oxygen and they get mad at me, too. But why waste someone's time looking after me? I'll be dead soon.'

The carpet is an unbearable brown, with patches worn through from the legs of chairs. Curtains hang unevenly in their thick and dismal colours, keeping out the world. It is neither hot nor cold inside, and Lou feels the oppression of the room, as if it were an antechamber, a place to sit watching the ticking of the clock, awaiting the end.

'Let me take you outside. The sun is shining out there. We'll both feel better, I'm sure of it.'

They sit on a wooden bench with the oxygen canister perched between them, and the sun warms their backs.

Lou tries once more. 'I'm not just talking about help around the house, Giorgio. There are palliative care services. Help make the end not so terrible.'

'Lou, maybe my end's supposed to be terrible. Maybe then I get to pay my debt before going up there.' He raises his eyes skywards.

This time she holds his hand before she speaks. 'I've seen David, you know. Up in Wittenoom.'

As if he knows he needs to conserve oxygen to reply, he simply stares at her, his jaw slack.

She continues, 'I don't think he knows you have mesothelioma. That you're dying.'

He shakes his head in slow motion. 'I never understand why he go up there.'

'Giorgio, I think he went there for you, somehow.'

More tears leak out. 'Look at me,' he says, wiping them away slowly. 'I never used to cry. And now I can't stop. Maybe these are all the tears I should have cried before.'

The warmth of the sun suffuses into Lou's back, and it feels benign, mellow. It is as though it's a different star to the one up north. Different worlds, she thinks.

Giorgio appears to gather strength. 'We just yell a lot in our family, never cry. Well, that's not true. David, I know he cry a lot when he was little boy. All through school it's so hard for him. He was such a big boy, so healthy, strong like me before I start to waste away. But he couldn't read and he couldn't write, and it seems that the only way to make this better in those days was to yell at boys to make them work harder. My wife, she did most of it, the yelling. So I know he cry a lot in his room, where he think nobody knows.'

XIII

Giorgio holds a hand to his chest, as if willing himself to breathe steadily and get these things out.

'He can't finish school. He try all sorts of jobs, none of them last too long. And he's unhappy, like all of us. The only time I see him happy was with his girl, Lacey. They were going to have a baby, and I knew that this was the time, finally, God say, Giorgio, I'm going to let everything be alright for you. You have so much bad time, that I give you a grandson and everything can start over. And David, we make everything so he can be happy, too. But it doesn't turn out that way.'

Lou can hear a cough welling up inside him and entreats him to rest a little. Just sit and enjoy the sunshine.

'Yes, maybe you right,' he says before the hacking erupts. 'But maybe better if you do the talking, Lou. Maybe you have some secrets you can tell a dying man.'

The Safety of Enclosed Spaces

'A secret?' Raymond said. 'Such a word.'

'Please,' Miss Rosa said.

'Yes. Of course.' The inevitable had entered the room, positioning itself between them. 'Before I came to Wittenoom—'

'No, not out here,' she interrupted him. 'In here.' And she gestured to the closet behind where the desk now nestled. She slipped around the table and opened the door. The cupboard was of decent size but unclear purpose, like many of the crannies in this building. Mostly empty, without drawers or shelves, it contained a few items for cleaning, and an unevenly stacked pile of stationery. Two people could stand inside with little effort, by the looks of things.

Miss Rosa walked straight in. Raymond hesitated for a moment, and then followed her.

He stood intimately close to her. Taller than Miss Rosa, his chin grazed the top of her hair in this cramped space. He was glad he had shaved that morning, as he could sometimes miss a day. Even still, his whiskers grew with a torpor resulting in a smoothness not often found in other men at this time of evening. So many things for which to be grateful. Not the least of which was this warm fug of a cupboard.

She waited, expecting him to continue what he'd started, and, as he was unsure of any other move to make, he did exactly that.

'I failed a boy.'

Miss Rosa tilted her head upwards, watching him.

'Quite badly, I'm afraid. Let him down.' He felt a shrinking of the space around them. 'And he died because of it.' Wanting to put his arms someplace, but not knowing where, he carried on talking instead. 'I had to fill out the death certificate, late at night, on my own, and I couldn't put the truth on it.'

'Was it really your fault?'

'I believe so. I didn't listen. When I should have.' He looked up towards the ceiling of that confined space, steering his words away from Miss Rosa. 'I should say I did listen to many things. I listened to the experts and the words of textbooks, but I didn't listen out for the truth. I couldn't hear it, the pings and the reflections of it. And, finally, once I'd found it, I never spoke out. Truth's a slippery thing, Miss Rosa.'

'That would have been very difficult.'

'Not as difficult for me as for that wretched child.'

And Raymond could still feel the growing panic of those last days, when his ignorance had followed him round like a demon in the shadows. Whenever he had found a chance he would leave the miserable clinics and go to check on the boy. He had hoped to find him alone, at least once, but the mother would always be there, sitting in the same chair, clutching her overstuffed handbag or sitting with it clamped between her feet. On the occasions he had tried to slip in at night, he had been barred by the gladiatorial night nurses. He hadn't insisted.

'Have you figured out what's going on, yet?' He winced at the venom in the mother's tone, recoiling when he heard her speak. It was as though she took pleasure in throwing darts at him and his inadequacy. She exuded the impression that she knew what the problem was, but planned to torture the medical staff until they figured it out for themselves. Which was, Raymond knew, ridiculous, as well as unfair on the mother in this unenviable position, frantic about her son's unexplained maladies and simply lacking the social graces to demonstrate it.

'The consultant will be around later,' Raymond found himself explaining, not for the first time. 'He has a few new theories about your son, I believe.' Raymond turned to the boy and softened his tone. 'How are you feeling today?'

The boy put out an unsteady hand and clutched a handful of bedcover.

'Please … Doctor …'

Raymond's thorax suddenly tightened. 'What. What's wrong?'

'What's wrong?' the mother yelped. 'He's terrible. Can't you see?' She pulled up his shirt. 'Complained of tummy pain all night. And this morning. Not that anyone was listening. He hasn't eaten a thing. Look at his stomach. Have you ever seen anything so swollen?'

The boy's abdomen did appear inflated that morning, and was covered in linear scratches, like he'd tried to claw away the discomfort during the horrors of the dark. 'And now he can't even walk. Look at him.' She spoke loudly, projecting to the entire ward, as if it were important that they all heard this conversation. Raymond inhaled as she hauled at the boy to make him get up, but he didn't stop her. She yanked at her son with hard movements, looking around as she did, ensuring that all in the ward bore witness to how sick her son was getting, and additionally to invite them to take note of the medical staff's incompetence.

The boy couldn't stand. Not without assistance. He swayed and grasped onto the flimsy sheets at the end of the bed. His mother beckoned for everyone to watch by way of an exaggerated frown and raised eyebrows.

The boy fixed his eyes on Raymond. It was a porous, grappling look – a plea for help. Raymond was desperate.

Slowly, the boy lifted a flagging arm and made one simple motion with his fingers, as though he were putting a spoon to his mouth, and then he left the pulp of his index finger on his lips. Raymond stared, not understanding. The mother snatched away her son's hand and pushed him along, propelling him so that he would display his gait for all.

Raymond closed his eyes for a moment, suspending the image of guilt in the shape of this unsteady child. Several days ago this boy had been standing, lined up against a wall. Now, he could hardly put one foot in front of another without tripping over himself, as though he had forgotten the mechanics of lifting his feet. Raymond reopened his eyes, compelling himself to watch. As the boy lurched, Raymond reached out and wrapped an arm around him – he had no weight at all despite his bulging belly. The boy hung onto him, his grip feeble. Even with Raymond as a frame, the child only managed a few steps. His legs lifted like a marionette's, making a slapping sound when his feet hit the floor. The boy stared up at Raymond and managed a nod. It was as if he was saying *you know what to do now.* Only Raymond didn't. He was simply aware of the thud in the cage of his own chest.

They sat heavily back on the bed. Raymond rose and started to tuck the boy's legs back under the covers. The mother took over, elbowing Raymond out of the way.

'See?' she said.

The consultant was lingering on the ward's horizon. He must have spied this attempt to walk because he came striding over.

'There. That's it!' He pulled off the shroud of covers. 'I knew it!' He stood back, crossing his arms. The cut of his coat moved with him, bunching up at the shoulders. A hush fell across the entire room. 'After *extensive* consultation of the most current medical literature, I have been able to come to the conclusion that all of your son's symptoms are due to a rare condition, only recently described. It is porphyria,' he announced with a flourish. 'Acute intermittent porphyria.' He smiled, allowing a theatrical pause. The audience was growing in number. 'I was only sure when I saw him walking. Foot drop, you see. Classic.'

The mother didn't move. She continued to stare at the consultant, who was beaming, as though he was posing for a photograph.

'Are you quite sure?' she asked.

'Quite,' the consultant said with a nod. 'All we have to do is wait for him to pass a urine sample, then pop it out in the sunshine to watch it change colour. And, presto!' He took in the gathering. 'If there is any sunshine, of course,' and he smiled at his act of generosity, making a quip under such serious circumstances.

'Are there any other tests you should do,' she asked, 'to be sure?'

'No. The urine colour is quite specific. It's what all of the textbooks say.'

The mother's gaze did not move from the consultant. Raymond watched her from where he stood, hunkered down in his own den of ignorance. How could he have missed such a clear diagnosis? The image of the boy's finger on his lips came back to him and, in a way, Raymond understood it as a reproach – you know nothing, and you speak no truth. You must listen to those more knowledgeable. Understand your place. Your questions have only complicated matters.

In the immediate aftermath of the revelation, however, Raymond became curious about the mother's reaction. After all this time, to not be smiling, congratulatory, relieved. She did not even ask about treatment. Not at that point, anyway. The consultant turned, his leather shoes creaking, and he left, throwing a scatter of orders at Raymond like confetti.

'And, was it?' Miss Rosa asked. As he spoke, she continued to look up at him. Her nose, elegantly slim, almost touched his mouth.

'Was it what?' Raymond was finding it harder and harder to focus. He felt her reaching under his coat, which was all of a sudden too hot, too heavy in this humid space.

'Porphyria.'

'No,' Raymond said softly. 'Not even close.'

'Porphyria,' she said. 'That sounds good.'

'I beg your pardon?' Raymond asked.

'An impressive diagnosis. Porphyria.' The boy's mother appeared as though she was swirling the word round in her mouth, tasting the novelty on her tongue.

A piece was missing, Raymond was sure of it. A decoder. An answer buried deep. He thought back to the finger on the lips.

He wanted to be alone with the boy. Start over. Try to ask the questions he should have at the beginning. Find a doorway into the child's mind. But there she was, standing between them, an impenetrable barricade. The only thing he managed to say was, 'I'm not sure we should be rushing into anything.'

'Oh, but he seems so reliable, this *consultant* of yours.'

'He is, it's only that …' Raymond trailed off, unsure of what he wanted to say. 'Well, let's just look at the urine, then.'

'Yes,' she said. 'Let's.'

Vial after vial the boy produced, under the strict supervision of his mother. Each time the pots were placed outside, Raymond watched them. They never changed colour, except for the occasional suggestion of a shift in hue, sparked by the passage of the hours. By the end of the day, Raymond's vision was blurred and he returned to his quarters, tired and beaten. He pulled down his text-books from their shelves, and once more opened them across his tiny table. It was all there. Porphyria. Symptoms of abdominal distress and bloating, mental agitation and confusion, generalised weakness, and there, the defining criteria of nerve palsies, causing wrist, or more commonly, foot drops.

The next day the consultant blared further. 'More urine! That's what we need. There is no other single diagnosis in all the texts that have ever been written that would say otherwise.'

But the boy was becoming weaker and more confused. He stopped looking up at Raymond. His mother continued to wheel him off to the lavatories, and with his head lolling to one side it looked like she was parading the wounded up an aisle to receive a medal. One of the last times Raymond saw him conscious was as he was being manhandled into the chair to be pushed off again to produce.

Miss Rosa absorbed it all. Although he directed his words up to the ceiling, they fell intimately down, settling warmly upon her.

'Porphyria,' Miss Rosa said. 'Sounds like the lover from a Keats poem.'

'You've read Keats? Miss Rosa, I continue to underestimate you.'

'Not at all. I may have helped myself to your small anthology. I hope you don't mind.'

'Of course not. I am delighted that you felt you could. That's from *The Eve of St. Agnes*, I'm quite sure. *Meantime, across the moors/Had come your Porphyro, with heart on fire/ For Madeline.*'

The richness of the poetry filled the strange cupboard further, hanging warm and viscous in the air. They could have been standing in the chamber of kings, designed with ornately carved wood and high celestine ceilings.

'He was misdiagnosed too. Keats,' Raymond said.

Miss Rosa didn't speak.

'I kept thinking what I knew of Descartes' teaching. I was missing something, some way of thinking about the problem, something I could not see, or something I could not divine. Whatever it was seemed just beyond my grasp. Descartes had warned us against trusting our own senses, recognising that they can be deceitful. I knew I had to go beyond them and find the problem in the mind.'

Miss Rosa slowly moved her hands down his waist.

'Descartes impelled us to consider the two separately – the infinite thoughts of the mind and the sensory inputs of the body.' He stopped himself. What had he said? Had he accidentally said sensual, instead of sensory? He was becoming flustered.

'And I thought,' a bead of sweat trickled down Raymond's temple, but he did not wish to reach up and wipe it away, 'that in this was the truth. And it was up to me to decipher the battle going on between these two things, in order to discover how to wage peace. I still believed in it after he …' Raymond moved in a fraction closer to her. 'I actually thought I didn't believe in those theories *hard* enough. So, I followed them all the way out here. To try again. To really convert them to action, and uncover a purity in the way we practise …'

At the word 'purity', they both looked at each other, dead straight and true. Miss Rosa reached up underneath Raymond's coat and slid her hands past the waistband of his trousers, down through the cleft of his buttocks, and left a finger resting gently on his anus. He didn't move, apart from tenderly closing his eyes. He continued talking, one slow word after another.

'But I know now that I was wrong. I was wrong about which mind was the problem. I was wrong about so many things. Had nothing right at all. Not then, and not over here. Maybe nothing, until now.'

'Poppycock,' the consultant said, several times, in response to Raymond's attempt at a debate. 'It's not the role of the physician to look into the weakness and disability of the mind. Just because the theologians and philosophers have abdicated their responsibilities, it doesn't mean we should be picking up the pieces.'

'But for hundreds of years, some of the world's greatest intellects have tried to understand the interaction of the two components, to discover whether they're entirely separate or interdependent. It's just that I wonder if this might have something to do with the case. Whether we're so focused on the physical presentation in front of us that we can't see what else is going on, something more important, vital, but perhaps less tangible.'

'Witchcraft and quackery.' The consultant leaned towards Raymond. 'If you want to play with those theories, I suggest you go a bloody long way away and try them out. Not here where we do proper medicine. You're on thin ice, Filigree.'

By the next afternoon the boy was dead. Blue-grey and cold. The mother's recriminations rang out through the wards, down the corridors, through the clinic and into the chill air outside. There was so much more rage than grief.

Raymond stood at the bedside, struck dumb, letting the accusations blister into his skin, where he felt them scar, deep and angry and permanent. As the mother foamed and roared, he saw the consultant in the distance, washing his hands and walking off. Raymond thought he heard him say to one of the nurses at the far end of the ward, 'That's just what happens with porphyria.' And as the mother gathered up her things, in a world of apoplexy, Raymond could see into that oversized handbag and saw that it was bulging with paint peelings. Hundreds of strips of paint from walls. Lead paint.

'And you didn't say anything?' Miss Rosa enquired softly.

'I tried to. She knew I'd seen right into the depths of her and her bag. By the time I'd worked out who to inform, she'd got in first. I never found out exactly what she told people. By the next morning, I had the director's assistant knocking at my door. No one would give me a straight answer, only that I would have to work under supervision from then on. When I met with the consultant to tell him what I'd seen, he closed the door in my face, appalled, he said, to have been working all this time with someone with those sorts of tendencies towards children. If I put even a toe wrong while I was there, including filling out my fairy stories on the death certificate, I'd be lucky to sweep the mortuary for the rest of my career. Even my resident colleagues shunned me. I was out of the program. It was too late, anyway. Nothing would have changed for the boy. I knew the best thing I could do was leave and find some place new. Start afresh. Even find somewhere to develop my theories. Oh, I had so many plans.' He inclined into Miss Rosa.

She had moved her hands and they now cupped his buttocks. Her head rested on his chest and the heat in the room nestled them both. Raymond emerged from his story, freed, finally, to talk. 'I can hardly believe that I've been so ineffectual out here. That I've failed again.'

Miss Rosa withdrew her hands, leaving behind a cool vacancy where they'd been.

'What?' She stepped backwards in the confines of the cupboard and placed her hands on the crests of both his hips. 'What on earth do you mean by *failed again*, Raymond?'

'Well, here. In Wittenoom. What am I, really, me and my plans?'

'Oh, my dear Raymond. You are perhaps a little blinder than I thought. Firstly, it wasn't you who poisoned that poor child, so you need to move on from that. But here, in Wittenoom? You're the closest thing to a saviour some of these people have seen. I believe this is the opposite to failure, Raymond. Open your eyes and see. And once you've done that, you'll be able to speak out, clear and strong, and this time, this time people will take notice.'

Raymond said nothing more. The bonds that had shackled him for so long simply sublimated and floated off, slipping out of the cupboard unnoticed. He leaned back himself, just far enough to free his hands but not uncouple from Miss Rosa's grasp. With a winding pleasure that made hours of minutes, he reached a finger to her face and slowly trailed a path around the oval of it. He then traced lightly down her nose and outlined the curve of her lips, intently watching his finger as he did so. He drew around and around those lips until he finally let his index finger sink down the line of her chest. As gently as he knew how, he drifted his open palm across one breast, and then the other, and then mapped the perfect contours of both of them. Her eyes stayed closed, lost. He eventually slid the flat of his hand up behind that impeccable hairline, where he cradled the back of her head. She opened her eyes and they looked at each other. After many slow, ticking minutes, she moved into him and again let her head lay on his chest. And they stayed standing, just as they were, connected in the warmth, until the food outside was long cold, and the town slept with hope on its breath.

XIV

Why poison a man already dying?

'We all have secrets, Giorgio.' Lou bites her lower lip. 'Mine are nothing special.'

They limp back inside. Lou throws open the dank curtains and a corner of the room lights up, as if a lone match was struck. Settling him in, she arranges his crooked, wheezing body into a chair and lays a crocheted blanket over his legs.

'Stay alive for a bit, Giorgio. You've got unfinished business.'

'Have I?' He grasps onto her arm.

'David,' is all she says, and he nods.

He tells her where to look for his wife's new phone number. She finds it in a tattered exercise book in the kitchen next to the phone, and she scribbles it down.

'She'll know how to find him,' Giorgio says.

Lou leaves with a promise that she'll try.

On the train back to her apartment, Lou watches the suburbs streak by. Flashes of houses are visible through the train window, the pulsing stills of them contained and neat. None have garden beds of toxic waste, or the groan of generators, or the smell of diesel wafting in through their windows late at night. Images of advertisements playing out on neon television screens burst from front rooms in glimpses while the train rushes by. As the engine slows, pulling into a station, she sees somebody engrossed in a game show, and she can make out a host with orange skin and plastic teeth pointing at numbers. The same program is visible with its silent roar in the next house along. People sit motionless in front of the screens.

A family clambers in to the carriage, and they sit noisily opposite. Some of the children stare at her. They are all drinking orange juice from cartons and they drop chocolate wrappers on the ground.

She looks down at her shoes. Her runners are still streaked with plum red; the thin clumps of Pilbara dirt clinging to them, having nowhere else to go in the concrete of this city. As the train pulls away from the station, a metallic shriek echoes down the aisle of the rocking carriage and she stands. She no longer wants to be on this train.

Lou alights at Karrakatta, across from the acres of forest-like gravestones. Low clouds are sneaking across from over the ocean, mercury-coloured and full, rolling in like wet marbles into a game. The weather has different ideas from those of the morning.

She wanders aimlessly at first, but then she orientates herself and finds the overgrown laneway that houses her father's headstone. It's in a cul-de-sac of plain tombs, an out-of-the-way secular section with none of the elaborate crypts of the Roman Catholic corner nearby. They'd all argued about how much money to spend on the stone carving, which had been distressing to them all, and pointless in the end. He was dead, and underground, and nobody visited the weedy gravel hideout. She hasn't been there since the funeral. There are no flowers on his grave. The inscription is simple: a name and a date.

She picks up what she thinks at first is a shrivelled bone, but she sees it's simply a petrified leaf. Her father would have loved having this near to where he rests, and he would have sold it a story, hours long. 'Everything has a tale, Lou,' he always said, 'you just need to know how to tell it.'

The thunderclouds scallop the air, and the shades of the headstones descend into darker hues of grey. She watches overhanging trees drop an occasional copper-coloured leaf. An eddy of wind picks up the discards and tumbles them across the narrow paths, where they settle on the lees of the ground.

Lou has a sudden image of what this little corner of the earth might look like if the top layer were stripped off, perhaps if she had some type of X-ray vision. There would be tiers of orderly skeletons, she guesses, some with their arms crossed, the way they were farewelled in their funeral homes. All of them finished with the business of living, no longer feeling pain or the burning distress of being unloved or the harsh crepitation of disease. How many of them are underground because medicine hadn't saved them when it ought to?

Several bloated raindrops fall onto the path ahead of her and one thumps onto her head. The wind quietly moans among the boughs of unkempt trees. There is no human noise. Nobody else still drawing breath is here today. Perhaps they are all at home watching gameshows, she thinks, sheltered from what looks like an unexpected storm.

She picks up several of the leaves and bunches them together like they were a bouquet, then places them on her father's grave. She should try to contact her own mother, again, maybe just go round there for tea, but she can't face sitting in the front room with the doilies and smell of Dettol and the disapproving sounds that come from putting down her cup in the wrong place. Lou knows she will look at her mother's face with its permanent eyeliner and immovable hair that's set every Friday at eleven, and she will feel nothing but guilt for the distance between them.

So, she boards the next train back home, picking up the journey where she left off, and makes her way towards her narrow void of an apartment. There she sits on the kitchen bench and eats tuna out of the can with a spoon. The notebook is still there for her, however. She tears a page from the back to write a letter.

The Letter

'What do you think, Miss Rosa?'

The letter was simple and straightforward, and Raymond had written it out in his large, looping scrawl.

'I think it's perfect,' she said. 'Nobody could take umbrage with this. All you are doing is voicing some general concerns about the level of protection provided. I like the way you have focused on the future health of the workers and laid no blame upon a single person. And Pliny! Who would have thought?'

He sealed it, smiling. 'Miss Rosa – would you be so kind as to find the address of the mine's head office?'

'That will be no problem. I wonder though, whether a phone call might be even more expeditious. There could be no excuses about lost letters or lengthy delays that way. Why don't you just phone Sydney. Repeat these concerns and invite them to visit.'

'Brilliant. And by the time they come, I will have had a look at the mine sites myself.'

'That reminds me,' she said, 'I have an old camera that I thought you might like to use. It's rather special to me – having accompanied me through the many ups and downs of life. One of my few constants. The flash is a little unreliable, but it still works, and I have two rolls of film. It might just be the thing.'

And as simple as that, plans for a late-afternoon raid, first to the mines and then to the mill, were hatched. A phone call was made, and even though Raymond could not climb higher than a secretary to lord only knows who up at the offices in Sydney (Sugar refining? How curious. Why were they running an asbestos mine? What would they know?), he was confident that his message, that he was seriously concerned about safety breaches occurring, and that men's health and perhaps even lives were at risk, would be passed on. After all, what decent man would not want to hear the truth about his own company?

The early part of the afternoon saw a thin stream of workers enter his office, most by the back entrance, and all giving a covert history while extracting from Raymond a promise of confidentiality. As anticipated, he heard not only their stories, but also listened to lungs swimming in fluid or battling the slow build-up of scar tissue. He grew weary of recommending that they immediately leave their job and return home. 'Not possible, Doc,' was the usual reply. 'Got nowhere else to go, nothing else to do.' Protection, Raymond realised, would be the only answer, and he recorded this, in capitals, in every single patient note he made. Mrs Italiano methodically filed them all, in deft alphabetical order.

Raymond would have liked to wear something a little more suited to stealth, but his choices were limited to serge and his dull, red-dusted brogues. Hardly espionage attire; however, nothing here had been as he'd imagined, so why worry now?

By four-thirty he was steeled. As he stepped out, he saw the unseasonal clouds again gathering. Miss Rosa promised to cover for him at the hospital, if anyone came looking.

By the time he'd arrived at the entrance to the mine site, he was weighted with sweat. The low clouds had filled the air with moisture and he felt like he was walking through gelatin. Slung over his shoulder, the bag containing an exercise book and Miss Rosa's precious camera was awkward and heavy, and it slipped repeatedly as he hiked.

The circumference of the mine site itself was fenced off, encaged in a filthy honeycomb of wire with rusted barbs lacing the top. A single entrance round to one side of the pound allowed not much more than a single man to pass through at one time. Another entrance further up, wide and presumably to allow the passage of machinery, had an industrial padlock hanging from its latch.

Raymond pulled out his handkerchief and wiped his forehead, and then slipped in amongst the narrow counter-current of dust-caked men walking in and out through the gate. Soot rose in clouds from their feet as they stepped. Several of them looked at him without saying a word. A man he recognised from earlier in the day began to speak, but Raymond made a hurried gesture, shaking his head and holding up a hand. They seemed to understand.

Raymond progressed to the mine entrance itself. He was as Jonah, he thought, entering the whale. The maw of the mine opened up to take him in, into the vestibule – a reprieve of an area where the men could have their last moments upright before having to hunch into the stopes, those tunnels wheeling off this main cavern like entrails. Even the struts inside here looked cetaceous. They were arched and oddly white, and he had to stop himself from thinking of them as bones, curved and holding up the carcass of the body around him. The ground reverberated underfoot, as if the mine were living, speaking back to him.

Inside this chamber, the air was like gel. Not only densely humid, but every particle seemed to hold dust within the water. He fancied he could see the microscopic fibres dancing their macabre waltz inside each droplet. How could one breathe this for an hour, let alone ten, even if it were for the only pay a man might see? Each thick breath added to the nausea of being in there, but he had a job to do, and he swallowed – a particulate-full gulp. The shudder and groan of some type of machinery out of sight vibrated the walls and the floor. He felt the quaking of it in his ears.

Just beyond, in the main shaft leading away from him, Raymond saw a great lip of rock hanging precariously from a ledge. A tongue of unstable rubble, poking out at anyone who walked under it.

He set down his bag and pulled out the notebook. First thing to document – the air quality. After that, the men inhaling that air – without mask or respirator or the thinnest pretence of protection. And then, he would turn to practices – what does a day of crouching and crawling through these hellish tunnels do to a body? He saw himself being able to fill pages of depositions. Following this, he intended to medically examine each of the workers. His jitters began to still. A plan always does that, he thought.

He reached into the bag and extracted the camera. Steadying it against his eye, he focused the lens and began to take photographs of the entrance. Even in the viewfinder, he realised that the images would be damning – the air was visibly fouled, its minerality shrouding the unmasked and unprotected men. Each of them wore not much more than shirts and shorts, their exposed faces smeared with grime.

As he lowered the camera and prepared to move further in, the flash began to fire off of its own will. It made a buzzing sound and sparked its magnesium flare three times in a row. The cavern burst into brilliance each time. He fumbled with it, grabbing his bag at the same time, hoping to shove it in and hide it away.

'Oi! What are you doing here?'

Momentarily blinded, Raymond couldn't see what was producing the booming voice. As his vision returned, he saw a man striding towards him, waving great truncheons of arms. 'You're not permitted in here! You were told.'

Raymond recognised the ox-man, even more a colossus in the enclosed space. He took a step backwards, but the heavy man simply walked over, grabbed the camera from him and hurled it against the wall. It splintered, quite slowly it seemed, into myriad black, mechanical pieces. The film sprang out and flew unfurled into the dust of the ground. The men about him stopped still and Raymond held in a yelp.

'You are going to get out, right now, or I'm going to make you.'

Although a few watched him – what would he do, this doctor? – others resumed their motion and industry, men with their eyes trained on the earth.

Raymond held up his hands in surrender. Water poured in rivulets down his wrists into his shirtsleeves, and he knew his face was pulsing red.

'That,' Raymond spoke clearly, 'was unnecessary.' He stepped over to the scattered pieces of camera and picked them up one by one, placing them carefully in the bag. Once he'd finished with this unhappy task, he pulled out an edge of the notebook, just to show the ox. Words cannot be thrown against a wall, he showed him. And if you do, then new ones will sprout in their place.

And Raymond limped back to the hospital, his trembling hands clutching the sorrowful bag of parts, to get those words down, as fast as he could.

In less than an hour, the deputy manager stood at his door. Strangely he was wearing a hard hat, the first time Raymond had seen one donned in this town. Behind him, again, was the huge minder.

The conversation was brief and one-sided. Head office were sending out two representatives. They'd be in Wittenoom on tomorrow's flight. They would be followed by an officer from the Department of Mines, maybe in a day or two. When Raymond tried to speak, to explain his position, he was shut up. The deputy manager seethed with every word he spoke.

'And, *Doctor*, if you're going to stir up a hornet's nest,' the deputy manager concluded, both of the men's bulk blocking out the last of the evening light in the doorframe, 'you'd better hope that your own laundry is clean. Very squeaky clean.'

XV

4 October 1997

Dear Dave,

I've started this letter a hundred times over. I don't know if it should be an apology or an explanation. Perhaps it's both.

So, firstly, I am sorry. I've spent a few days with Giorgio. You were right, of course. His story needs to be written properly. I understand the obligation you felt under – I can feel it, too.

You should come down and visit him. He has mesothelioma – there's no nice way of putting it. I suspect he doesn't have a whole lot of time left. I'm going to look up your mum – Giorgio tells me she'll know how to get hold of you, to get this letter to you.

As for the explanation, how much time do you have?

The story is in my notebook. It's all buried in there. It was supposed to be some type of narrative therapy, I guess, but it hasn't turned out the way I thought. I wanted to get a few things that happened to me at work down on paper – write it out of me – but somehow it's transformed into something else, altogether. I wonder if it might be better if I put my account of what occurred, the things that turned me into this train wreck, down straight and simply, rather than disguised and garnished.

Lou stops and makes herself tea. Her apartment, with its high, useless windows, is always cold, even when spring has budded into life on the doorstep. And dark. It's an unhappy place, she thinks. An apologetic mess, not much better than Giorgio's, and she's taken to writing at the kitchen bench, sitting on a high stool, as she can't find room at the table. The wall clock provides the only sound, a rhythmic cracking noise – a glacier, on the move. She sits back down, staring at the page. Where does one start a tale like this?

Remembering the specific details is harder than she expects, and feels like beating through cobwebs with a stick. But she labours past it, and one by one, the images start to flare in the front of her mind.

She shouldn't have died. She was just a little girl. It was my fault. All of it.

'What was your fault, Lou?' She pictures Dave asking her, him leaning back propped up by his arms somewhere warm, where nobody else is around to listen in.

'I'd gone out to the little department to help out,' she would tell him. Helping out. She shakes her head. Thinking she was of value, that she had something to offer. Working through a backlog in that small second-tier hospital, a place out of sight of the major institutions. She'd been a patient-processing machine that day, and they loved her for it. Patients in, patients out; so efficient it felt irrational. Hardly the minuet with pathology she aspired to, but still, it was service of a sort. Nothing terribly exciting came through the door, anyway – mostly sniffles and certificate requests and mild anxieties. Where one gets complacent with the banal and lazy with ease.

Her apartment feels like it's dimming and the happenings all stream back to her, as though it's a movie reel, rethreaded and cranking up to full speed, showing all the details in full, brutal colour. The weak sunshine of the morning fighting through the few windows to form great squares on the department floor, the biting smell of morning coffee in the air, the sound of the well-rehearsed joviality of the team of nurses, the snake of patients from the triage desk through the clinical areas then disgorged out the other side. And amid that production line a girl about five years old.

'She fell off the swing at home and hurt her arm. Now, she's not moving it. I wasn't going to bring her in,' the mother's words were impatient – nothing out of the ordinary for this factory of unwell, 'but she was complaining of pain at school, and the teachers said I should bring her in here. Get her checked out.' She looked up at Lou and made a snorting sound. 'I've already waited an hour, though.'

Lou bristled when this mother, this heavy-set woman with wiry yellow hair and nicotine-stained fingers, eyed her off. Inside the confines of the cubicle, a sour cocktail of sweat and cigarette smoke was nothing less than assault. It was difficult to see behind her bulk to the gurney, but on the stretcher, instead of the patient, was this woman's oversized handbag, a green, cracked vinyl thing, and the little girl was perched on a chair off to the side.

'So, if you wouldn't mind hurrying it up.' The woman's voice was soaked in scorn, and Lou felt a heated indignation rise in her throat. Who was she, to treat a doctor this way? You spend all day giving of yourself to the community, and this is your reward. She could feel the urge to bite, but she checked it and pushed past the woman to the little thing in the corner.

The child appeared sullen, looking down at her dirty, chewed fingernails. She didn't respond when Lou greeted her. Lou sighed loudly, sensing the queue of patients outside waiting to be seen, the endless roll of the needy – she did not have time to squander.

The mother made an opaque face at Lou and opened up her handbag. Lou could see inside, to scrunched-up food wrappers and a half-empty cigarette packet.

Lou couldn't help herself. 'You know that smoking around children damages their lungs.' A broadside on the offensive. 'It worsens asthma.'

'She doesn't have asthma.' The mother pronounced her words slowly. 'She's here for her arm. Because the teachers told me to bring her. Did you not hear me?'

Anger needled into Lou. She turned with exaggeration and spoke to the girl. 'What happened?'

The little girl had hands like a doll's – tiny, really, for a five-year-old. Maybe Lou had got the age wrong. She didn't have the chart with her. In an attempt to be efficient, she had slipped in without the notes. Lou hadn't even looked at the girl's name. It was just too busy. The girl had a china face and thin, dark hair knotted into two long plaits. Her school uniform was the generic kind; a bleached yellow shirt and a blue skirt, grubby with patches of ink and dirt, the tumble of the playground signed into her clothes.

Looking at the floor, the girl said nothing, and Lou's impatient words hung unanswered in the cubicle. Lou was tired – she'd been on shift till midnight the previous night, and had come home wired and buzzing. She'd watched forgettable documentaries until two, eating ice cream straight from the tub. For some reason, the images of one of the programs came to her head – pelicans and seagulls, pipers and hummingbirds. Lou was distracted by the memories of birdsong and the flight of free birds.

The mother spoke up. 'I told you. She fell off the swing. And she's shy. She won't talk to strangers.' The mother pronounced the last word like a schoolyard insult.

Lou shrugged and peered at her watch, ensuring the movement was clearly visible. Raising an eyebrow, she reached out to examine the girl's twiggy arm. The girl flinched, drawing it away. 'She doesn't like being touched either,' the mother said, plucking crisps out of a miniature packet.

Lou angled herself round to answer the mother. 'Well, she seems to be moving it, now. And it's not deformed. So it's not likely to be broken, is it.' Lou heard her own disparaging tone, and while she didn't necessarily like it, she knew that she was at least serving out her frustration on someone deserving.

The little girl watched the clipped exchange between the two women, and Lou could sense her attention, this tiny, silent bystander.

Not much I'm going to be able to do, then, is there, Lou wanted to say, *if she doesn't want to speak, or be touched. Not sure what you expect me to do.*

For a flickering moment the girl peered up at the doctor towering over her. Started to move her lips as if trying to speak. Nothing came. She wiped her mouth with the white back of a bitty hand, and jiggled from side to side with diminutive, twisting movements. It was strange. Lou was thrown by it, and then the little girl looked up and straight at Lou, inside Lou – odd, for such a shy child.

The mother grabbed her bag and said, 'Well, what did the X-ray show?'

'I didn't know she'd had one. Did the nurse order it?' Lou was still learning the ropes of this autonomous little place. Pictures first, ask questions later, it seemed.

The mother's mouth wormed into a sneer. The air felt tight, like the bow as it's drawn.

At that moment jumbled noise began to encroach into the narrow space.

'Dr Fitzgerald, we're going to have to get a wriggle on. There's an ambulance bringing in a sickie in a few minutes.' One of the nurses, efficient, decisive, popped her head into the cubicle. 'I've already ordered an X-ray here. It looks fine to me. If you could check we can free up some space.'

Lou stepped out to a frisson. Somebody commented that they were glad it was Lou on shift; not everybody instilled such confidence in them as a team. Momentum was building, that tensing of warriors at the battle cry. It was always like this before a critically ill patient hit the door. This is what she was trained for, and she tasked her team with the calm of ordering breakfast. Time-wasting nonsense could just wait. She spritzed by the X-ray and nodded to the nurse that she was correct – the X-ray was entirely normal. Pulling on a gown and gloves, while an assistant tied her up at the back, she instructed someone to put a bandage on the girl, she had no idea who, probably just spoke into the air.

She saw the mother hustle out the child, without a bandage, or sling, or even words of explanation. Lou saw the scowl from where she was but didn't care. Someone shoved a fitness-to-return-to-school form under Lou's nose, a request from the mother, apparently, which Lou signed with her gloved hand, not even bothering to read it.

The patient rushed in by ambulance was unquestionably sick. In the chequered winter sunshine, ahead of the team of nurses, Lou strode out to the ambulance bay and threw open the vehicle doors. A woman in her early eighties lay inside, clutching onto the whitish tendon of life, groaning in pain from her distended, pulsating belly. Lou made the diagnosis on sight, and she sensed the admiring nods behind her. A ruptured aortic aneurysm, its final, catastrophic haemorrhage imminent and the patient's death preparing to accompany it. But not that day, no. Not with Lou there, marching around, calling the shots, ordering the interventions. She conducted the resuscitation like an orchestra: inserting intravenous lines, cross-matching and organising blood and phoning the bigger centre up the road in readiness for transfer. The woman needed an operation, and Lou put down the phone with a clunk, nodded to the team, and said, 'Yep, we're good to go.' Lou jumped in the back of the ambulance with the patient (God, did she even salute the staff as they roared off down the road?), and asked the driver to flick on the lights and sirens. She stood swaying over the patient for the entire trip – one hand on the pulse and the other hanging onto the intravenous pole. They blazed through the doors of the big hospital, eschewing all help, and paraded off with the patient, bestowing her on the waiting operative team like a gift. All great. Very satisfying. Really heroic.

By the time she returned by taxi to the small hospital down the way, much of the patient load had dissipated. A few short hours were left in her shift, and Lou spent them basking in the praise and esteem of those who rarely saw such excitement. One of the nurses sought her out.

'I've left some notes for you to write, if you get a moment.'

Lou raised an eyebrow, a conspiratorial gesture. Paperwork? Leave the paperwork for the desk-johnnies. That's not for those of us who rescue people from the brink of death. Not going to be bothered with that.

The nurse turned to Lou and said, 'And well done. We don't get many cases that sick coming through, but you were fantastic. So in control. That will be one grateful family. How often do we get to truly save a life?'

Lou smiled and thanked her. 'You were all great.'

The warmth of magnanimity can cosset like a quilt, and the soft comfort of self-deception feels just as cosy.

'And thanks for sorting out the loose ends while I was gone.'

'No problem at all, Dr Fitzgerald. Did you see those bruises on the little girl? I'm sure you did. Quiet little thing, wasn't she. And what a dreadful mother.'

Even then. No alarm bells. Nothing. She wished she could say that she had the good grace not to sleep well that night. But she simply dreamed away the hours, bathed in a nocturnal salve of self-congratulation.

The next morning she returned to that little department – her last rostered shift there before heading back to the mothership. The day was a savage winter one, with no bowing sunlight streaming inside, just a rough-edged wind and low sodden clouds. She arrived bang on time – eight o'clock – and she entered into the strangeness of an empty department, cold and fluorescent and smelling of antiseptic.

XV

A lone nurse scurried past her, with her arms full and her face grey. She glanced up when she saw Lou standing there. As she hurried by, she mumbled something Lou couldn't make out, but Lou could see that her eyes were teary. An echoing sound bounced off the walls. All the trolleys were empty, all the staff gone. She watched the nurse carry on, out into the back where the resuscitation bays were situated. From the heart of that area, the sound of agitation leaked out. Lou crept over, confused by the oddness of the moment. It became clear that all of the staff were inside, and the drawn curtains were damping down the frantic sounds, rendering the noise into just a low moan where Lou stood.

As Lou approached, she heard the noise grow, but then all of a sudden stop. It left a terrible vacancy of sound – an auditory concussion. She went to pull back the drapes, after all, surely she was needed if there was a resuscitation going on, but she felt as though she were moving in a dream, all treacly and slow.

She saw, inside the curtains, the final act of a failed resuscitation. People sunk over a scant, lifeless body. The first things on view were the bone-white little legs, angled in the middle of the large bed. And it was clear that this was the moment the end is called, after all efforts are exhausted. The defeated staff hung like weeping trees over the tiny patient. Tubes and lines and miniature puddles of blood were spread over the floor. A few of the nurses were hugging each other. Several of them looked up and saw Lou. They glanced at each other, then turned away. She edged in closer, into a sight so appalling that it branded its memory onto her retinas.

There she saw, lying broken with her skull cracked like an egg, one eye blown up and distorted, leaking out oozy haemorrhage that had streaked down her neck, and oedematous swelling bloating up most of that petite face, the little china doll from yesterday. Her frail, bruised body had already begun its death mottle. Had probably started a little while ago. Lou's gullet closed off and terror reared up inside her chest, kicking to get out.

'What?'

Nobody answered her. Grimly, they commenced the chores that were so horrendous yet so routine for a death in the department. Turning off the monitors, shutting down the ventilator, pulling a stained sheet up over the body far enough to tent over the wilting tube coming out of the little thing's mouth. An oil slick spread through Lou's mind, coating her vision and turning her thoughts to liquid.

'What happened?' was all she managed. Still nobody spoke. Lou gulped, taking fish-like swallows. She backed out into the emptiness of the department, into a bench, and she leaned into it, no longer seeing. A crushed man in scrubs came out and walked over to her. During the hideous early hours, when the child had roared in by ambulance, still clinging onto the last heartbeats of life, the staff had called in one of the senior doctors to help with the resuscitation. He was now sunken-eyed, his face pasty. He picked up the notes, the chart from the night, as well as the ones from the day before. He tossed them at her.

'Have a look in there.'

Inside was an envelope, the seal broken. Lou pulled out the letter it contained. It was addressed to the examining doctor, dated the day before, marked private and confidential. A plea from one of the teachers at the little girl's school. Said they had quite a few concerns about her. Said they had nothing really to go on, not enough to go reporting it to the authorities (they'd been burned before, the letter said, with this family), but they would be very grateful if perhaps the emergency doctor who saw her could have a good look at her. Perhaps they could sort something out – admit her, get the authorities in that way. They didn't want anything terrible to happen. This was an opportunity, a moment of hope for little Milly. She's such a bright young thing, so lovely, such potential. Thank you so very much. We have confidence you'll be able to intervene. Signed and slotted into the medical notes. The notes that she didn't write. A letter she hadn't read. The time she hadn't taken. A voice she hadn't heard. Her name was Milly.

The exhausted night doctor spoke. 'She came in a few hours ago. Beaten to a pulp. Cerebral haemorrhages, ruptured spleen, pneumothorax, broken ribs. Some new, some old. The police have already been here. They've taken both of the parents into custody.' He took the notes back from her. Set his teeth. Clenched his jaw. 'This letter was here yesterday. In the empty notes. Your notes. Yesterday …' He seemed capable of short words only. 'Yesterday. That opportunity. Your opportunity.' He pressed his fingertips into his hairline and massaged his forehead. He started again. 'Lou, you're off the floor. But don't go anywhere until the police come back. They want to interview you. Then you may as well just go home.' He started to say something more but stopped himself. Just shook his head and disappeared back behind the curtains. And that was that. That was what it was.

Lou reads through the letter. Unlike her story, this is garbled and scratched. The kitchen has grown gravid with dark. She shakes her head and screws up the paper with the useless words, tossing it into an already full rubbish bin.

The Picnic

They turned up with family in tow. And a photographer. Word filtered through to the hospital that to honour the company's visit, there would be a picnic. Mrs Italiano filled in the rest. It would be a grand event, she told Raymond and Miss Rosa, paid for by head office. The school would close before lunchtime, so that no child would miss out.

'The place is abuzz,' Mrs Italiano said. 'They're assembling a marquee and lining up trestle tables. I hope the weather holds for them.'

Raymond was unsure how to take in this turn of events. He trusted that the inspectors would come and find him before any festivities – surely the purpose of their visit was serious, and transcended the frivolity of picnics and party tents. He'd spent the night making a clear deposition of his concerns, which he intended to present formally. He would also ask to accompany the gentlemen on their tour of the premises.

Miss Rosa said nothing, simply clucked around the clinic straightening up the already tidy room. Gathering his papers, Raymond slipped them into a manila folder, then into his briefcase. He'd felt shamed when Mrs Italiano mentioned the photographers, having apologised many times to Miss Rosa about the loss of her camera. The details of the threats he'd skimmed over, still unsure of their significance, but he had a feeling Miss Rosa could fill in the gaps herself. Her ease of forgiveness was heartening, and he made it clear that he wanted her by his side when they turned up to the spectacle looming down the road.

Just before noon, with only a rim of red sun visible through the swathes of opaque cloud, Raymond and Miss Rosa walked over to the mines. A circus-like buzz filled the forecourt. Men and women were laying out rugs and erecting all sorts of structures – shadecloths, tents, as well as long, teetering tables. Children were running around, chasing each other and dodging under the trestles. Others were playing a heated game of cricket, with empty beer bottles for wickets, and several more were clambering over the hillock of tailings to the eastern side of the entrance fence. Women in patterned dresses were arranging food and drink, whilst others were sitting in clusters chatting, and colourful streamers – blue, orange, white – had been strung up along the wire fence. The revelry was confusing for Raymond. Hesitantly, he gave Miss Rosa's arm a squeeze. What sort of merriment was this, he implied. She nodded with understanding.

Behind one of the tables, Raymond spied the deputy manager, talking to what must be the gentlemen from head office, men as at odds with the locals as animals behind bars in a zoo. White shirts such as those won't last the day,

Miss Rosa whispered to him with her light smile. She was looking forward to seeing how they held up by the end of it. The festivities seemed to lighten everybody's mood, even Miss Rosa's. Raymond, however, remained wary. The deputy manager could be seen speaking close into the ear of the clean-cut men and then he pointed to Raymond. After a short consultation, filled with elaborate hand gestures, the two company men strode over to him.

'Dr Filigree, is it? I'm Dudley Pemberton, and this is Jim Drinkwater. We're the representatives from head office.' There was a ritual shaking of hands, which was particularly lacklustre, Raymond thought. The pair looked so similar they could have been issued from a factory line – middling height, dark Brylcreemed hair, and sturdy black-rimmed glasses. Their white shirts were indeed blinding, finished off with narrow ties the colour of cyanosis, and both men wore shorts held up by gleaming leather belts. They sported long white socks and disturbingly shiny shoes. 'We're here to reassure everybody that the mine is quite safe and that everything here is in shipshape.'

'Well, I'm not sure that it is,' Raymond started, and he pulled the folder out of his portmanteau, 'which is why I called—'

'Oh, look, here're the little tackers,' Dudley interrupted, as two boys of about seven or eight tore between them, chasing a dusty tennis ball. A third, taller, child followed behind them. 'Boys. Meet the doctor of the town. Filigree.' He gestured towards Raymond. 'Unusual name, isn't it? Filigree?'

The children looked at him for a moment, the smallest throwing him a carefree smile, and then they scampered off again. The older boy ran underneath a braided pink-and-yellow streamer, which had been strung up between trees, and leapt with the spring of a gazelle in order to pull it down. The small crowd burst into short, muted laughter and watched as he ran amongst them, trailing the colours like a kite. People strolled around with hats and parasols, while more women arrived, bearing wicker hampers. The entire town must be here, Raymond thought.

Over the frolicking racket, a voice discharged from a loudspeaker. It was difficult to understand, and Raymond saw that it was coming from the ferret-like man who had visited him a few days prior with those slotted eyes full of intimidation. He was now holding up a megaphone in his scraggy hands. Dudley wandered back to his compatriot.

'Thanks to the generosity of head office in Sydney …' Raymond couldn't make out much more. He asked Miss Rosa if she could, and she said that all she'd heard was that they'd have the picnic and games first, and then the visitors would have a chance to give the mine the once-over.

'This was not what I was expecting,' Raymond said, bafflement not yet giving in to disappointment.

'And something about the photographers,' Miss Rosa said. 'That if we are lucky these might end up in a newspaper somewhere. Apparently, we're to show the country what the backbone of it is up to.'

Raymond saw that the ferret man expected a cheer, beaming his thin-lipped grin, but only scant applause filled the silence.

'Anyway,' the scratchy voice continued, 'enjoy this profusion of hospitality …'

'I can't listen to any more of this,' Raymond said, and he strode over to where the two office men were strutting around the bounteous tables like peacocks, with the deputy manager in obsequious tow.

'I'd like a word, if I may,' Raymond said.

'Of course, Doctor, although if you don't mind, it will need to wait until after this.' Dudley pointed to the pile of tailings, where a large group of children was gathering. 'That's my son there. Excuse me, I need to make sure the photographer gets a decent angle.'

In front of the gigantic heap of tippings, this mammoth grey-white shape that cast a shadow onto the outermost of the trestle tables, were two of the visiting boys. The smallest of them was busy making some type of construction. Knocking into Raymond, the largest of the lads shot past like a scalded rabbit to join in the fun.

Raymond looked on with horror as he saw that the child was gathering large mounds of the cottonwool waste, great handfuls of the powdered discards, and was fashioning it into, surely not, yes it was. A snowman. The two visiting men were calling out a commentary and encouraging him to make it larger, greater. Dudley produced a carrot and a trilby hat. He must have brought them over specifically.

'Come on, son! Bigger – just the way we'd practised. More!'

The boy was sweating and layers of dust were sticking to him, making his cheery little face floury. He was working hard.

'Get that there, will you!' Dudley called orders to the photographer. 'The papers will love it.'

The crowd murmured uncomfortably. Presumably mistaking this for boredom, Dudley yelled, 'Make him fatter! Give him his nose.'

From several viewpoints, the photographer clicked away, capturing the boy at work. Finally the monstrosity was produced, a lopsided, hardly recognisable snowman. The crowd continued to watch warily. Dudley walked over and ruffled the boy's hair. A plume of grit and dust exploded into the air, and the boy beamed at his father.

Raymond felt a tap on his shoulder, and while everybody else was looking with confusion at the filthy homunculus and the posing of the city children in front of it, and Miss Rosa had wandered off to chat to Barry, who was partaking generously of the beer outside a yeasty tent off to the side, he was led away by the deputy manager and his weaselly partner, out of sight of the mob.

Raymond clutched onto his manila folder. He saw that the deputy manager had one of his own.

'You can't say we didn't warn you, Doctor.'

The short crony took the deputy manager's file from him and flicked it open, making a show of reading its contents.

'This is the last time we'll make you an offer, Doctor. We can exchange folders here and you can make your way back to the hospital.'

'Where you belong,' the deputy manager added.

'Exactly. Not here. Which will let us get on with the job of ensuring that everything is above aboard. There'll be no secret chats with our distinguished visitors. No slipping them your letters, or your depositions. No making your amateur noises. Plus, we will need to see all of your patient files on all of our workers. In the meantime, Dr Filigree, if you just quietly turn around and go, you can have this.' The file was waved at him.

'I'd like a look in there, thank you,' Raymond said. He was in the crossfire of weapons he did not even recognise.

'I have no doubt you would, Doctor. So, all you need to do is hand over your file, and we'll do the same, and you can walk away.'

Raymond shook his head. 'I cannot stand by and watch the health of the workers being compromised. I've seen the safety equipment withheld. I know what's being done with it – being siphoned off on the black market somewhere for unlawful profit. And the asbestos dust – even with the best safety equipment in the world, that stuff is lethal. Anyone who condones the breathing in of it is committing their employees to a slow, breathless death. It's willful negligence, and surely there would not be a court in the land that would look favourably on this. On you.' There. It was said. His fistful of words were now out in the open. He inhaled deeply.

'Is that a fact, Doctor.' The stoat of a man wore an odd expression; a snarled, distorted smile. 'Because, accusations as big as this would want to come from someone trustworthy.' He looked down at the file. 'Not from someone who, say,' and the deputy manager watched Raymond intently while his partner read out, '*has a history of interfering with children.* That's why you left your last job, we were told, Doctor. Wasn't hard to find out about you, you see. A quick phone call to your last employer and the stuff came flooding out. Hardly surprising he's making trouble down there, were the exact words of one of the consultants you worked under.'

Raymond's tongue was dry. The chest which he had newly filled with plans and steel-strong hopes had been opened to reveal that they had turned to ash.

'But that was a lie,' Raymond said. 'An utter fabrication, by ...' He heard his words hollow and weightless as he spoke them.

'Of course they were, Doctor. Although that seems to be at odds with what a former matron of here said when we contacted her. Seems she's willing to fill out an affidavit as to your soundness of mind. Now your file, thanks.'

Raymond stood, his feet forged into the iron earth. The term *unquenchable* came to him. He saw Miss Rosa walking over to him, and he gestured for her to stay away, imbuing a simple hand wave with more substance than was possible.

He shook his head. They could not cut out his tongue. 'No, I'm afraid.'

Neither of the two men answered. The stand-off would have remained, this enraged silence, for a good deal of time, were it not for the eruption of gaiety and action behind them.

'Hop in, kids!' Dudley had enlisted the services of the ox-man, and the two were standing beside a battered, rectangular steel trolley, with sloped sides and trundling wheels. Several children were being lifted up like feather pillows and deposited, laughing, inside. The boys from over east stood in the front of the cart, as though they were roving sea-captains. 'We're going for a ride.'

'There's room for more!' Jim called out. 'Come on.'

Raymond ducked away, gripping his file, and strode over to the performance, as the beefy man heaved the ore cart full of its giggling load towards the mine entrance.

'Hang on,' Raymond called out. 'You can't take the children in there. It's not safe.'

But he was ignored. A number of the townsfolk were holding back their own children, hanging onto hands, or clutching them to their skirts, but several older ones who had jumped in, plus the three belonging to the out-of-towners, whooped with joy inside the cart as it pitched off and was pushed out of sight. Dudley and Jim trailed in behind the human carthorse, and the voices of the children faded from earshot.

The constrained carousing outside petered off. Townsfolk returned to their blankets and tables, and nibbled at food with little enthusiasm. He heard one of the children prevented from going on the joyride saying he wished they had ice cream. Snails of turbid clouds amassed above them. Miss Rosa found Raymond standing crookedly, watching the empty entrance to the mine, and a shifting wind blew behind her, the type which brings with it fearsome weather. Oily dust settled on the menisci of teacups.

Raymond simply shook his head at her. 'I think I ought to go, Miss Rosa. This picnic is not the place for me. Although …'

He could have predicted it. In fact, afterwards, he blamed himself for not doing so, when the obvious had been hanging from the rooftop. From inside the mouth of the mine, a crescendo of noise thundered out. First a rumble, then a crash, then a welter of screams and shouts.

The townsfolk looked up to see Dudley running from the entrance. His arms flapped, his face was frost-white. 'Rockfall! Get help!'

Everybody galvanised within seconds, hats and parasols dropped. Raymond joined a group of about twelve men and women who barrelled their way inside, jostling to get there quickest.

That lip of rock above the main tunnel had split, cracking and bursting its seam, with some of the largest chunks landing directly on the cart. Boulders were piled on top, others heaped on both sides. Formless shouting and crying filled the cavern, and uninjured children from the back of the cart were climbing out into the arms of the volunteers. The air was thick with plumes of dust, like a mighty bonfire had just been lit, and it was difficult to take a full breath without coughing.

'How many are under?' Raymond yelled. 'How many?'

Dudley was trying to heave off one of the larger rocks. 'My son's under there! Help! Help, please.'

'Everybody to it,' Raymond shouted. 'All hands.'

'I'll call the firies,' a man answered.

'Get Barry to bring the ambulance,' Raymond yelled.

He sensed everybody working together, a coordinated rescue of superhuman strength. Rocks were lifted off the pile, one by one, some from angles that defied physics. Pasty, spluttering, crying children were pulled out until the last two remained. It was the out-of-town boys who were trapped. The oldest was slate-coloured, his leg flexed unnaturally, pinned under a vast hunk of rock. He was slumped into the furthest corner of the cart and was cradling the head of his younger brother, the imp of the snowman scene. Into the granitey dust that coated the cart side behind him, an expanding orb of red was spreading, a thick, bloody bloom. The young boy was unconscious, drooped strangely across the older one, the blood coming from the side of his head. Fruitlessly, stroking his younger brother's face and whispering for him to wake, the older boy did not look up and did not answer the hysterical pleas from his father.

Eventually, with a synchronised grunt, the last boulder was hauled off the boys. The ox-man, silent and painted in the dingy powder, reached in and single-handedly passed first one boy, and then the other to the waiting crowd, who began to carry them outside as a team.

'Be gentle with them,' Raymond called. 'Watch their necks.'

The older boy howled briefly with the agony of it, and then slipped into a stoic silence. The younger one made no noise. And then the convoy emerged into the light, sliding by the horrified, wordless crowd, delivering the boys into Maude, where Barry raced them, and Raymond, back to the infirmary. This time, though, any fear had left Raymond. He had an intravenous line into the younger boy, despite the bounce of the truck, before they'd even arrived. He was ready.

In the operating room, with the anaesthetic machine pumping away, Raymond's actions were slick, as if the episode of a few days ago had been simply a rehearsal.

The older boy's leg, shattered and buckled, was so pliant it was easily splinted with rods, and it was then wound and finished off with bandages. Both Beatrice and Candace were ice-quiet and superb. Raymond hardly had to utter a word. They then moved the boy back to the ward to join the smaller one. The younger brother had regained some degree of consciousness, and was now groggily responding to command. However, a boggy, putty-like swelling over his left temple greatly concerned Raymond; a possible harbinger of a temporal fracture, lacerating the blood vessels leading directly to the brain. He had to get the boy out to a surgical centre, quickly, that much he knew. But how?

Dudley burst through the doors of the ward, accompanied by Miss Rosa. His colleague, Jim, followed them, nervous and wide-eyed, keeping his hand on the door handle.

'How are they, Doctor?'

'Your eldest will be fine – requires an operation, but he's out of the woods. It's the little one I'm worried about. He may need the services of a brain surgeon. And soon.'

Dudley blanched. 'Please, do what you can, Doctor. How do we get them out? Do you have the Royal Flying Doctors out here?'

'Royal Flying who?' Raymond asked, looking at Miss Rosa.

'The RFDS,' she said, 'but they don't come out here. Something to do with safety, our landing strip, or their planes. I'm really not sure. It always seemed to be a different reason.'

'Perhaps let me make some calls,' Jim said quietly. 'If you could direct me to a telephone.'

Once he left, Dudley crouched down next to his youngest. 'What can I do, Doctor?'

Raymond told him there was nothing, consoling him as best he could, although he spotted his own file of concerns and appeals where he'd dropped it. He should demand the man read it – payment of a sort. But he watched the father with his wrung hands and body twisted over his son's, and Raymond knew he did not have the heart.

As Miss Rosa returned to the ward, a deep rumbling sound, felt, rather than heard, shook the windows.

'Thunder,' she said. 'Can I get anything here, Dr Filigree?'

He was distracted, watching the boy. Things weren't right – he'd begun to slump again, and had stopped answering Raymond's questions. Dudley, in his agony, called out the boy's name, over and over, getting less of a response each time.

'Emery. Emery son. Can you hear me? What's wrong, Doctor. Why won't he answer?'

Raymond shone a light in the boy's pupils, sluggish but still reactive, he observed, and then he counted the boy's respiratory rate.

'Things are progressing, I'm afraid,' he told Dudley. 'It's urgent that we get him out.'

Emery's hair was soaked through, and his chest retracted in and out between his ribs. A wandering line of dribble spilt from one corner of his mouth.

At that moment, Jim appeared. 'They're coming. From Port Hedland. Took a bit of persuading, but they're on their way. Should be here in half an hour.'

A mighty flash lit up the room, and fat rain burst from where the sky gaped open, bucketing down on the tin roof. From the window Raymond could see the deluge of rain thundering over a torrent of people, townsfolk rolling up the hill to the hospital, surging in like stormwater.

'A flood coming,' Miss Rosa said. 'They'll all be here to help.'

And true enough, the front room became a seething, steaming shrine, a berth for vigil and solidarity. Raymond slipped out to see and reassured them that they weren't needed, but nobody wanted to move. An urn of boiling water had been brought in, and one of the ladies was making quiet cups of tea, handing them around as though they were gifts of the Magi.

In one corner, he saw the deputy manager and the crony, hidden amongst the crowd. He squinted – they were going through his patient files. Raymond drew himself up, about to shout across the swarm, when Beatrice slipped in from the ward and pulled at his sleeve.

'Dr Filigree, you'd better come quick. Emery is seizing.'

Raymond turned, glancing once more at the men in the corner, and hurried off to the ward. Candace stood over the tetanic boy, holding his jaw. Dudley himself was rigid with fear.

'Phenobarbitone, Beatrice. And quickly.'

She bolted to the pharmacy cupboard, and Raymond turned the boy onto his side, where he then weakened into a limp, unconscious heap.

Speaking loudly, to be heard over the roar of the tempest outside, Raymond had only a few words for Dudley. 'Time is of the essence, now,' as Emery snorted into the mattress – the sheets wet with the life seeping into them. And as Beatrice returned with the oily syringe, and Raymond was whispering encouragement into Emery's ear that nobody else could hear, the boy began to convulse again – a screaming, frothing seizure that looked as though there could be no coming back from.

XVI

Lou's appointment with the hospital's legal department is at nine-thirty. No one at the office was clear about the support they were required to offer her since she'd officially quit her post, but they agreed to see her, anyway – after all, it wouldn't just be her reputation up on the stand; the whole hospital might come under scrutiny.

But she turns up, nervously, at nine, not realising that such departments work on a more urbane schedule and the door is decisively locked.

To pass the time she wanders into the charade of a hospital garden; a tight square dotted with frail, anaemic trees, their bark peeling like cheap paint, the ground carpeted with a thick undergrowth of cigarette butts, smoked to the quick. She sits on the single bench, which has graffiti scrawled in neon layers, as though they were chapters of some street bible, overwritten daily.

Singing floats in from the nearby chapel, perhaps a choir rehearsing. She stays, listening, herself an orphaned stone statue in the grounds. She'd like to buy a coffee, but doesn't want to run into anybody she knows. Their pity, their poorly disguised gratitude that it was her, not they who had stumbled down a lethal rabbit hole, would be quite visible.

The music is angelic, harmonised and note perfect, and she drinks it into her ears. It makes her think, for the first time, *maybe I could come back*. She wonders if it would be possible, in any way, to return to medicine. It would have to be at the bottom again, of course. And a different hospital. It couldn't be here.

Here she would never outrun the talk, the looks. The aftermath was worse than the incident in some ways. Word got out so quickly, painfully inflated ones at that. The retelling grew horns and gathered contagion, until people would hardly look at her. She knew that it was probably her hubris in the face of the elderly woman with the aneurysm that had done her in; the way she'd worn her glory like a cape. The woman had died the next day, of course. Let go by the surgical team. A complaint had been filed about that, too; the patient had written a directive about her end of life which had not been seen, and Lou had saved her against her wishes. After that it was all downhill, with Lou increasingly lost and myopic. She couldn't trust herself to see anything right, having been so blind when it had mattered most. And over a short period of time, a grey fear had begun to consume her, obscuring her vision every time she saw a sick patient, wondering when something like that first incident would happen again, and the barbaric, the unthinkable, would jump back into her headlights. One girl she should have saved, one entire life with its branches and ripples and possibilities. And it had warped her, so that every time she spoke, to a patient, or a colleague, it was guarded and unsure and eventually just plain hopeless. And plain in other ways. There was no poetry, no magic left in medicine, and she wonders whether there ever had been.

She sits listening to the women singing hymns in the chapel of a dirty, inner-city hospital. Wondering who they are, with their saintly song and celestial voices. Pouring out verse with purpose, bequeathing something positive, as simple as it may be.

At nine-thirty, she discovers that the medico-legal department have conferred and have changed their mind; since she is no longer employed by the hospital, it is now a civil matter and they are not obliged, or covered, to represent her at the coroner's hearing. She'll have to go it alone tomorrow. The door is closed firmly behind her.

And as she has nowhere else to go, she perches herself on the lawn of the park opposite the emergency department, and watches the coming and going of ambulances, seeing the syncopated disgorging of patients from their rears to then be swallowed up by the hospital. The vans drive away empty, off to ferry in more of the city's unwell. It's like the story of Sisyphus, never ending, never reaching the top. When she's had enough, and everybody starts to look the same, she spies a cachectic, bluish man, bundled in rugs, knotted up in oxygen tubing, clunked out on a trolley and wheeled inside. It is Giorgio, she sees. Unaccompanied by anyone but faceless paramedics. She can taste the loneliness of the scene from across the road, and she watches him being sucked through the department doors.

Flight

Sheets of dark rain fell, like an ink storm. Thunder followed so close on the heels of the lightning that Raymond wondered how anything outside would be left standing. He didn't like the chances of any plane landing in this weather.

With the help of anticonvulsants and oxygen, Emery's seizures temporarily burned out to a simple tremor. Raymond positioned his head as best he could. Then, in what felt to be only minutes, a new, mechanical rumbling could be heard between the brief gaps of thunder. The plane.

All eyes focused on Raymond. He put down his stethoscope.

'Right,' he decided. 'The most expeditious way of transfer would be if I take our patients out to the strip. We'll save precious time that way. Barry can drive, and I'll sit with the two boys in the back. Load Maude's front seat with equipment, Candace. Miss Rosa will help.'

His orders were followed in an instant, the crew moving as one, and the boys were packaged into the rear, helpers holding umbrellas and other makeshift covers over them as they did. There were so many solemn volunteers, Raymond could not have counted them. The rain continued to pour so heavily it could not percolate into the red earth, and it looked as though the land, like some of the people above it, was weeping. He heard a few say they'd never seen such a storm in March, and there was a question whether it was a foul, or perhaps even divine, sign.

'We are going to do our best, Dudley.' Raymond put his hands on the watery-eyed visitor's shoulders before squeezing into the back. He turned to the small crowd, 'And thank you all. You've been brilliant. Crucial, in fact.' The throng pulled back.

'Drive,' he said to Barry, who booted the jalopy into gear.

As they tore down the road to the airstrip, Raymond supporting the jaw of the now deeply unconscious boy, the thunder began to miraculously roll away, wrapping up to the east. The rain slowed to a shower, and then, as they reached the edge of the airfield, dwindled to stray, sporadic drops. They sped inside the gate. There was no airport to speak of, only a tattered windsock, currently hanging sodden and limp, and a listing, open shed. Threadbare tyres, painted a cracked white, marked both ends of the strip. They parked underneath a crumbling sign, which did not appear to have been repainted since its installation. *Welcome to Wittenoom. The Home of the Future.*

The rain had turned the ground to soup, and the dirt alongside the tarmac was difficult to negotiate. The ambulance slid sideways through the sludge. Asbestos, heaped up like that, might be perfectly flame-resistant, but was as useful as newspaper in the wet, Raymond thought.

The aeroplane was buzzing circuits.

'Trying to work out how to land on this piece of crud,' Barry said grimly. 'God knows how the milk run does it.'

Raymond jumped out of the ambulance and his feet sank into the muddy clay. Shielding his eyes, he looked up at the twin-engine aircraft, banking tightly only a thousand feet or so above the ground. He waved madly. *Come down. We need you.* His shoes sucked into the ooze with each step, slapping back on his feet when he lifted them. The sun broke through the clouds, its burning rays beginning to dry the mud like a kiln.

A thumbs-up signal appeared from a side window, and the plane passed over crosswind and descended onto the strip, jolting to a rather elegant landing, all things considered. Two men jumped out, both dressed in khaki shorts and shirts, and tough mountaineering boots. One had pilot's insignia sewn into the shirt shoulders.

'G'day. Sounds like you've got a bit of trouble out here.' The man with the unadorned shirt spoke first. He had a light and breezy tone, which all of a sudden was desperately reassuring. 'I was expecting more flies out here,' he looked around. 'It'll be the rain that's got rid of them. I'm Bob Harvey, Flying Doctor. And this is Sven, the pilot.'

'Greetings,' the pilot said, his accent stretched with Eastern European vowels. 'It's no wonder we don't come out here too often. Not so good an airstrip, yes?' He pushed a pair of sunglasses up onto his head.

'Thank you so much for coming. My name is Dr Raymond Filigree. Medical Super. Been here a week. And I've got a head-injured boy in the back. Extradural, I think. Can we get him some place with a neurosurgeon? And quickly?'

'Absolutely, my friend. Let's go.'

The three, assisted by Barry, carried the young boy, his breathing now stertorous, through the side door of the plane, followed by the older boy. The two doctors spoke succinctly, swapping notes and making plans. With every sentence, Raymond felt hope rise within him. These men were competent, efficient, and had obviously done this many times before. The sky continued to lighten and the sun bore down on them, back to its old ferocity.

As the patients were being strapped in, Raymond ventured, 'I just wondered why we didn't see you before. You know, with the explosion. For the burnt, the injured.'

'The what?' Bob stopped at the buckle and looked over at Sven, who was doing his walk around.

'The explosion. On Friday night. The dynamite at the store. Several dead, lots injured.'

The pair looked at Raymond, incredulous. 'But we heard it was something minor,' Bob said. 'A small fire.'

Sven had a hand on the wing, not moving. 'We weren't needed.'

'People dead?' Bob said. 'You've got to be kidding, mate.'

Sven's eyes were wide, and he didn't move.

'I'm quite serious,' Raymond said. 'And then ambulances just turned up to take the wounded away. I didn't even know who organised for them to come. I thought it must have been some official response.' He watched as the two men slowly shook their heads.

'Just take all the patients away without being called?' Bob asked.

'That's no official response,' Sven said. 'That's …' He looked like he was searching for an appropriate term.

Raymond's optimism was cleaved by a new sense of shame. How hadn't he known? Why didn't he make the calls then? 'I didn't know what the process was.' He spoke stiffly, and climbed into the back of the plane to help make sure everything was ready, lines were secured, airway was intact.

'Don't you worry about that, Raymond. You're new to the system,' Bob said. 'What bothers me is that we didn't hear. Nothing official at all. Talk was it was just a little incident. Only a few minor casualties. All in hand, they said.'

Sven added, 'Yes, all in hand, they definitely said. We're used to this place being a closed shop, but that, that's …'

Bob rubbed both sides of his forehead. 'Jesus bloody Christ.' A sound, like tinnitus buzzed through the air. It was probably cicadas getting fired up again, but to Raymond it sounded like disbelief.

'Several dead?' Bob repeated. 'That's a major bloody disaster. I heard a brief company release on the radio down in Perth. It said there was a minor fire in a deserted warehouse and nobody was seriously hurt. No mention of any deaths. No major injuries.' He put his hand on Raymond's shoulder. 'Why the hell didn't we hear?'

'Bastards,' Sven said quietly. 'It was a big, bloody cover-up.'

'Unbelievable,' Bob muttered. 'And you dealt with all of this on your own?'

Raymond nodded, unsure of what else to say.

'Well, it's time you got some help. Let's get these boys down to Perth. Sven?'

Raymond clambered out of the aircraft and Bob climbed in. Sven swung himself up into the pilot's seat.

'Before you go,' Raymond said, 'could I ask who you think I should speak to next? This place is more than a closed shop. It's a bunker. And a cataclysm waiting to happen. There's no safety equipment, no extractors, no masks, and the conditions, in both the mine and the mill, aren't fit for the devil. The miners, the wives, even the children, they're going to pay the price for decades if things aren't cleaned up. I'm not getting anywhere speaking to the people in charge here, and the company directors don't seem to take any notice, either. I don't know where else to turn. Somebody needs to listen to the health risks here. I'm happy to write a thousand letters if that would help.'

The propellors chugged into life, and Bob had to shout above the roar. Bob assured him that they'd do everything they could to help. 'Keep writing,' he said. 'Get it all down. Leave no bloody stone unturned.' Bob knew the Director-General for Health. Although he was still officially part of the bureaucracy, he was a good man, and might be able to slice through the layers of moral illiteracy that seemed to infest the tiers of people below him. Bob said he would get the letters to the director himself, as soon as he was able. The first step to accountability. Time the truth was told.

Before the plane door closed, Bob reached out to shake Raymond's hand.

'You're a bloody hero, mate,' he yelled. 'A regular Renaissance man.' He reached out to the door handle. 'A Newton of the north. A Da Vinci of the dirt.'

Raymond smiled, and Sven bellowed from the front. 'A Descartes of the dust.'

And then the plane was taxiing back through the muck. It took off, banking gracefully to the south. Raymond felt the weight of acceptance settle over his shoulders like a brother, and he waved until he could no longer see them. Barry opened the door of the ambulance and ushered him in like a king.

XVII

Lou knows the back way into the respiratory ward. This hospital is labyrinthine, a rabbit warren, built upwards and outwards by impulse, added to on whims. Throughout its history, renovations to the building had always been done sporadically, expediently, usually for bursts of political advantage, and never in the order needed. The lung ward always seemed to miss out, though, while the building around it was dressed up in new season's fashion. Its past life as a tuberculosis sanitorium proved tenacious, however, and it has stayed looking as if it still belongs to that era. The result is a long, tired ward with an enclosed verandah, the walls a stale beige, a floor of powder-blue linoleum, and a twenty-four-hour soundtrack of coughing and wheezing.

Lou sneaks through a back entrance, knowing he will be there. She looks down the row of patients, the cadaveric men grunting, all tied to oxygen tubing, many with yellowing hair from their steadfast marriages to nicotine, some veiled by wafts of nebulised steam, puffing away like miserable, hoary dragons put out to pasture.

She can see him, Giorgio. He's been admitted to the verandah area. She knows, from the days when she worked the wards, that this is where the patients who require less intensive treatment are admitted. Sometimes, it's because they are only mildly unwell; a little bronchitis here, a lump for investigation there. The other group are those that are dying and there is little left to be done. It's a rather peaceful spot, really. The buttery light that filters through the windows in the afternoon is comforting, and it's quieter than the main part of the ward. Welcomed here are veterans of all types – occupational, as well as those from the tickertape of war. Asbestos victims are frequent users, a queue of breathless camaraderie, and Lou thinks it wouldn't be the worst place to meet death. She imagines the spectre of it, death with its signature look and swift collection process, visiting silently during the night – surely it would not always be unwelcome. But then again, what if some of these deaths could have been postponed, denied this prematurely dyspnoeic and gasping exit? If the letters of the great men – Saint, McNulty, others – had been heeded, not lost, made public? The ones that now sit tucked away on file in the backblocks of unpopular libraries. How many lungs could have remained undefiled? It's the eternal speculation: what if?

Two nurses fuss over him, a male and a female, clipped and clean and efficient in their uniforms. They are settling him in and arranging an IV infusion. He looks exhausted, and Lou does not want to add to his burdens. So, she writes him a note and promises that she will return to see him. She sneaks back the way she came, and is grateful, at least, that she can still slip through unseen.

Whisky and Words

Miss Rosa sat with him all afternoon. As he drafted depositions, she read alongside, offering suggestions, corrections and a general stream of support. Unbeknownst to him, she had been busy dredging up historical documents. It turned out she still had a friend or two down in Perth, one of whom worked as a filing clerk in the State Library, and the pair had spent several hours on the phone.

Neither of them was bothered by the soaking humidity left behind by the storm, and they worked with pertinacity, Raymond filling page after page. He knew that, in all likelihood, with his unrepentant words, he was writing himself into exile, but he was finally fortified and was prepared for what might follow.

By the time he'd returned to the hospital, the two men from head office and their remaining boy had left – taken a truck owned by the mines and headed across to Port Hedland, where they knew they could find a flight down to Perth. The rest of the crowd also gradually petered out, retreating to their homes, the camps, the tumble of the town. Raymond and Miss Rosa were left alone. A gentle breeze blew through the open window of the front office, and from somewhere distant, they heard music, a sweet ribbon of sound, flowing into the room.

Somehow, Miss Rosa had procured a bottle of whisky and two crystal-cut tumblers. She poured short measures into their clinking glasses, half full with ice, which they touched together each time a letter was completed. Miss Rosa addressed the envelopes: to the company over east, the Department of Mines, the Minister for Health, the *West Australian* Newspaper, the Medical Board, the Office of the Premier. His final missive was to the Director General of Health, a copy of which they would post to the Royal Flying Doctor Service, for backup.

Dear sir,

By now it must have come to your attention that an epidemic is looming, its epicentre the mines and the mills of Wittenoom. It will be a plague of our own doing, and it will be irreversible if we do not act immediately. We, those that run the mine, those that profit from the mine, and those that stand by, are permitting lungs to fill with asbestos fibres. You will be quite aware of the extreme lethality of even scant exposure. Pliny first wrote about it as BC turned to AD, and since then the consequent pneumoconiosis has been documented time and time again. I refer you to repeated concerns throughout history: the British Lady Inspectors of Factories in 1898, the UK Parliamentary Commission into the asbestos industry in 1906, even the Americans were fighting in court for compensation for asbestos-related lung disease in 1927. Yet still, here we are, without a skerrick of protection, in 1966, letting men breathe the stuff like oxygen, putting their lives at risk every day both down the ratholes of the mine, as well as in the bagging mill (not to mention the irresponsible dumps of tailings all throughout the township).

The mine executives either sit oblivious to history, or are willfully ignoring it. I, sir, can do neither.

I have examined the chests of the men. The hallmarks of disease are present already. There is no question that this will only get worse. The time bomb is ticking, the fuse has been lit.

There is a singular lack of accountability amongst those in charge of this mining venture. I also have concerns that records of inspections may have been falsified, documenting attention to safety issues, which are simply not true.

Mark my words, sir, if we do not insist that the highest-quality protection is provided to the workers, immediately and scrupulously, then we shall all be culpable for the impending catastrophe. It will be an environmental calamity never before seen – hospital wards will fill for years with the consequences.

I beseech you, sir, to mobilise assistance. The very least is to mandate compulsory protective equipment and environmental control. I will assist myself, in any way possible.

I remain, your humble servant,

'Scratch that,' Miss Rosa said. 'You are nobody's humble servant.'

He smiled and signed off,

Dr Raymond Principle Filigree,

Medical Superintendent,

Wittenoom Hospital

And the pair clanked their glasses together, again, and drained them in a mouthful.

At four-thirty, as they were sealing the last of the letters into envelopes and the air inside had cooled to perfection, a hesitant knock came at the front door. Miss Rosa opened it to the deputy manager and the ox-man, who looked rather less of an oaf since Raymond had watched him pull the boys from the cart.

'We'd like a word, Doctor. Alone.'

Raymond began to protest, but Miss Rosa had already cleared the glasses off the desk and was making her way out. He saw that she'd only taken with her the final letter, the one addressed to Bob Harvey, care of the Royal Flying Doctor Service. The rest sat exposed in front of them. He gestured for them to sit. Miss Rosa firmly closed the door behind her.

XVIII

Lou turns up on time for the two days that the coroner's court convenes. Dressed in a suit, she sits at the back of the courtroom, camouflaged by the blandness of her appearance. She speaks to nobody, and no one seems to notice that she's there.

In the end she is barely called upon. Her role is primarily as medical witness. The teacher who is present makes a brief point about the letter, but this is passed over quickly, and the focus remains on the criminal actions of both the parents and the failure of a government department expected to simultaneously protect children from the brutality of caregivers, whilst still upholding the sanctity of civil liberties. The impossibility of this task takes up all the copy in the newspaper covering the case, and leads to days of fruitless public debate. And then the appetite of the public turns elsewhere, to the corrupt use of credit accounts by unionists and another shark attack.

Lou walks down the steps of the courthouse, past the photographers jostling each other for a last shot of the social worker from the Department of Child Protection, and into the cool evening air. Her pace doesn't falter. She is free.

Shutdown

'They're closing down the mine,' Raymond said. The meeting had been brief, the details flung at him like bones to a dog. 'In fact, the whole town. Just like that.'

'Was it your letters?' Miss Rosa asked. Mrs Italiano was by her side, come on a visit, and they had linked arms at the news. 'But how?' Miss Rosa clutched onto the back of a chair with her free arm, willowy, as if a puff of wind taking fancy could topple her without effort.

'Nothing to do with me, it seems.' Raymond closed his eyes and shook his head. It had all been so preposterously sudden. He'd like to call it incomprehensible, but he knew that the ways of men such as these, when viewed from the correct angle, are easily understood. 'Although they would have liked to blame me, somehow. No. I gathered, from listening between the lines, that the mine was running at such a loss – there hasn't been a profit in years – that it was simply not worth continuing. Throw in a top executive's son's head injury, and it became the perfect time to chuck the whole thing in. Tomorrow. Can you believe it. The buses are already ordered. Families will be told at daybreak.'

'Everyone?' Miss Rosa was struggling to speak.

'All the menfolk?' Mrs Italiano asked. 'Losing their income?'

'Exactly. And not a penny of a payout to a single soul. Broke, was what they said. Nobody's buying asbestos anymore. Some major deal with the British cancelled on the quiet. I almost felt they were trying to pin this one on me, but they just ran out of steam and whitewash.'

'Oh, Raymond. What about all the immigrants, those that came here to work? Are there any guarantees?' Miss Rosa asked.

'They're probably only guaranteed of one thing,' he said. 'As they left, they picked up all my letters. Swiped every one of them. I was too surprised to do anything. Of course, I can rewrite them, but I guess they'll have a different focus, now. It was the only thing I managed to say, to be honest. That the company's responsibility will not end with a closed sign.'

'And what did they say?' Mrs Italiano asked.

'They laughed at me. Said I was a misplaced fop and a dreamer.' He smiled. 'I expect there are worse things to be.' He ran a hand through his hair. 'And then they were gone. I don't even think I saw them walk out the door. They disappeared like a magic trick.'

Mrs Italiano said, 'I don't know if this is a tragedy or a godsend. All I know is that there will be rafts of people going hungry. Perhaps it's time for me to step up. Everyone will be widows of a type by tomorrow. I'll find a way to meet with the womenfolk, form some sort of support group.'

'You're a leading light, Mrs Italiano. Go and shine.'

She took in the room. 'Although, and I know this sounds odd, I will miss this place.' Walking over to the mostly bare bookshelf, she ran a finger along the shelving and over the meagre stock of books. 'I know those monsters killed my Federico, but still …' She looked at her finger, then blinked, holding it up for Miss Rosa and Raymond to see. It was plastered in dirt, and where she'd run her finger was a deep crevice, a canal in a thick badland of dust. Miss Rosa marched over to look herself. She did the same, drawing an index finger through, and demonstrating that the bookshelf, indeed, was caked in centimetres of dirt.

'How very peculiar,' was all Miss Rosa managed.

'You've always kept this place so clean, Rosa. How is …?'

An odd tinkling noise filled the silence behind them, and they looked around quickly, thinking they must have missed something.

'Candace? Beatrice?' Miss Rosa called out. She still held onto the letter.

'Barry?' Raymond added.

No response was returned. In fact, for a long minute, there was an absence of any noise at all. And then a strange scraping noise scuffed into the room, which seemed to come from a separate part of the hospital. Miss Rosa wondered if it might be the call of a bird, but unlike one they'd ever heard before. They stayed still, listening. Quiet, once again.

The trio moved a few steps to the front window. Outside, along the wire fence, was a curious sight. The snowy chickens, which had always remained a pure white despite the marauding red of the earth, were skirting along the weave of the thin metal fence, waddling in single file. They made no clucking noise and they looked like they meant business. The gate to the rest of the world was open, and as Raymond, Miss Rosa, and Mrs Italiano peered together through the window, they saw the fowls walk one by one through the gap, then scatter, then disappear. The three shrugged. What did it matter, now?

In the distance, where Raymond would ordinarily have seen the sparkle of lights of the township coming on, he saw nothing. The town remained dark, hollow-looking.

Mrs Italiano looked quite suddenly pale, perhaps even ghostly. When Miss Rosa asked if she was alright, she only answered that she was simply exhausted. All of this excitement, surely.

'You must go, Mrs Italiano. Do nothing tonight. Go sleep the sleep of the woman whose deeds have been, and will in the future, be counted as courageous. Somehow you will be written in the stars, as sure as history.'

Miss Rosa embraced her in a hug and then, with Raymond, assisted her to the front door. The pair both watched as she slipped through the gate, the gravel path seeming to close up behind her as she went.

With Mrs Italiano gone, the room seemed to echo. 'The bookshelf,' Miss Rosa said. Her voice had taken on a rich timbre, as though she were a character on a stage. In the minutes that they had farewelled Mrs Italiano, the dirt seemed to have piled higher on the few books that were there. Where was it coming from? Looking around, even the furniture had layers of dust, laminating everything in a gritty reddish-grey. The tinkling sound recurred, glassy and persistent this time.

Miss Rosa walked to the bookshelf, pulling out the Keats, and blew a storm of powder from it. The motes danced through the air, catching unseen draughts.

'It's been rather lonely there,' he said. 'I never managed to fill up those shelves. My books never came.'

'Yes,' Miss Rosa said, 'but still, there's so much hope, so much promise, in a single book.'

Raymond said, 'True, although it didn't help much out here.' He formed the smallest of smiles. 'Maybe the happenings in this world are too strange, even for books. Too complex for non-fiction, too absurd for stories, and absolutely too brutal for poetry.' He laid a soft hand on Miss Rosa's arm. 'I want you to have it. Please. It's no use to me.'

Miss Rosa clutched it to her chest. The lights flickered. They looked up and the entire room sparked. The main lightbulb went dark. An ancient, untraceable smell filled the room, and the pair looked at each other, neither understanding. Beyond the door to the hospital a crash rang out.

'Let us go look, Miss Rosa,' Raymond said cautiously.

She nodded, and they walked to the door.

XIX

Lou battles her way to the reception desk, past bottles of hand sanitiser and laminated notices on stands warning anybody visiting the ward to be simultaneously hygienic, quiet and brief. 'He's going to be shifted out to a hospice today. They're getting him ready for transfer. You can't go in. I wouldn't bother waiting, although I can't stop you.'

Lou takes a seat in the waiting area. It's hemmed-in and the plastic covering the chairs and the floor has a dizzying, matching lime colour. It's nauseating to look at it, but perhaps it's the sickly smell from the ward; something disturbingly sweet, a thick sorbitol odour. Families come in and out; sitting, hanging off the edge of chairs, leaning against the walls, most sombre, a few bored and fidgety. Some stay for an hour, others only minutes. Lou has brought her notebook, prepared to wait, and she continues to write, watching the story end, unexpectedly and swiftly.

XIX

The ward clerk eyes her up and down several times, and then returns to answering phone calls in her iron voice and painting her nails. Lou plans to keep waiting and writing.

She has also written to the medical director of the hospital. Requested a meeting. What she'll say to him she hasn't yet planned, but she needs to start somewhere and it may as well be a plea to resume somehow, in some capacity.

Her mother had read about the coroner's hearing in the newspaper. As Lou had not even rated a mention, her anonymity amazingly secured, they were able to talk about it on the phone.

'Disgusting human beings,' her mother had said.

Lou had agreed with her, and the surprise of actually doing so felt like a thaw between them. They made tentative plans to have dinner together the following week, somewhere neutral ('and not too expensive thanks, unless you're paying'), and Lou had booked a table at the local Chinese restaurant.

The waiting area empties out while she scribbles. It'll be past visiting hours, soon. Lou puts up her feet on the seat opposite, as the ward clerk has now gone home, and there is no one around to tell her off. A change of nursing staff sounds like the current coming in. Lou hears a well of discussion and handover and greetings.

And then the drift brings in Dave. He appears abruptly, and in an instant the room is full of him and his wrinkled clothes and blocks of boots and the smell of dust and mint.

She stands, but neither of them says a word. She can see the might of the Pilbara in his outline; the licking flames, the cavernous nights, the sky lit up like tinsel, lone birds calling out the song of the free, gravel roads so straight and long they looked like they might reach the edge of the planet, the echo of abandoned buildings, the spinifex, the dirt. The images are massive in this confined, drab waiting space.

He nods at her, but it could mean anything. And then he heads off down the corridor, to the verandah where his father is living the minutes that now have numbers assigned; the last clock ticks of life. Now that she has her own minutes back, she will use them, but tonight she will leave them to theirs. She decides to walk home through the muted colours of spring, crunching through grass, running her hand along railings. Somehow, she has her own ending to unearth.

Dustfall

The tinkling noises began to arrive in slabs, muted crashing noises erupting, growing louder, from somewhere in the infirmary. Each caused the pair to jump.

Creeping towards the door, Miss Rosa spoke quietly, in affirmation. 'Yes, Raymond, we ought to have a look.'

At the door, they paused and grasped for each other's hands, as if preparing for a swan dive, a tandem leap into the uncharted. Together they pushed open the door leading back into the hospital. A strange breeze blew up their legs and right over the top of them.

They trod slowly, lifting up their feet, even their footfall whispering disbelief. Leaves rustled towards them, reeling over their shoes, blowing across the floor and collecting in corners. These were strange, foreign leaves – brownish, speckled, patterned things, the type that are dumped by a hurried autumn. Although, there was no autumn up here in this tropical semi-desert. And no deciduous trees, either. And yet, here they were; chestnut-and-cinnamon leaves buffeting over the empty concrete floor of the infirmary. Raymond and Miss Rosa peered down at the curious things amassing round their ankles and rolling through the corridor. Cool currents of air heaved through the room, buffeting into them, which they felt, as if they were a solid pair of hands, pushing them along.

It was utterly perplexing, and they carried on, turning into the empty first ward. Neither spoke. Odd pieces of paper, scraps of bandages, torn gauze, and all sorts of sweepings blew across the floor, carried by the invisible wind. They squinted, looking upwards, and saw that the clinking noises had come from broken glass, hailed down from ruptured windowpanes.

As they progressed through the room, they saw that almost all of the windows were broken. Some were simply cracked, with the loss of a little triangle here and there, others were shattered, the entire frame empty. Splinters and fragments as well as great wedges of panes were smashed and strewn all across the floor and on top of the empty beds. Shards were caught up in the bedding, where the sheets hung slack and dangling, without bodies to keep them on. In some of the twists of linen, leaves and dirt had also become trapped, heaping into the creases.

A crash behind them caused Raymond to start. They turned to see a smashed bowl, its pieces now littering the floor. Miss Rosa bent down and picked up a ceramic triangle, a sharp-edged chunk of white, lined with blue, and she rubbed its surface, trying to understand. Wan showers of dust blew in through the gaping holes, and the flecks swirled above them; a weightless floating circus.

Raymond walked up to a wide yawping frame, his steps apprehensive, and he shielded Miss Rosa behind him.

They peered out and downwards. Long tentacles of grass had started to creep up the walls and into the building. He looked blankly at the incomprehensible scene.

'It wasn't like this …'

'What has happened here, Raymond?' Miss Rosa's voice was the smallest he had ever heard it. He felt the clutch of her thin hand at the back of his shirt.

The light outside had shifted gear. It was dark and somehow purposeful, as if the sun had also disappeared in search of its own denouement. The draught bowling through the corridors had honed itself a sharp edge, and was rapidly cooling. Raymond and Miss Rosa crept along the hall and into the operating room. Miss Rosa, whilst looking around, distracted by disbelief, crouched slowly and placed the Keats, along with the envelope and its letter, underneath a pile of medical journals that sat in the corner. She didn't see that the journals had turned pale, faded and waterlogged. Raymond extended a hand and assisted her up, and they carried on through to the children's ward, where the mural was so dim and discoloured it was almost impossible to see. They slunk through into the kitchen.

The back door of the hospital was swinging open and shut, creaking and slamming. In here the windows were also mostly gone. Looking closely at the voids of window frames, the pair saw that the circumferential wood had gone soft and begun to rot. Back behind them, the rest of the hospital seemed to be opening up in front of their eyes. Sections of the walls around the doors, and even the walls forming the buttresses of the building itself, were beginning to crumble. On the eastern aspect, half the wall had broken away, leaving a cavernous hole, wailing in the wind.

The pair edged along, not wanting to make a single sound, so unsure of the situation were they. They inched through to the kitchen. Piles of crockery were coated in solid dust and grime, the metal utensils dull and tarnished. A bottle of vinegar standing on the bench had turned a thick black, and the smell of plant decay wafted to them in soft bursts. They didn't speak until they had made their way through that back door and out into the dark. Only the heavy moon provided any light, now. The remains of the hospital were black and eerie in silhouette. The pair took several steps away from the building and looked wordlessly back to where the dilapidation seemed to be continuing, carrying on in front of their eyes, in its own time, with its own agenda.

Miss Rosa eventually spoke. 'Well, there's nothing much left for us here, Raymond.'

He almost laughed. 'That, my dear Miss Rosa, is an understatement.'

Despite the bewildering circumstances behind him, he could not help but think of the practical. What does one do with a dismantled life? How could he continue, or even re-enter, the life he had left behind? He couldn't imagine doing anything now that didn't include the dwarfing red earth, the still creek beds, those massive blue-and-gold skies, and the responsibility of a town. He wanted to belong. There was no going back to the bleached-out existence he had led before.

'I would like to see the gorges, Miss Rosa.' He turned to her. 'Shall we go and visit?'

She swivelled to him and smiled. 'What an excellent idea.'

'I shall bring a torch.'

'And something warm.'

'And you.' He reached out and grasped her hand.

And they made their way round to the front of what was left of the hospital and out through the front gate. Some of the wires were broken, jutting out and poking through the fence, leaving holes where there had been none before. Raymond closed the gate behind him, firmly and deliberately, and he took a last look, not at the crumbling hospital, falling apart, brick by brick, but at the hinge of the gate, which had rusted through.

In the distance, the nocturnal howl of a dingo rose up and welcomed them out into the night.

XX

The meeting is nothing like she anticipates. She'd paced around the hospital perimeter, rehearsing lines for a good half-hour beforehand, picturing the hermetic chill of the director's office. Under tape, between fencing, she'd ducked and weaved through construction sites – everything outside the hospital was always being primped up as well, an endless cycle of buildings being torn down, as they were not quite modish enough according to the fleeting local councils, and being replaced by edifices no more aesthetic, but certainly shinier – and this provides an unending variety of routes to walk. Nothing's permitted to be static, she thinks, and she wonders how she can work this into conversation.

The rest of the world is oblivious to her and her turbulent internal dialogue. Women holding coffee like myrrh, wearing joggers paired with skirts, powerwalk in pairs around the nearby cathedral, jackhammers clatter and pound, a long-established group of homeless men and women shout at passers-by – mostly innocuous, almost singsong catechisms about the intestines of the city, horns toot, air conditioners hum, the sun shifts. After circling the place twice, she enters the administrative annex of the hospital, where those with prescribed lunchbreaks and clean shoes are housed.

The director is unexpectedly conciliatory.

'Yes, well I've had the chance to review all of your files. We may be able to organise a provisional position, as long as it's back here, and in a fully supervised capacity, until you can be signed off.'

Lou breathes. None of her appeals had been necessary.

He continues, 'Sometimes, I wonder if we don't do enough when …' Then he changes tack. 'We'll expect you to visit the hospital psychologist, of course. You'll need a sign-off from her, as well. My assistant will arrange the details. Here, take her this.' And he scribbles down a list of items: dot points of conditions that form a life – her re-entry into medicine, back to her job. A comedown from the days of before, that's for sure, but still, a renewal. Or perhaps a rebirth, she thinks.

She shakes his hand and walks out into the drifts of sunshine.

Back in her unit, she picks up her notebook. She has all afternoon and a word processor, and she types it out, every word, until the moon rises up to join her.

Epitaph

The water flowing through the gorges of the Pilbara has always been ice cold. It's been that way for eternity, no matter what fiery temperatures consume the ground above. Standing on the ridges of those transcendent canyons, the chill diffused up and out, onto the flushed faces of Raymond and Rosa. He shone his torch down, locating the narrow natural staircase created by climate-hewn stone and tree roots. Both were reluctant to let go of each other's hands, but the confined path forced them to walk in single file. Miss Rosa mostly clambered down behind Raymond, hooking her hand into the belt loops of his trousers.

The floor of the gorge was flush with running water. It poured in waterfalls, wound around natural dams and bubbled over boulders. The air smelled pure; of the spritz of citrus and of aniseed. No hint of metal or fume ash was detectable down in this cavern out of sight of the world. The cool air rushed through their noses with each breath in, and it made them both smile. Having reached the base, they were unable to walk far, as the ground was so overgrown and lush. They found a huge, slanting stone, and they climbed up onto it, sitting close together. Their knees were crouched up, leaning into one another. Underneath them was a blanket of soft dirt and pliable leaves. Raymond reached his arm behind Miss Rosa's back, so that she might have something strong and dependable on which to lean. They sat, letting time curve around them, and then they watched it float off again.

Raymond spoke into the nightfall. 'This is the place for poetry, I would think. Not in books, or in bodies, or on cold sheets of paper. It's here that deserves the most lyrical, precious verse.'

'Are you able to recite me some?' Miss Rosa asked.

He inhaled her proximity, and it was ambrosia.

'Keats. After all, he is my favourite.'

Raymond could only recall a few lines, but he offered them up to be carried on the black breeze of the night.

When I behold, upon the night's starred face,
Huge cloudy symbols of a high romance,
And think that I may never live to trace
Their shadows with the magic hand of chance.

Miss Rosa closed her eyes, drifting.

'Funny how such parallels can be drawn time and time again through history, isn't it.' Raymond moved in very close, so it was just the two of them and his whispered words. 'Keats wrote this out of fear that he may fail to achieve love or fame in his short lifetime.' He reached over and outlined the circumference of Miss Rosa's ear, and drew his finger over the angle of her jaw. She remained perfectly still. 'One can never predict how one's life will turn out,' he said. 'How our existences are shaped not only by major events, but by the smallest of things.'

This was now the most comfortable place in the world, the most luxurious, and the most warm, despite the cold brought in on the wind. They sat forwards, their hands entangled, examining each other's as reverently and closely as if they were the scrolls of ancient lands.

'That is true,' said Miss Rosa. 'But, Raymond, what will you do now? Where will you go?'

'I don't know. I think perhaps we should stay right here. You and I. Forever.'

Miss Rosa laughed. 'Yes. Frozen in time. Like characters in a book.' They both giggled at the absurdity.

'That would be wonderful. And in years to come, people could visit this place and look upon us, and imagine the tale of Raymond and Miss Rosa, and how they came to be statues on the floor of this magnificent gorge, bonded together like petrified tree trunks, while the rest of the little town behind them withered away dead.'

'How delightfully ridiculous,' Miss Rosa said.

'A ruin,' Raymond said. 'I've always wanted to be a grand ruin.' He swung the beam of his torch in a drowsy arc across the water, into the rock caves hidden in the walls of the gorge, and then up across the ageless trees. The wind suddenly dropped, and all the silhouettes were still. No branches moved. No leaves rustled. 'I want you to ruin me.'

And there they did bond. Together, with exquisite slowness, they removed each other's clothes and discarded them without care, except for Raymond's suitcoat, which finally became useful to cushion the angular back of Miss Rosa. He traced a line over every wrinkle and every fascinating creamy corner that comprised the story of her body. He re-encountered that warm tongue, and together they explored every part of each other, both outside and in. As they discovered a cadence, they searched each other, finding what may have been a breathtaking beginning, or a climactic closure. The moon, which had watched over so much pain, hung full and quiet, letting this moment last as long as possible. Elsewhere, tides could rise and fall, births and deaths could occur, but here, these two could have sanctuary for as much time as they needed. And, along with the rush of the waterfall, and the song of the dark, they joined in the rhythm of the earth, until the conclusion of the night found them cold and solidified and wrapped as one.

XXI

She watches the two of them. At first, Lou thinks that Giorgio must have passed away – he is slumped in the wheelchair and she can see no movement in his overburdened chest. But then she sees that he nods occasionally in response to something Dave has said.

The garden of the hospice is everything one would imagine, like a preface to paradise. Artfully arranged benches and unobtrusive statues scattered about (no angels, Lou notes, nothing so crass, just serene children and unassuming animals). The hedges are handsomely trimmed and intensely green, while lush, orderly trees rim the perimeter. Gentle music is piped through discreet loudspeakers. It ought to feel corny, but the effect is reassuring and calm. She wishes her own father could have taken that last gulp here.

When she approaches them, she is holding out the bulky envelope in front of her as though it is a white flag – an offering.

'It's just a version,' she says. 'But it's for you.'

XXI

Binding it up, she'd been unsure how to title it. In the end she'd scrawled a word on the front. *Dustfall.* The story will be something different for Giorgio as for Dave, just as it was for her. She hasn't made a copy for herself.

She lays it gently on Giorgio's withered lap, and wipes a thin layer of dust from the cover, only visible under a rogue shaft of light. Summer is coming. The sun is shifting south. Blossoms have landed in the cup of tea gone cold by Giorgio's side. She smiles at Dave and he returns it. And then she walks through the weeping branches of the willows, out of the hospice, directly into the day.

Author's note

Dustfall is a work of fiction. Although inspired by the true history of the asbestos mines of Wittenoom, much has been modified in the crafting of this novel. Time, in particular, has been stretched and pulled around like toffee.

I stumbled on the abandoned shell of the Wittenoom Hospital in mid-1991. It had drawn its last breath only the year previously, living out its final days as an occasionally staffed nursing post. It was a ghostly, evocative ruin, with scraps of gauze still on the floor, waterlogged journals stacked on broken shelves, and a strangely gleaming anaesthetic machine in the corner of one of the rooms. The hospital was not signposted, and there was no mention of it anywhere in the town. At that time, small pockets of the township were still peopled, even thriving on the back of the curiosity of hardy tourists. The population was listed as 45. The following year the grand dame of Wittenoom, the Fortescue Hotel, was shut down, and in 1993 the grotty old aerodrome, damped down for decades with beds of toxic asbestos tailings, farewelled its final plane.

Between then and 2007, when the town was officially degazetted, almost all of the remaining buildings were pulled down by men in moonsuits. The population had fallen from 20,000 at its peak in the mid-sixties down to, at last count in 2016, three. My most recent visit was in 2014, and by then most of the signs of human habitation had been consumed by the red dirt and the spinifex. The valiant citizens who still remained were nowhere to be seen.

The parallel stories in *Dustfall*, in 1997, and in 1966, have both taken necessary liberties with these facts.

Regarding the story of compensation for the victims of asbestos mining in Wittenoom, the court cases were certainly long and gruelling, with many of the affected dying before an outcome was reached. Bitter legal battles are still ongoing.

In the novel, Dave says of asbestos's lethality, 'it is and it isn't'. Mesothelioma is a complex malignancy, and the explanation of this line in the book is beyond the scope of these brief notes. Suffice to say there is thought to be a unique individual susceptibility to the development of mesothelioma, and in those most at risk it is possible that a single fibre may indeed initiate the disease process. However, in any individual, exposure to a massive burden of aerosolised dust and tailings such as occurred at Wittenoom, may be sufficient to cause cancer to grab hold, if enough time passes.

For further reading about this dire chapter in the history of Western Australian mining, I recommend the websites:

http://www.asbestosdiseases.org.au

http://www.australianasbestosnetwork.org.au

Thank you, again, for reading *Dustfall*.

Michelle Johnston, 2017.

Acknowledgements

Acknowledgements feels too bland a word for this list of people, a group to whom I would much rather profess my profound and deep gratitude. *Dustfall* required far more than me to sculpt it into a book. Under my own steam it was simply a morass of wild ideas and a puddle of heartfelt words. The champions in the non-exhaustive, unordered line-up below played pivotal roles in bringing *Dustfall* to fruition, and for this, and every supportive step they took, I thank them.

- Terri-ann White, Director at UWA Publishing and all round tsarina of the Western Australian publishing scene. Thank you for scolding me in the kindest way possible, and believing that I could write a better manuscript.
- Clive Newman, my agent, who made me redraft the damn thing more times than anyone else.
- Kathryn Heyman, mentor extraordinaire. She, the queen of the quiet sigh during our Skype sessions, not only pushed me to write and rewrite to the highest standard of which I was capable, but also performed invaluable psychotherapy for my characters, and was a role model for what an author could be.

- Alexandra Nahlous, editor and eagle eye. Thank you for your military work reigning in what was a rather out-of-control party of commas.
- The other wonderful staff at UWA Publishing: Charlotte and Kate.
- My writing group: Louise Allan and Jacqui Garton-Smith, who demonstrated patience beyond the saintly in their re-reading of the same scenes over and over, and who never wavered in their belief in *Dustfall*.
- Early readers, of whom there were many – each of you provided some new angle, something unseen, a kick of gravity, or a well-earned chastisement. Mostly though, you all believed in me, and I thank you: Marlish, Loralie, David, Amy, Mark, Aidan, Scott, Jon, Carolyn, Tim, and Steve. Plus Anita, who read every, and I mean every, version, and never once complained.
- The glorious people at Hachette Australia and the Queensland Writers Centre. Winning a place at the table for the Manuscript Development Program was the first match strike that allowed me to see the road to publication. I am indebted to you for getting me on that road in the first place, with special mention of the fabulous Robert Watkins.
- My most beloved of family members – Richard, Isabelle, and Julian. You trusted I could do this from the beginning. Thank you for coming along on the ride, and swimming with me in the fantastic, unending pool of literature. We all agree: books are quite simply the best.
- The huge cast of other people of influence: Ernesto and Fulvia, for their stories about the heyday of Wittenoom and the excellent tiramisu, Robert Vojakovic AM JP, President of the Asbestos Diseases Society, for donating his valuable

time, Jeff Prothero, for the evocative photo of the mine access hatch, and Ben Hills, author of *Blue Murder.* There will be many others I've left out. I apologise for my appalling memory.

- My parents, Judy and Ted, for your patience and support over so very many decades. You really are good eggs.
- And you, the reader. This book is, of course, for you.